THE
DUVAL
CONSPIRACY

For my fellow committee man, Joe Popeski! Best wishes!

THE
DUVAL
CONSPIRACY

BY THOMAS C. DAVIS

Thomas C. Davis

MARSHALL JONES COMPANY
Manchester Center, Vermont
Publishers Since 1902

©Thomas C. Davis, 1995
All Rights Reserved
Library of Congress
Catalog Card Number 95-80929
I.S.B.N. 0-8338-0225-9

Dedication

This book is dedicated to the memory of my mother, Corinne Eastman Davis, who left us the beautiful poetry, but then was gone before she could finish her novel; and to my father, Governor Deane Chandler Davis, a master storyteller, who cared enough to protect the mountains, the valley land, and the lakes, rivers, and streams of Vermont.

Prologue

Three men gathered in the small room off the main ballroom.

Outside the closed doors of the carefully guarded room, the five hundred or so guests drank, nibbled on exotic hors d'oeuvres, smiled, mingled, and moved about in the grand tradition of the American cocktail party. Men and women elegantly dressed and coiffured tried to appear unmindful of the flash of cameras. Outward charm and cordiality were a mask for everyone, yet they knew one another well; they were part of Washington. They came from Nebraska and Oregon and Texas and from all over America; many had come with a dream that they would make a difference. But if any of those assembled had descended on Washington with an idea that they would somehow remain unchanged by the town, the heady aura of power quickly dispelled that quixotic notion.

The huge birthday party for one of the United States Senate's favorite octogenarians was taking place at the Capitol Hilton on Connecticut Avenue. To the three men gathered behind closed doors off the main hall the Washington party scene was routine. The memories of the hundreds of similar parties they'd attended were reduced to a blur.

Inside the soundproof room, Alex Konig was addressing two men: one, an older man, white haired, and a longtime figure on the Washington scene; the other, a tall man, equally imposing, and about fifteen years younger.

Konig went on, "... of course the transcendent issue, and our real dilemma, is how to manage the business of the people over a period of time when the standard of living for middle-income Americans is declining. Can a free society truly manage this? No evidence exists suggesting that it can. And of course putting our future on a credit card as Congress and the White House have been doing for years simply has to end or we face collapse.

"We have survived the last ten or fifteen years by diverting people from the real issue — their pocketbooks. It has been done by stirring up issues like school prayer, equal rights for women and gays, the race issue, abortion, flag burning and the like." Alex Konig was lecturing.

In a manner unparalleled in the annals of American politics, Alex Konig had become the most powerful person in Washington never to have been elected to office. The acceptance by the two men of his invitation to meet with him on this evening of celebration was a symbol of the political power Konig had accumulated and a further signal that he was ready to harness his considerable resources to use that power.

Alex Konig had sky-rocketed onto the American political scene seemingly from nowhere. A self-made billionaire, he made his first fortune with a small development company which over time branched out into both commercial and residential real estate. He recognized early that the price of land world wide was on the way up, and Konig had the patience to wait and add to his acquisitions when prices stalled or fell temporarily.

From this position of financial strength he then identified blue-chip American businesses that had become inefficient, top-heavy, weak, and increasingly non-competitive on the international scene. In the grand style of other American corporate raiders he moved to gain control of a number of such American companies; he succeeded, and then by selling off or closing down weak divisions, and taking advantage of all available tax loopholes, he made an even greater fortune than he had already accumulated while the stock market showed its approval.

All the while, Konig was nurturing a benign image. He purposefully avoided the notoriety lavished on other ego-driven corporate raiders. When he was playing hardball with the executives of companies that were his targets, or with communities that would become devastated as a result of corporate decisions to close down or sell off major divisions without notice, he saw to it that other people received the blame. Publicly he skillfully disassociated himself from the less than pleasant aspects of free-enterprise buccaneering.

He created a non-profit corporation known as For the People, which established national grant and loan programs to small businesses and entrepreneurs as a way of demonstrating faith in the free enterprise system. The favorable publicity he received for this effort more than matched the resources he committed to the project. For a while he was a favorite of the Sunday supplements and even found himself featured in one of the weekly news magazines, a periodical, it might be added, in which he had a sizeable stock holding.

It was about this time that with a minimum of publicity he combined the forces of several of his and other corporate entities, both foreign and domestic, and established Multi-Corps International which in a very short time became the largest business conglomerate in the world.

He received a presidential appointment to serve on a commission established to make future recommendations on the financing of health care. He was often asked to testify before legislative committees in

Washington. He accepted every opportunity and began to hone his public skills, some said with an eye to running for the presidency.

Konig never considered a run for the presidency. While information about his childhood had been sketchy — he claimed to have been brought up in a foster home in Los Angeles — he knew that if his political future were riding on the information researchers would easily uncover the fact he had been born in Hungary and was thus constitutionally precluded from serving in the nation's top office. As a foundling in native Hungary Konig had survived his early years through the use of his wits, and had in fact taken the prideful name of Konig for himself at age ten. He found his way to the United States by fleeing Hungary following the revolution of 1956.

Within the past two years Konig had written and published a book entitled, Econo-Democracy, A Plan for America. *The book spoke to the concerns of the average citizen, offering a unique if not well described theory of how to solve America's nagging economic problems. The book was neatly tailored to the urgency many Americans were feeling about their country, and by simply expressing these concerns, Konig's book received widespread attention. People wanted to believe what Konig promised, namely that a country that had lost its way, could, by returning to the old values, be redeemed. The book seemed to have answers — and revived the promise of the American dream.*

Konig's thesis was that modern nations were of their nature inefficient, incompetent, and in most matters not up to the task of managing the business of the people. Ultimately these nations, left alone, would doom the world. His book went on to describe recent research demonstrating that economies of scale were not subject, as used to be held as gospel, to any principle of diminishing returns. Konig's premise was that the future of mankind rested with the growth of massive international conglomerates unfettered by government. The book suggested that as international business enterprise became more pervasive and more powerful, nations would increasingly be unable to undertake the wild political gambles that so often led to instability, and thus to war. With financial and political power vested in massive business enterprise rather than government, war would become an impossibility. The petty arguments of nations would be subsumed under business planning, and war as a means of stimulating the economy of a single nation, or propping up a wavering leader, would be a thing of the past. Business interests would be paramount and nations would no longer be allowed to carry on the destructive international relations which they had so poorly managed in the past.

To move toward what he described as an econo-democracy in the near term, Konig prescribed giving the American President vast new powers to deal immediately with the problems of the deficit, restrictive environmental controls, the dangerously weak dollar, and the drain on the treasury engendered by Social Security, Medicare and other social legislation. To do this, of course, would require a very different Congress than currently was guiding the nation.

In a little-noticed epilogue to the book, Konig announced that he was forming a new organization that would assist in carrying this message. Borrowing from the name of his charitable grant-in-aid program, For the People, *he named the new organization,* For the People — Now.

Reactions to the book were mixed, though better than one might have anticipated. The persistent lethargy of the American economy, and the inability of any administration to reduce crime, unemployment, or to halt the deterioration of American cities created an atmosphere where new ideas were given license. One critic said, "Konig's book is the most globally significant new idea in the latter half of the twentieth century," and "a vision that must be pursued ... technology is taking nations, democracies and otherwise, toward an uncertain future with poverty, unemployment, and instability becoming a way of life across the globe."

Strong reactions of an opposite kind came from those who saw in Konig's book "a kind of dressed-up fascism, that was nothing new at all, but something that had failed time and time again, leaving misery in its wake."

On this spring evening in Washington, with the scent of cherry blossoms in the air, Konig had invited the two men sitting before him to this meeting for the purpose of revealing to them a part of what he had planned for the future.

He continued, "Gentlemen, we don't have to agree on everything in order to agree on some things. I approve of your program to reduce the deficit. Without this, and it will take years of course, there is nothing good for America down the road. But you and I know that, with the present composition of Congress, you cannot pass a program that increases consumption taxes, reduces environmental controls, eases the capital gains burden, reduces Social Security and health benefits for the elderly, and encourages off-shore drilling for oil and the exploitation of our other natural resources.

"In addition, if you expect to get the job done, you need to create an environment that will make it possible, even necessary, for the president to take unto himself vast new powers, powers critical to managing the economy, but unheard of in the past.

"You know with the Congress we now have, all of this is impossible. What I plan to do is intervene to assist those candidates running for Congress that, based on my research, will support deficit reduction legislation, if necessary by creating emergency powers for the president. Candidates who will support strong executive action are critical. I will also target for defeat candidates who would most likely resist all or important parts of the deficit reduction program, as well as those who would resist the transfer of important powers to the chief executive."

As Konig held forth, the two men said nothing, casting only an occasional glance at one another. Finally the younger man spoke up: "F.D.R. tried it back in the thirties. He tried to take extra-ordinary executive powers to get the country out of the depression and the Supreme Court ..."

"Bah, the Supreme Court! A very different time. The legal system in this country is a joke — attorneys vie for the riches of each other's clients, the poor go unrepresented, and a string of second-class appointments has reduced the court to a debating society on abortion. These days if the president assumed new authority, by the time a challenge was brought before the Court it would be too late. People want strong leadership. Ninety per cent of the public wouldn't care a whit for the niceties of its legality. It would be too popular to thwart; the people are desperate to see public policy get off dead center; this Court would never have the courage to act."

"What do you propose to do that will give us a Congress we can work with?" inquired the older man.

Konig stared at the others a long moment, and just as a brilliant professor might dismiss students who were not up to a given task, he replied, "I propose to take off the gloves, and do what has to be done to win."

"You mean ..."

Again Konig interrupted the older man, "What I propose is a program of direct intervention. I will undertake whatever actions are necessary to discredit candidates that need to be defeated."

"I don't think we need to ask our friend Alex any more," interrupted the younger man. "He is not asking us; he is informing us, and I appreciate that."

A short time later the two men left; Konig remained seated, reflecting on the conversation just concluded. They had agreed with everything he said, as he knew they would, for it served their interest. Responding in self-interest with scarcely a nod to ethical considerations was second nature to most politicians. Konig had counted on that.

Powerful as they were, the two men who left the room had no real understanding of the far-flung resources that Konig could bring to bear on the enterprise he had briefly outlined to them. Through the years Konig had made friends and contacts throughout the federal establishment, including the courts, the federal criminal justice enforcement system, the CIA, as well as a host of governors and mayors throughout the nation. Along with these major figures, and for Konig's purposes of almost equal importance, he was acquainted at lesser levels of government with people whom he could use for some of the messier, more unpleasant undertakings he needed to accomplish. These things would be done, of course, in ways that made it impossible to trace them back to him. All of it had been years in the building.

This evening's meeting would not be the end of it. Konig, while seeking a sympathetic Congress, had little hope that the current cast of characters occupying the White House had the wisdom or the ability to carry the day on deficit reduction. He knew, too, that the voters, disillusioned once more by inaction, would look next time beyond traditional political boundaries for leadership.

Alex Konig would be ready. For the People — Now *was ready.. to act when the word came down.* For the People — Now *had money and a voter data base second to none. Perhaps most important he planned to instill in this organization a missionary zeal and an a religious fervor that historically had always proven necessary in times of revolutionary change. If the country failed to follow this plan, Konig knew it would be only a matter of time before they would turn to him to lead the country out of the morass in which it found itself.*

It was all in the plan.

Contents

THE
DUVAL
CONSPIRACY

Chapter One

Ben Willey left the restaurant and drove to the lot in front of the supermarket. He parked the Lincoln in the center of the lot and got out. The store was located off Main Street in the center of Brunswick, Maine. It was after nine o'clock and the warm summer day was at long last yielding to darkness. Willful June moths attracted by the overpowering neon lights were frantically thrashing about, noisily battering the window. Willey entered the store with the intention of buying only basic necessities — milk, coffee, and orange juice. Later he left with a large bag, having succumbed to the merchandising prowess of the food chain, fifty-five dollars poorer, but with food for the freezer and some of his favorite tiny rib lamb chops.

Walking from the store back to his car, he noticed a gray Dodge van that had pulled up alongside and parked next to his Lincoln.

Closer than it should be.

Glancing about uneasily he shifted the groceries to his left arm and walked around the back of the van in order to see the license plate. Alarmed at his finding, he felt a quick knife of fear. His pulse quickened.

Virginia plates! Damn! He hadn't wanted to see Virginia. Or Maryland. Or D.C. That could mean he had company. He wasn't ready for company.

There was no sign of anyone inside the van. Willey squeezed between the two vehicles, digging in his pocket for his car keys as he edged in. He remembered a trick he had learned, and he juggled the bag of groceries and then held his keys in such a way that the end of one of the keys jutted out between his second and third finger. If anyone were to attack him, he could now slash at them using the keys between his fingers as a weapon. Or so he hoped. It was all he had.

He unlocked the driver's side door quickly, squeezed into the Lincoln, and shut the door quickly simultaneously snapping the power lock.

Filling out the retirement papers at the office, closing down his town house, loading the car with all it could carry, and the uneventful trip north had all seemed much like a vacation. But alert now, Willey once again became deadly serious.

Could they have gotten onto him already? Impossible, he reassured himself. If the van was on "company" business, then they would have had to be watching him for several days.

He inserted the key in the ignition for a moment, then paused.

Perspiration broke out on his forehead. He looked at the empty van again. A bomb — maybe rigged to his car? No, that didn't make sense.

He turned the key.

The Lincoln started, purring smoothly.

Ben Willey inhaled deeply and blew out as though exhausted.

He looked around in all directions and began to back up. Easing the front of the car past the back of the van, he slipped the car into drive and pulled out heading toward the parking lot exit that led onto Main Street.

Walking toward him as he headed out of the lot was a young couple with three small children trailing behind. The man sported an inch-long beard, and was dressed in cutoffs and a dirty T-shirt. The young woman wore oversized shorts and a wild shirt celebrating a rock band Willey had never heard of. After they passed, Willey pulled the Lincoln to the side of the lot — stopped, positioning himself so he could observe the van through the side mirror.

The children ran ahead to the van and waited impatiently. The man unlocked the rear door, sliding it back so the children could scramble in. Then he went to the front door and got in, reaching across as he did to unlock the other door so the young woman could enter.

Still Willey waited, the Lincoln idling. The van started up, backed out, swung around and drove out of the lot oblivious to the now thoroughly alert Ben Willey.

Moments later, Willey also exited onto Main Street and drove the short mile and a half back to his condominium, angry that his imagination had overwhelmed his judgement, but nonetheless convinced not to waste any more time.

He needed to get the envelopes he had brought from Washington into safe hands where they could do some good.

Fifteen hours earlier, shortly after six o'clock that morning, Ben Willey had backed the fully packed Lincoln out of the garage at his town house in Alexandria, Virginia, and into the heat and humidity of the morning. Within minutes he was on I-95 North out of Washington D.C. The Lincoln warmed easily to the challenge of the trip; the air-conditioning held the sticky, ninety degree heat at bay.

Willey had always liked the trip north. He'd traveled this way many times. If he wanted, he could cover the almost seven hundred mile trip without ever leaving I-95. But he preferred to by-pass Boston traffic by picking up I-84 at New Haven, Connecticut, passing through Hartford and connecting with the Mass Pike. On the Pike a ways, he then exited onto I-290 following that until he reached I-495 around Boston. I-495 ran into I-95 north of "Beantown" just past Salisbury Beach.

He'd taken only what he could carry in the car. The movers would be coming later for the rest. He'd have to return to Washington to arrange for that and to sign the papers when his town house was sold, but for all practical purposes, Ben Willey had left the District for good.

On Sunday night, when he loaded the car with the suitcases and boxes he was bringing with him, he slid the three thick manila envelopes under the carpeting in the trunk of the car, and piled suitcases and boxes over and around them. He knew that hiding them there wouldn't fool anyone who knew how to search a car, but it made him feel better to be cautious. Eventually they would find out what he had done — but not right away. Not before he reached Brunswick anyway, he reassured himself, chuckling as he realized that he, the serious, impassive Ben Willey, was not immune from a little whistling in the dark.

Out on the Jersey Turnpike heading north that morning, Willey glanced at the gas gauge which showed the tank a quarter full. He pulled the big Lincoln into the right lane, and a mile or so later spotted one of the look-alike rest stops/gas stations located every few miles on America's major highways. He checked the mirror as he pulled off, taking special note of any other vehicles exiting at the same time. But neither the passengers in the battered pickup truck driven by a very old, very black farmer, nor the young woman with four children in the back of a mini-van appeared to pay any attention to him. But he had to check.

No one could know about the materials in the envelope. Not yet.

He parked the car and got out and looked around. He stretched his five foot nine inch frame, feeling the usual aches and pains of a man in his mid-fifties who had been sitting in a car for a couple of hours. Willey was balding and had a round face framed by glasses that at times gave him an owlish look when he was concentrating. While his body had begun to thicken through the middle, he hadn't gained any weight in ten years. He grabbed the coffee thermos from the car, flipped the power lock securing all four doors, and headed inside.

Back on I-95 with the car full of gasoline and the thermos full of coffee, Willey turned on the radio, and adjusted the dial to where he was able to pick up classical music on his favorite New York radio station. He set the cruise control at sixty-two miles an hour, settled back and was pleased to find the the New York station playing Mozart — one of the early symphonies he couldn't identify right away. But Ben Willey figured that if on Monday morning of your first day of retirement, you find Mozart playing on the radio, then all is right with the world — for, he reflected, there is no bad Mozart!

Retirement. He thought he'd feel different, like he'd finished something, or arrived somewhere — attained a destination. But the only feeling he had right now was a feeling of relief.

Of what he wasn't sure, even with the information he'd put together and placed in the three padded envelopes. In the hands of the right people there was no telling what might happen. The Agency was like an octopus, lots of tentacles.

Brunswick, Maine is a neat, orderly town located about thirty miles north of Portland. The centerpiece of this pretty New England town is Bowdoin College, a picture-book New England college with a beautiful campus, huge trees, and staid stone buildings that registered permanence, stability, and as evidenced by the spacious residences in town, old money.

Brunswick is also where, at the age of nineteen, Ben Willey met and fell in love with a young girl named Kathleen Farr. Kathleen's family, who lived in West Hartford, Connecticut, was visiting for the summer. Kathleen was a couple of years older than Ben and during that wonderful summer in the early fifties she won him in every way; teaching him to talk of himself, to trust, and to make love. In the fall, the Ben Willey who returned to Burlington for his junior year at the University of Vermont was a changed young man. But in less than a month, he received a letter from Miss Farr. It seemed that for her their summer affair had been a mistake. She wrote that she had become reunited with a former love and hoped that Ben's memories were as warm as hers would always be. He never spoke of her again, and withdrew within the personality of the shy, brilliant young man he had always been.

Willey spent most of his career in Washington and decided long ago that when it was time to retire he would return to Brunswick, Maine; he could do almost everything he liked and still live in the small coastal town. If he wanted to travel, the highways were good and the Portland airport would be just a few miles away. Boston, New York, and Montreal, Canada were all within easy reach.

Following his graduation from the University of Vermont, Ben Willey pursued an advanced degree at Princeton. During this time he was recruited by and joined the CIA, where he would spend his entire federal career. In the beginning he served time in the field, including stints in

Brazil, Colombia, and Argentina, all the while learning the complexities of information-gathering.

When he returned to Washington he was assigned to the Special Documents Division, and within five years had become the Chief. He managed documents necessary to agents, contractors and free-lancers that could not be obtained elsewhere. These included false papers, doctored photographs, and a host of other materials necessary to sustain field operations and "special field projects:" the highly secret interventions into the political affairs of other countries that some members of the intelligence community found so intriguing.

A short while ago, when Willey's superiors had approached him regarding early retirement, they made it sound like a bonus, which financially it was. They explained to Willey and hundreds of other Agency professionals that the early retirement program was being implemented for cost control reasons. But Willey knew the other reason. The real reason.

Vietnam, Watergate, Iran-contra were a sad legacy for the time Ben Willey committed to the Agency and to his country as he saw it. During his years there, he managed to establish and maintain strict rules and procedures for the Special Documents Division. Because he ran a tight ship and could deliver what was needed, when it was needed, he had, over the years, become well-known to Agency professionals. If someone wanted documents of any kind, Willey required that they have authorization to obtain them. Otherwise it was no-go, for Willey played by the book. Along with other career people, he resisted the ideological push and pull of the ever-changing political leadership of the Agency. For most of his years at the Agency, this had been possible.

More recently, things had changed. The shenanigans of a now deceased, and thoroughly discredited director had left the true professionals caught between the terrible choice of breaking the law or of being branded disloyal to Agency goals. During the late director's political reign, the Agency became rampant with animosity and distrust even among old friends.

The scandalous Iran-contra fiasco led the director's office to terminate most of its clever little operations which had bypassed the established systems of Agency approval. Willey, and other old timers had been encouraged for a while.

But with the new director, Bill Richards, the dirty business had begun again. Richards was widely supported in and out of the Agency. Soon Willey began to receive requests from "upstairs" to ignore a necessary approval, to fashion or provide fake materials without appropriate accompanying documentation, or to provide such items for people or companies not authorized to receive them. With or without the new director's knowledge, people in his office were once again back to mucking around in operations.

As before when this had happened, Willey insisted when asked for special favors that he know enough about the operation to be sure of its legality. If other systems of approval were breaking down, Ben Willey was determined that his division would not be involved. As usual this created tension between his office and the director's office as well as conflict with political appointees. After a while it was clear that top brass wanted someone serving in his position who would "go along to get along," a phrase that Willey detested.

But with all his best efforts he knew he was being compromised, drawn in whether he liked it or not. To the surprise of everyone, when top Agency officials approached Willey again with an early retirement offer, he accepted.

Arriving in Brunswick in the early evening Ben Willey had driven directly to the condo he had leased. He had made the arrangements while visiting in Maine the previous winter, knowing that retirement was not far off.

A developer undertook the project a couple of years earlier on a prized piece of property close to both the campus and downtown, and Willey had been the first customer. He selected the far end unit with a heavily wooded area in back. It would be a secluded location, but near enough to walk to the library, downtown, and the summer music theater located on the college campus.

Willey drove through the parking lot and noted that another unit, one in the center of the complex, was now occupied. The parking lot itself was recently paved, with the landscaping mostly completed. To Willey the grounds appeared scalped, artificially neat as though waiting to grow up. Tools and equipment in evidence on previous visits were now gone.

It was still daylight when he pulled up in front of his condominium. He had parked the Lincoln, ignoring the bags and boxes that needed to be taken in, and gone up the steps, bringing only his briefcase and now anxious to see his new home. Slipping the key in the lock, he opened the door and entered.

Uneasy for a moment, thinking of the three envelopes buried beneath the bags in the trunk, he paused, wondering if he should retrieve them before he did anything else. They were safe enough where they were he decided. He searched for the light switch, found it, and snapped it on. He sniffed the air, but the people he had hired to furnish and set up the apartment had done a good job. No hints of mustiness or stale tobacco smoke were in evidence, only the fresh smell of paint and plaster.

The layout was thoroughly functional, as he remembered. He still liked it and congratulated himself on his choice of a place to live. There were two bedrooms, a bath and a half, a living room that flowed into a dining room, and a small kitchen. Willey admired once again the ornate chandelier which hung over the dining room table. Little things sell real estate, he reflected; the chandelier was one of the first things that had attracted him to the place, by lending — he whimsically reflected at the time — an old world feel to modern American living.

He checked all the rooms and found them prepared as he had asked. He'd opened the cupboards; dishes had been put in place, but no food. He told the maid he would stock them himself. He wished he had picked up coffee and milk on the way in. Not to worry. He needed to eat dinner anyway, since he seldom ate much while traveling.

On this initial visit he had postponed unloading the car and instead hopped back in the Lincoln and headed into Brunswick to pick up a few groceries and to search out his favorite Italian restaurant conveniently located in the center of Brunswick.

He had feasted on antipasto, followed this with a delicious serving of an unusual veal dish accompanied by a side of very thin linguini, fresh Italian bread with more butter than was his custom, and topped it all off with strong coffee and dark chocolate ice cream. Sometimes, he reflected as he leaned back in the chair, when one dines out not everything is exactly what you hoped for; but occasionally, only occasionally, everything is just right.

Last week on Friday Ben Willey had called Charlie Gleason to ensure that the three copies were secured in the padded envelopes and ready for Willey to pick up. Gleason had replied that everything was ready to go, or, as he put it, "I wouldn't let you down now, would I, guy?"

Charlie Gleason had operated his photography and special services shop barely on the right side of the law for twenty years. As a young man Gleason had gone to jail for extortion. Slight and wiry, Gleason was no match for the thugs he ran into while in jail. He was bounced around, beaten up and raped several times. Charlie Gleason didn't like jail. A year and a half later he was back on the street. He decided he wasn't going to go back behind bars regardless of what it took. He opened a small photo shop near his home on thirteenth Street, in downtown Washington, D.C. The sign over the door and on the window advertised film developing, enlargements, passport photos, and special printing services.

He was barely surviving until Ben Willey came along. But Gleason was the kind of man Willey was looking for, someone outside the Agency he could work with, treat well, and hopefully, over time earn the man's confidence and trust. That was what happened. Over the years Willey engaged Gleason's services by subcontracting to him many of the documents and photos that needed to be created or altered. Willey also dealt with other subcontractors, but Gleason got the bulk of this kind of business. It worked well for both of them, and if it didn't make Charlie Gleason one hundred percent honest, he stayed clean enough to remain out of jail.

When Willey walked into Gleason's shop that last time before he left Washington, he was greeted with the familiar, gruff, "How aw yuh?"

Willey nodded, and again asked, "Everything ready?"

Gleason went into the back room and returned with three large manila envelopes and put them on the counter. "Send the bill the same place?"

"Yeah, I've arranged it — there'll be no problem."

Willey had been with the CIA for thirty years, in charge of his division for the last twenty-five. Gleason inquired about the bill because Willey had told him two weeks before that he would be retiring, and that someone else would be coming by to do business with him. Gleason wanted to know more. Willey tried to explain that a reorganization was underway at the Agency and Gleason would have to wait to find out who he'd be dealing with.

Charlie Gleason didn't know about reorganizations. He didn't have a clue what went on in large bureaucracies. Willey's explanations meant nothing to him. Earlier Willey had told him not to worry, " They can't get along without you!"

Gleason only grunted.

And began to worry.

Chapter Two

"Jack, what's the picture on that award dinner on Friday?" Congressman Alan Duval was calling from Washington to ask his top aide in Vermont about a forthcoming dinner at which the congressman was scheduled to receive a special award.

Duval would invariably call Jack Marston before attending the various events to which he was invited. Marston and his small staff attended to constituent and political chores for Duval in Vermont. "What's the picture" was code for how large a crowd could be expected, what was the political composition of the crowd, was the press expected and if so what would they be asking about, were there special problems associated with the event, and were there any people apt to be on hand who would need special handling. Occasionally, Marston would check with his sources to determine if demonstrators might be on hand, and if so he would plan how Alan Duval should respond to them. Sometimes he would need to find a way for Duval to avoid them altogether when entering and exiting an event. It all depended who was demonstrating and what particular axe they had to grind. Observers often noted the easy matter-of-fact way Duval dealt with such confrontations, but it was a professionalism born of a lot of practice and the advance work of Jack Marston and his staff that made it possible to face each situation of this kind without committing any major gaffes — gaffes which the media and especially TV would appreciatively and dutifully bring into the living room of Vermonters.

"It'll be a love-in, Alan." Marston said, replying to his boss's familiar question, "Should be some decent press, there's nothing else going on, and the *Burlington News* will send a photographer to a Friday night event if they don't have to travel too far from downtown Burlington."

The familiar joke among Vermont politicians and their "flacks," whose job it was to get their bosses good press coverage, was that if the world came to an end after twelve o'clock on Saturday, Vermonters would have to wait until Monday to get the story. Such was the frugal reputation of the once-proud *Burlington News* which a few years earlier had been acquired by a highly profitable national newspaper chain. The focus of the local paper had shifted to the bottom line of the financial statement and local news suffered a loss of coverage while the paper, protesting loudly to the contrary, abandoned any sense of community responsibility. Management, intentionally or otherwise, had destroyed the institutional memory of the paper by transferring, retiring, or otherwise ridding the paper of its best reporters. Burlington's television stations did little better, and saw fit to push the "hold" button at noon on Saturday, returning to the real world on Monday.

On Friday night, Congressman Alan Duval was to receive the Vermont Leadership Award from the prestigious "Vermont Way Council." It was the first such award the council had ever given. The Vermont Way Council had been set up as a permanent organization to carry on the work started by a special commission of the Vermont legislature, which prior to his entry into elective politics had been chaired by Alan Duval. It was from this position that Duval had gained state-wide prominence.

Information on the approaching awards dinner had been provided to Duval through staff memos which he read thoroughly. But like every politician of this and other generations, Duval hated surprises. To avoid them he always checked his sources, verifying his information in every way, and never relying on a single source.

"Anything new on Meacham?"

"I heard he's going to travel around the state in one of those travel homes. He's found a large one — twenty-six feet, I heard," replied Marston leaning back in his chair, his right foot resting on a drawer partially pulled away from the desk for just that purpose.

Ex-Governor Brad Meacham who everyone thought had retired from the political wars was called out of retirement to run against Duval in his bid for the U.S. Senate. The seat was soon to be made vacant with the retirement of its venerable incumbent, eighty-four year old Austin Grover. According to most observers Meacham would have his work cut out for him.

Duval had provided Vermonters concerned with the environment with a special leadership prior to going to Washington, and his work since his election to Congress had only enhanced his reputation. Knowledgeable insiders in the state were unanimous in predicting his elevation to the United States Senate in the fall election.

Jack Marston, special assistant in Vermont to Congressman Duval, was a square-faced, solidly built man around five feet ten, with slightly graying brown hair. Now in his early fifties, Marston knew his way around the state and around Vermont politics. He'd grown accustomed to the probing banter of his boss, and even enjoyed getting the last minute calls from Duval, most often while Duval was at the airport waiting for his plane to be announced for boarding. Duval wanted to know what was going on, and it was Marston's job to keep him informed.

"Jack, how are the crowds reacting to Meacham?"

"I've seen him a couple of times — he's no better than he ever was. That's his major problem, always has been — can't stir the crowd. The party knew that when they asked him to run. He's better in smaller groups — he knows the issues, especially state issues. They picked the right guy, he's tough, experienced, and he won't help us by making any big mistakes. In fact, their whole idea is to be ready to pounce if you blow one or screw up in any way. They know they can't win otherwise."

"Yeah ... well make sure our campaign people and the volunteers don't get too cocky," replied Duval, challenging the good news as successful politicians often do when the source of the good news comes from within their own organization. Duval was ever wary that an incipient complacency might be setting in. Pausing for a moment Duval continued, "Jack, the numbers have been moving ..., some of the others don't need to know, but you do. I've slipped six points since March."

"On favorability? Did you measure head to head against Meacham?"

"Favorability. Still fifty-eight to thirty-eight against Meacham. A lot of guys would kill for those numbers, huh Jack?"

Marston had turned in his chair and was gazing out at the lake. The news didn't particularly surprise him. A six point drop in favorability was something to think about, but early on Duval had been in the high seventies and couldn't be expected to maintain those lofty numbers until the election. In addition the economy had turned soft in Vermont and that always worked against incumbents. Marston had been around long enough to know that the concern he heard in Duval's voice was a more serious finding than the numbers themselves. He trusted Duval's instincts. Marston often said to others that the best political brain on staff was the congressman himself. "They are good numbers — but Alan, you've been out among the natives the last three weekends, how does it feel to you?"

"I thought I had more depth than I do ..."

"People want to vote for a simpler world, Alan, and no politician alive can deliver on that, that's why you guys have to fight just to hold on to what you have."

"Well, Leland and Company say I'm still a winner ..."

"By what?"

"They say I'll come in six to ten points over Meacham."

"Damn — that means you'll be slipping some more and the press will be running stories on your deteriorating poll numbers all summer."

"That's the real problem. It'll bring him money, people, and worst of all he'll have some momentum. I worry that our consultants at Leland don't understand what momentum can do in Vermont."

"Alan, you know what I've always lobbied for — "

"Yeah, plan B. You were right, Jack, it's time to broaden the base. Time to get beyond the enviros and pay a little attention to our other friends," Duval conceded.

"I'm glad the Washington experts finally agree ... it takes that crowd a long time to figure it out!" Marston, who had little respect for Washington-based political consultants, leaned back in his chair and smiled to himself. He wasn't really worried about him losing the election, but he had always urged Duval to take a more inclusive approach with other constituencies. Duval's support was broad, but so far he had no passionate loyalists except among the environmentalists. "A mile wide and inch deep," one pundit had quipped while commenting on the depth of Duval's strength.

The environmentalists were in place — they'd lay in front of tanks in the street on Duval's behalf, Marston mused. Other groups remained luke-warm. The business community, the bankers, construction trade unions and the farmers had never felt they received enough attention. Educators and the social service community also were uneasy about Duval's less than wholehearted endorsements. Duval, however, had always believed that the rewards of special interest politics were suspect, arguing that the lives and the point of view of most voters cut across a variety of different concerns. He believed that he could best serve Vermonters by looking broadly at the general interest. So far his fresh approach had worked, helped along by some imaginative political organizing and a superb record of constituent service.

But now the economy was softening, the markets were nervous, the huge national debt held interest rates high just as it had for years. Hostility was building against incumbents. Duval, while not an incumbent of a Senate seat, was the third member of the Vermont delegation in Washington. Earlier in the campaign his political consultants had urged him to promote his Washington experience in his advertising. D.C.-based consultants always put more value on Washington experience than did voters in the hinterlands. Now with the economy cooling, Washington "insiders" were more likely to be identified by voters as the problem, and surely not the solution.

"Alan, we look forward to seeing you, and with the rave notices you're going to get from that award dinner they'll never lay a glove on you." Marston hoped his enthusiasm would be contagious.

Nobody wanted a candidate losing confidence.

Chapter Three

Following Ben Willey's Friday visit, Charlie Gleason brooded all weekend. A tough weekend; a long weekend.

Too many cigarettes, and too much booze.

Gleason liked to say, "Mrs. Gleason didn't have no dumb kids." This Monday morning he wasn't so sure.

"Somebody'll be in touch with you," Willey had said on Friday, the same thing he had said earlier.

"Yeah, like when?" Gleason said aloud to the empty shop.

When Gleason had started doing business with Ben Willey nearly twenty years ago, Gleason correctly figured that the Agency had very deep pockets. He saw early on that Ben Willey was as good as money in the bank if he, Gleason, didn't screw it up. No second class work, no late deliveries, and no loose talk. So Gleason tried; he did everything he could to keep Willey happy — didn't pad bills; did it right. And it worked. Building and maintaining this mutual loyalty was one of the few things Charlie Gleason ever did right. And because of it, he made a nice living and stayed out of jail.

When Willey had first talked with Gleason many years ago, he had insisted on being Gleason's only contact with the Agency. If Gleason got a call from anyone else in the Agency Willey wanted to know about it. Gleason was to call him. This happened a couple of times over the years, and each time Gleason had notified Willey. For that Willey rewarded Gleason's loyalty, and steered increased amounts of business his way.

But now everything was changing.

Willey never talked much anyway about business or anything else, but now that he was retiring, Gleason found himself on Monday morning tired, hung over and without a contact at the Agency that had provided fifty per cent of his business.

"Someone'll be in touch with you ... Bullshit!" Gleason said aloud as he paced the floor of his shop early on Monday morning, the smoke from the ever-present Camel cigarette hanging heavy in the air. The only other person Gleason knew at the Agency was Edgar Steele. He knew Willey didn't trust Steele. In the envelopes Willey had picked up Friday had been copies of the stuff that Steele had Gleason produce. As Willey always told him to do, Gleason called right away and told him of Steele's orders. Gleason could see that Willey had been onto Steele for some time.

Now everything was changing. There'd be no Willey to take care of him.

The way Gleason figured it, he did everything Willey asked — and now the bastard had gone off and he'd never see him again.

Gleason pulled a bottle out of the bottom of the old desk and poured himself three fingers in an orange juice glass. He tossed it off without a chaser and shuddered. He lit another cigarette from the stub he held between his thumb and first finger, sat down and stared at the wall, unconsciously rubbing the stubble of his now nearly white beard.

Goddamn Steele, the guy was a real talker. Gleason wondered, was he a big shot or a nobody. Smooth bastard, dressed sharp, but that didn't mean shit.

The more he thought about it, the more he felt Willey had let him down. He poured another drink. Again to no one in particular, he said aloud, "He could have at least given me a name."

Acting on impulse — something he had fought against all his life — Charlie Gleason dialed Edgar Steele at the special number Steele had left for him.

"State Department." When Gleason asked for Steele a special operator told him that Steele would call back.

Phones at the CIA are invariably answered this way. It is impossible for the average person to telephone the CIA and have anyone answer "CIA."

When Steele returned the call, Gleason said impulsively, "We got to meet — right away."

"Okay, after this week I ..."

"No, no. Today — now," said Gleason, his voice rising.

Steele heard it. Fear. "Later today I can ..."

"It's about Ben Willey ... something you don't know about ... a lot you don't know about."

Steele, immediately uneasy, said, "I'll be over in twenty minutes," and hung up.

When Steele arrived a short time later, Gleason locked the front door, grabbed the bottle from the desk, and ushered him into one of the back rooms where he kept his cameras, copiers and other special equipment.

At home in Brunswick, Maine, Professor Herbert Kleinerman was sitting at the beautiful handmade chess table in his den. The table was a gift from a rich young chess enthusiast. Kleinerman had once traveled to Los Angeles to direct a tournament sponsored by a company owned by the young man's family. The table was made of mahogany and the board itself was a parquet of bird's-eye maple and pecan which provided a beautiful contrast between the dark and light squares.

A close friend of Ben Willey's, Herbert Kleinerman had lived in Brunswick for many years. A full professor, he taught political science at Bowdoin specializing in international relations including a much-sought-after course on the history of European foreign policy, 1885 to the present. Kleinerman was also a leading chess theoretician, as well as a noted author of two books on the chess opening, written specifically for tournament players. Because of his calm, even demeanor and worldwide reputation, he was constantly in demand for the role of tournament director at important national and international chess tourneys in North and South America, and in Europe. Willey and Kleinerman became friends through their mutual interest in chess, and both men looked forward to a joint project they had agreed upon years ago, namely to write a book on the history of the royal game. With new information in hand, they hoped through further study and research to clear up some of the errors and omissions that had crept into recent histories.

Sitting quietly before the chess board this Monday evening, Kleinerman was trying once again to establish the theoretical justification for a line in the French Defense that in recent years had fallen out of favor. As a young man he had used the line with the white pieces to gain a win with the international grandmaster, Boris Nabokovsky. That had been over fifty years ago, and for reasons he could never explain, he wanted to see the line used once again in master play. Romantic nonsense, he admitted to himself, but for those who loved chess such romance was understandable, or so his friend Ben Willey had once written in a letter, revealing a side of the man that Kleinerman had never before seen.

The phone rang.

It was Ben Willey.

Kleinerman had been expecting the call. "Wonderful to hear your voice, my old friend." He spoke with the slight German accent he had never lost. "Come over in the morning, I'll have a large pot of the good coffee, perhaps some bagels, eh?" As Kleinerman listened to the response, a slight frown appeared on his face. He then said, "I don't have any commitments until noon — come at nine or nine thirty, and we'll have time. It's good you are in town now, I look forward."

Chapter Four

During his twenty-mile trip home that evening, Jack Marston had been thinking again about Alan Duval's upcoming election. Duval, he knew, was worried over his slippage in the polls and Marston continued to ponder if the worry was justified, or if it was just the insecurity that politicians characteristically exhibit at the beginning of the election cycle.

Congressman Duval had scheduled a seven PM telephone conference call that evening among his key advisors. He wanted to talk about the campaign. Duval was looking for feedback; information, what was going on in the trenches. Washington-based politicos need this like the thirsty need water — perhaps worse, mused Jack Marston. He could think of nothing that had changed, other than the public mood, which was once again getting ugly, jittery. The economy was bad and getting worse. Not a good sign, especially in June of an election year.

The conference call would bring together consultant and pollster Eddie Fine of the Washington based firm of Leland and Company. Fine was located in Vermont and would remain here until the election was held. Also on hand was Bill Camilli, executive director for the state party; John Godine, Duval's campaign manager, and Marlene Brownell, whom Duval successfully recruited as chairperson for the Campaign Finance Committee. While the stated purpose of the conference call was to catch everyone up on campaign plans and information, there was a nagging piece of information that young Bill Camilli had uncovered and insisted on talking about with Duval directly.

And Duval would listen. The characteristics that had made him the person Vermonters wanted in Washington had served him in good stead. Over six feet tall with dark blond hair and a rugged outdoor complexion that would turn a deep red in the cold, his face was perfect for an ad in a hunting magazine. His robust good looks appealed to both men and women. Soft-spoken and seemingly shy, when he spoke about the things that were important to him, his convictions seemed ever the more real. And despite a serious nature, when he broke into laughter his perfectly white teeth and flashing blue eyes made him the instant center of attention.

As soon as he was elected for the first time, five and a half years before, it was obvious to most observers of the political scene that he had been born to it. For over thirty years Vermont has been foremost among the states in the cause for environmental conservation, almost regardless of which political party was in control. Duval had taken it a step further by not only working to preserve the beauty of the state and to encourage open land, but by being able to bring jobs to Vermont — not despite environmental controls, but as a result of Vermont's environmental leadership. Companies were now recognizing that quality-of-life issues were critical to top management as well as other employees and that the quality of life that living in Vermont offered was good for business.

Ten years earlier Duval accepted the job of Chairman of the Vermont Options Commission, a position loaded with a potential to self-destruct. While serving there, he had created the sophisticated computer model called the "Vermont Indicators." The model was capable of projecting the effects of various developmental strategies on aspects of the state's economy, including costs of education, highway, police and infrastructure costs that were a perennial problem in the state budget. Using his computer model, he was able to convince a cross-section of Vermonters and politicians appointed to the Vermont Options Commission that this type of computer modeling was their only hope for managing the present and future conflict inherent between development and the environment.

Duval's followers, and later his campaign planners, quickly seized on the opportunity to label him "Prophet for the Land." This lofty and pretentious slogan with the pun turning on the word "prophet" irritated his opponents, but they were powerless to combat the fact that he had been right — a quality environment would indeed generate quality development and bring the jobs to provide a better life for Vermonters.

Within a short time Duval announced for Congress.

His opponent in the first race was Judson Stearns, a well-known, well-liked Vermonter and a newcomer to politics at age sixty-five. Stearns appeared to be the favorite even three months before the election. But Duval plugged away, never showing discouragement or any indication of giving up. He talked consistently about environmental issues and what they meant to the state. He established a sophisticated voter data base, which he used for fund-raising, targeting voters, and persuasion polling. Perhaps more importantly, Duval was the first politician in Vermont history to use his French-Canadian ancestry to advantage, by coalescing the more than thirty percent minority — the largest in Vermont — into a viable constituent base.

Stearns had not anticipated strong opposition. And as is often the case with successful people who are neophytes in politics, Stearns was afflicted with a deadly sense of noblesse oblige. Three weeks before the election, Stearns' lofty image was tarnished by an in-state banking scandal.

His involvement was minimal and, had he faced it squarely, would have weathered it easily. But his amateur advisors were his final undoing; he tried to cover up, was quickly found out, and his standing in the polls plummeted.

Duval won with sixty per cent of the vote.

Congressman Duval received high marks from the public and the press in his first term. He was re-elected to a second term without serious opposition. From then on it was clear to political observers in the state that his sights were set on the U.S. Senate seat that would become vacant upon the retirement of the venerable Austin Grover. At age eighty-four, after serving six terms, it was virtually certain that Grover would step down.

Other Vermont politicians also began jockeying for the seat. But the favorite on everyone's dance card was the handsome young congressman from St. Albans, Vermont.

Jack Marston approached the turn to the mile-long dead-end road leading home. He felt the same anxiety, the same strange uneasiness that always seemed to appear as he neared his home. It had been that way since Ann died — as though he didn't belong there anymore.

He pulled into the yard, parked, and entered the English-style bungalow. Everything in the living room, indeed, everything in the house was exactly as he left it in the morning. He hadn't gotten used to that. It was as though he was the only person in the world. Nothing had been moved. Nothing. God, how he wished something had moved. Each time he entered the house, he felt like a stranger about to nap on another man's bed. It would be unseemly to get into the bed — to lay on it would perhaps be permissible. So it was with the house these days; he could use it, but never get into it. Ann and Jack had decided to buy the house the first time they saw it. It had always been "theirs," somehow it could never just be his own.

He put water in the kettle, set it on the stove and grabbed the instant coffee from the shelf — he never used to drink instant coffee. When the kettle whistled he poured the water onto the coffee crystals, stirred the potion, sniffed it, then set it back down and got milk from the refrigerator. He chuckled at himself and his preoccupation with such minutia. In the old days he would have made the coffee unaware of the process.

Picking up the portable telephone, he took his coffee and went outdoors to sit in the yard to wait for the conference call, drink the coffee, and probably, as he well knew, fall asleep. He sat a few feet in front of the cottage and looked down at the little pond located at the end of a short incline, a hundred and fifty feet away. Picture book. That's how he thought of it. It was one of the major reasons they had bought the place over twenty years ago. He noticed the vines climbing up the side of the cottage and the perennials gone wild from lack of attention. In another year the once carefully tended shrubs and flowers would have to be subject to some serious gardening.

Marston set the cup and saucer on the ground, enjoying for the moment the pleasant Vermont summer evening, the sun still high in the sky and a slight breeze keeping the heat at bay. He put his head back to rest and waited for the call. He dozed.

Chapter Five

Herbert Kleinerman lived in a large Tudor home adjacent to the Bowdoin campus. The house was larger than he and Greta needed, now that there were just the two of them. Their only son lived on the West Coast and was teaching at UCLA.

Less than a mile and a half away in his new home, Ben Willey had risen early, foregoing breakfast except for a glass of orange juice. He knew his friend Kleinerman would provide more than enough to eat as he loved to make a production out of grinding and serving coffee, accompanied always with bagels and cream cheese.

The bright morning sun greeted Willey. He squinted as he trotted down the steps of his condo, briefcase in hand. It was a short distance to his old friend's home. Robins and a variety of other lively birds encouraged by the warmth of the morning sun signaled their importance as Willey cut across the campus. Lawnmowers were already noisily crisscrossing the open green, leaving patterns in the grass, the special scent of the cuttings in the air; fresh symbols that another summer season was underway.

When he arrived at the Kleinerman's, Willey was greeted warmly by his long-time friends. Also as she so often did, Greta disappeared soon after he arrived, leaving the two men alone. Willey loved the house. It had that wonderful old world quality, as though it had always been here. The wonderful message of permanence, so often sought, so seldom achieved. Kleinerman went to the kitchen with Willey following behind, got out the special French roast coffee they both loved, reached for the coffee grinder and preparations were under way.

As the smell of the coffee began to fill the kitchen, Kleinerman sliced fresh bagels and placed several of them alongside a crock of cream cheese. He cleared a small table in the den to make room for everything. On the nearby table the traditional Staunton style chess pieces stood erect as though waiting for play.

The den had changed little since Willey's last visit. One side of the room was devoted entirely to chess literature. Kleinerman had installed some modern office equipment, including a computer, a rather large copying machine, and the newest addition, a fax machine. Willey wondered why his friend wanted to clutter the beautiful den with these machines, but kept his thoughts to himself.

In silence, Kleinerman arranged things so they could sit comfortably, only occasionally glancing at his friend as he moved a chair, adjusted the light, and tidied the desk. He sat down, leaned forward to look closely at Willey, and said, "Are you really ready to retire after all those years — no more connections there?"

Despite his slight accent words came easier to Kleinerman than they ever would to Ben Willey. Following this question Kleinerman picked up his coffee, sipped it, leaned back in his chair to wait for Willey to speak, willing to let the silence dominate.

It did for a while. Willey sat without speaking, staring straight ahead, his systematic mind ordering his thoughts. Then he leaned forward, placing the coffee aside, and began to speak. "It was time for me to retire, time to leave the Agency. No question. So much has changed, so much is wrong," he paused. "Pardon the history lesson, Herbert, but I've now lived long enough to know that history is the best teacher. "

Kleinerman smiled replying, "We all come to that, my friend."

Ben Willey then began to trace his years with the CIA. Much of what he said as he began talking had nothing to do with what he was going to ask of Kleinerman, but it was his way of gaining confidence on a subject so long bottled up in his own mind. There had been no one to talk to. He continued, "After Iran-contra, the next director lasted only a short time. He was honest, but he never had control. Then the blowup and all that bad publicity about the 'Everson Episode.' The Congressional hearings that followed drew attention to Bill Richards," he said referring to the former congressman who had chaired the hearings. "Richards was so much better at conducting a hearing than anyone had seen in a long time he became an instant hero. Like Senator Sam Ervin during Watergate, except Richards was younger.

"That was precisely what the administration needed. They got the bright idea of appointing Richards director. And you know, it *was* a great idea. His popularity made it possible for the administration to solve their problems not only with the public, but with Congress as well. He was everybody's choice. Everybody loved Bill Richards.

"The only problem was Richards didn't know anything about intelligence. He knew it in the abstract; he was a good legislator. But that sprawling morass we call the intelligence community would try the skills of any administrator — let alone one who doesn't know anything about it from the inside."

The "Everson Episode" that Willey referred to was a major security breach caused by an unstable renegade agent named Glen Everson; Everson had sold information which compromised at least ten field agents operating in South America. In addition he provided a remarkably accurate account of budget projections and outlays for intelligence gathering in the same region, the worst of it being that the financial information was published in newspapers both in South America and the United States, information that had never been made available to Congress, not even the oversight committees, and when the story became public all hell broke loose.

Willey continued, "One of the people I became suspicious of right away was a guy named Edgar Steele who is a special assistant to the director, Richards. He came to see me for a favor — I didn't know he even knew who I was. Political appointees like him come and go, and most of the time we find a way to work around them. We know they'll be gone sometime — hopefully before they destroy ongoing programs that are important to the country."

Kleinerman sat calmly, his hands clasped together resting in his lap. He recognized that Willey was coming to the important part.

Willey continued, "Steele wanted to get some pictures fixed up, suggesting that it was a joke for a class reunion. He said he knew we couldn't do it using inside people or resources, but he heard I had people on the outside who did this kind of work, and he just needed the name of one of the contractors I used. I just stared at him, and that really made him nervous, but he pushed me for a name.

"Did you refer him to someone?" Kleinerman interjected as Willey paused and slathered the second half of a bagel with cream cheese.

"I gave him the best guy I had for what he wanted, my friend Charlie Gleason. Charlie runs a shop on thirteenth Street. He does film developing, passport photos, specialty photography jobs — Charlie's got a talent for that sort of thing. So Steele went right down there, and ...," Willey gave a sly grin, "Charlie Gleason called me the minute Steele left and told me what Steele wanted. It's part of my deal with Charlie. I want to know everybody in the Agency that is bypassing my section and any other business Charlie is doing with the Agency. The first time Steele went there he was just testing Gleason. He took in some innocuous stuff — did that a couple of times. Then Steele made a mistake — an understandable mistake for someone not trained in intelligence work.

"Steele began to trust Gleason, trusted him enough that he took in some stuff I'll tell you about in a minute. But each time Steele brought stuff in Gleason called me, and each time I paid him for letting me know."

"What do you know about this Steele?"

"I know he's a politician by instinct. I checked him out and found that he spent several years at the State Department, followed by three years at the White House. Very bright, they say, and rumor has it Richards was told to hire him — by someone at the White House."

"Not unusual, really, those kinds of pressures ..."

"But a few weeks ago, Charlie called me and wanted me to come down to the shop. Had some things to show me. Our friend Steele had been in again, this time with something important. He had some very damaging pictures along with other documentation of a member of the House, who is now running for the U.S. Senate from Vermont. Congressman Alan Duval is his name. It looks to me like they're going to try and blackmail this man out of running for the Senate, or if he stays in the race, give this stuff to the press." Willey paused, waiting for his friend's reaction.

Kleinerman inquired, "Is it solid information or ... perhaps faked?"

"Faked or not, gathering this kind of information on a member of Congress is not even close to what the CIA is supposed to be doing. With what I know about the company, I've little doubt that they're doing a number on this congressman. His innocence or guilt is hardly an issue. Technology is at a point that it's nearly impossible to tell what is real and what is faked. At least some of the pictures were not faked according to Charlie — one shows the candidate with a major South American drug dealer; another one has him standing naked next to a very young woman — a very pretty young woman — also naked. I checked into it. The congressman, at the request of the administration went to South America to help forward their policies in helping preserve South American rain forests. This is an issue that Duval feels very strongly about — he's a very strong environmentalist. The documents that Steele had Gleason assemble, however, describe a clandestine side trip that Duval took to visit the drug dealer — one of the most notorious dealers in South America. It's written just like a press release; it claims the candidate's staff didn't even know where he was for a couple of days."

"Ben, how do you know he's doing this on his own? Is perhaps the director ... this Richards the one ... ?"

"I don't know for sure — I can't believe the director would be involved in this kind of activity."

"Could you go to him with this?" Kleinerman asked.

Willey sighed, "Even if I could get to see him ... no it's just too risky."

The two men sat for a minute in silence; Kleinerman refilled their coffee cups, then turned to Willey and inquired, "Did you get copies of these materials from your man Gleason?"

"Yes, I had Gleason make me three copies of everything that he put together for Steele. Then I drafted a long cover document. In the memo I spelled out exactly what Steele had Gleason manufacture for him. I also spelled out my concerns regarding Edgar Steele and perhaps others in leadership positions at the CIA. Together with the material Steele put together to blackmail Congressman Duval, it becomes a very explosive document. I've put together three copies of this material in large separate envelopes. I'm going to try to get an appointment with Senator Everett Stone — as you know he's Chairman of the Senate Intelligence Committee, and he's from Maine. I want to deliver this material to him. Congress is in recess and his Washington office told me Stone is in Portland. I want to give him one of the envelopes and have him tell me what to do."

"Do you know Stone?"

"Only by reputation."

"Then you know he's — how shall I say — an odd duck." Kleinerman smiled.

"Yes, I do know..."

"Wouldn't you have a better chance of getting to him in Washington? The staff of the Intelligence Committee would be handy for ..."

Willey interrupted, replying, "Hard to say, but I'm afraid the minute I walk into his office in Washington they'll tag me as an unhappy bureaucrat. They're a dime a dozen. Too many government employees use congressional offices as a wailing wall for petty stuff. Away from D.C. I think I have a better chance."

"Have you thought of contacting the candidate in Vermont, this Duval, to tell him about this?"

"Yes, but I want to get Stone's advice first. Actually I went to school with a guy named Jack Marston who's Duval's top person in Vermont. That's where you come in, my friend." Willey took his empty coffee cup, along with the plate bearing the small knife, and pushed them out of the way to the far side of the small table. He continued, "I don't think Steele or whoever else is involved has any idea that I have this material, or that anyone is even close. But you never know."

Reaching into his briefcase Willey extracted one of the three large manila envelopes, and handed it to Kleinerman. He looked directly at the older man as he did so, saying, "I hate to involve you — but I have to. I may never be able to get to Stone. That's why I've got three copies of the material. If at any time you don't hear from me for three days, seventy-two hours, you will have lost contact with me. Then if that happens, I want you to mail this envelope to Congressman Duval in Vermont. As I said, this is just a precaution."

"Of course, of course, you can ask me anything ... but you'll call me and let me ..."

"I'll call you every day," Willey reassured his friend, but if you don't hear from me for seventy two hours — three full days — just mail it." Willey smiled and leaned back in his chair aware now of how tense he must have seemed to Kleinerman, and he continued, "I realize that this may seem ..."

"Melodramatic?" Kleinerman interjected.

"That's the word," Willey replied grinning, "Melodramatic." Then serious once more, he said, "I don't see how they could know anything about what I've found out, but I've been around too long, seen too much to underestimate what could happen."

Kleinerman turned the envelope over in his hands and read aloud, "Congressman Alan Duval, Federal Building, Main Street, Burlington, Vermont 05401.

Chapter Six

"You never been back here, have you?" Not waiting for an answer, Charlie Gleason continued, "Had to see you right away — you need me, and I need you right? You want a drink?" He hadn't yet given Steele a chance to answer. His hands shook, he babbled on.

Steele listened, but between the booze and whatever had set him off, Gleason was barely coherent.

Steele listened and the story slowly emerged. Over the years Gleason had developed a special business relationship with Ben Willey. Now that Ben Willey was retiring, Gleason was panicking, fearing he was going to lose all of his Agency business. Willey's retirement could put Gleason out of business.

"I need to know who's taking Willey's place, who I'll deal with. Is it you?" He was pacing now, drawing deeply every few moments on the Camel cigarette.

Steele didn't answer at first. He listened. Probed. Accompanying the odor of alcohol and tobacco in the small room, Steele could smell the man's fear. A sixth sense told him there was more. He listened.

Finally Gleason, who had been babbling and continuously jumping from one subject to another, slipped and made a mistake. "... anybody who worked for the Agency, even you, come and want something, I had to tell Willey ... you know part of the deal I had with him." He stopped pacing for a moment, faced Steele and repeated as though he hadn't said it before, "It was part of the deal — anybody — anybody, from the Agency that brought work here, I got to call Ben. That's the way it was," Gleason continued defensively, "My meal ticket. I had to."

"This most recent material I've had you put together — did you tell Willey about that?"

"Yeah, er ... I had to ... he asked for copies. Part of the deal, like I said."

Steele's impassive face gave no indication of the rush of adrenaline he felt on hearing that Willey had copies of all the materials that he had asked Gleason to prepare for him. It all came out, including the fact that he had three envelopes he'd prepared for Ben Willey.

"Were the envelopes addressed?"

"No, he just had me put on these blank labels. He must have been gonna mail 'em — ya think so?"

With each new revelation Steele became increasingly alarmed, saying nothing, as all the while he could feel the tension building. He gave nothing away. He didn't let on to Gleason the seriousness of the situation. He would deal with Gleason later. His mind raced. He had to track down Ben Willey and get the copies from him before anyone else saw them. He tried to quiet Gleason, promising him a new contact at the Agency, and further promising that he would have as much business as ever.

Right now Edgar Steele needed a secure telephone. Rather than risk calls from Charlie's office or returning to his own, Steele told Gleason he'd return as soon as possible then left, jumped in his BMW and sped across town to his Watergate apartment. His mind was alive, working at lightning speed. Steele was in his element. He loved the challenge, the game.

He called his office and got Willey's Alexandria address. Someone had to search that apartment. He couldn't risk it personally. He needed a pro. Who else but "the artful dodger," Augie Brill, nicknamed as a result of various exploits he had carried out for the Agency at the direction of Steele and one or two other upper-echelon staff. Capable, smart, and totally without principle. An ex-drug dealer, Augie had one interest, money.

He called Brill and reached him right away. Steele explained what he wanted and hung up.

He called Willey's former secretary and said the director needed to locate Ben Willey right away. He'd learned the trick of making the bureaucracy jump by saying he was calling for his CIA boss, Bill Richards. Steele knew Willey was leaving town, but he didn't know where he was going. He made other calls, tied up some loose ends, and in less than an hour had set his plan for dealing with Gleason's bombshell revelation in motion. Finished for now, he took the elevator to the garage, and was soon back in the BMW headed for Alexandria.

Parking a couple of blocks away he walked to the nearby McDonald's where he waited for Augie Brill. Steele had met Brill when he had been working on the fringe drug operations tied in with the illegal aid the administration had been sending to the contra's in the mid-eighties. Some people were shy of Brill because he was an ex-addict as well as a former drug dealer. But Steele had found him to be closemouthed, smart, resourceful, capable of jimmying any lock, and frighteningly ruthless. Just the man for Edgar Steele. Steele waited in the restaurant ordering coffee he didn't want, while holding a newspaper in front of him he didn't read.

An hour later Brill walked through the door of the restaurant. It hadn't taken him long to get to Willey's condominium, slip the lock, and thoroughly search the vacant, near-empty rooms. Brill didn't find much. He did uncover some old but useless financial records and a carefully written note to the cleaning lady. But no address, or indication of where Willey was going. That was all. As Brill prepared to leave, he noticed the cleaning woman's supplies carefully clustered together by the door. On a whim, he picked up the pail, the mop, and finally a box of Brillo pads. Tucked in the box was a rolled up slip of paper. The cleaning woman had penciled in the address of Ben Willey's new condominium in Brunswick, Maine.

Steele had already obtained this much through his office but said nothing. Carefully he reviewed with Brill everything that he had seen or discovered at Willey's old address. There wasn't much. Brill had uncovered nothing new.

Still fiddling with his pad upon which he'd penciled in Willey's new address, he looked up at Brill and said, "Here's what I want — " Then it hit him. Unconsciously he had circled Brusnwick several times. He should have it spotted right away.

Brunswick, Maine!

Brunswick was the home town of U.S. Senator Everett Stone. Stone was chairman of the the Senate Intelligence Committee.

Steele now was pretty sure of where Willey was taking the envelopes he had with him, and he also knew that everything hinged on his own ability to stop Willey from getting them into the hands of others.

It was a matter of time.

He smiled at Augie Brill and said, "Have you ever been to Maine, my friend?"

Chapter Seven

It was just after seven PM when the obscene screech of the portable phone broke the silence of the summer evening yanking Jack Marston from a deep, uneasy sleep. He identified himself and the operator announced impersonally, "Conference call, Mr. Godine and Mr. Marston on the line ... ringing Mr. Camilli." Soon everyone was on the line, including Duval who came on last.

Campaign Manager John Godine took charge in bringing everyone up to date on the next month's schedule, information obtained from other campaigns, and the polling information Marston had gotten earlier from Duval. Eddie Fine the pollster/consultant remained silent, preferring as always to talk directly to Duval if he had anything to offer. Marlene Brownell chipped in with an optimistic fundraising report.

Good news on money is campaign Valium, and served to relax everyone for a few moments.

At that point John Godine brought up the slippage in their latest poll, but Duval interrupted saying, "Look, I know all that — we're slipping, but let's not make a big deal out of it."

Marston knew Duval hated going over old ground especially when it was bad news and he heard the impatience in his voice, so he interrupted, "Alan, Bill Camilli's got something he thinks is important, something you need to hear."

"Okay Bill, what is it?" Duval snapped, his nerves besting him for the moment.

Bill Camilli was young, and short on campaign experience, but he compensated with hard work and a ferocious intensity. Political campaigns are a mix of people, including those who dream of a better world in the future, along with those whose hearts have been broken too many times in political quest for them to dare to care too much. Marston and Godine, uncharitably called the neophyte Camilli, the last "true believer."

For his part Camilli thought the "old pols," as he referred to Godine and Marston, were lazy. Duval knew all this, and well understood that a quality campaign needed people with different kinds of talent and different backgrounds to make it work. This diversity of experience and age, and even the tensions created, actually proved to strengthen the campaign.

"Congressman," Camilli began, "my brother's girlfriend lives in D.C. She was at one of those fancy parties in Georgetown — her family is part of that scene — anyway she overheard two old "gray heads" deploring contemporary politicians, the direction of the country, and how good the old days were, that sort of thing. But her ears picked up — she's a political junkie like everyone else in Washington — when she heard one guy say to the other, 'There's some stuff out there on the record of several Senate candidates — candidates that everyone else figures to be easy winners — that we expect to come to light very soon.'

"The other guy asks how he knows all this, and the first man says, 'Some of us have decided to take responsibility for the outcome of certain elections — races involving candidates that are irresponsible ...' She couldn't hear any more of that part, but the guy went on to name some states involved and she's positive Vermont was one of them!

"She also remembered the one guy asking the other what they could possibly have on a guy as clean as you, Congressman. The second guy says, 'What could come out? Everybody says Duval is as clean as a whistle!'

"Then the first guy says, 'Today in American politics it doesn't matter what *he is,* only what *he appears to be!* And believe me, Congressman Duval is looking very bad, or will shortly!' Then he went on to say, 'We can make any of them look any way we want!' Then he said something like, 'The program is well under way ...!' That's all she got, but she said the guy was well dressed in an old money sense, and had that smug self-righteousness you get from the fanatics. But it scared her, he seemed so sure of what would happen."

"Did she get what other campaigns might be involved? What states — ?" Godine inquired.

"She thought she heard one of the Dakotas and Rhode Island."

"Small populations," Godine muttered.

"Yeah, but two seats in the Senate for Vermont or South Dakota or any small state carries the same weight as the two seats in California with fifty times the population," Camilli replied.

"The point is if someone really is trying to influence an election, it's far easier to do in a small state, and a helluva lot cheaper!" rejoined Godine.

The phone lines went silent, each of the conferees alone with their thoughts for the moment, deciding whether this was the kind of crazy stuff from out of nowhere that you hear in most campaigns, or whether maybe, just maybe, it was time to worry.

Duval broke the silence, the tension in his voice observed earlier replaced by fatigue, "Thanks Bill, we have to hear about that stuff ... if something's up, it's better to know early." He chuckled, "You know folks, I'm clean, I'm really clean! If this is for real, and frankly I'm inclined to believe it is, I haven't a clue what they're trying to hang me with. But I do think John," speaking to his campaign manager, "that we'll have to hold back some TV money for later in the campaign in order to be able to respond to any attack ads we hadn't anticipated."

"Two gray-heads at a Georgetown party, Jesus, that's not much to go on!" groaned an unhappy John Godine.

"Bill, any idea where these guys are coming from — left or right?" inquired Marston.

"She told my brother that they looked like State Department types ... expensive clothes ... pretty old."

At this point Marston headed off further small talk saying, "Don't start any rumors — be careful as hell — but Bill, call around the country and see if you get any rumblings of this from the party people ... I'll do the same with my contacts. Make sure you don't link any calls to Duval or the Duval campaign. Just find out whatever you can about any dirty tricks in other races around the country. We need to know if there's a pattern of this kind of stuff."

The time Ben Willey spent with Herb Kleinerman on Tuesday morning passed quickly. Shortly before noon he waved farewell to his friend and headed back to his condominium, somewhat more at ease with the knowledge that Kleinerman was now holding one of the three envelopes.

The next step, he knew, wouldn't be as easy, or as pleasant. He had to get in touch with Senator Everett Stone. Stone's state office was in Portland even though he lived in Brunswick. But Willey had no intention of trying to reach him at home. He'd have enough trouble getting through without barging in at the man's house.

He didn't know a lot about Stone. Although he had served in the Senate for three terms, to Willey he remained an enigma. Stone was said to be a man you could trust, but he knew of no one in the Agency who really felt they were close to him, including the new Director. Just as well. Willey didn't need a personality king, he needed someone who gave a damn, and who wanted to help — traits far more rare in the District than those not living there could imagine.

If he couldn't get to Stone, he would have to call his old college friend Jack Marston, and arrange to tell the story to Congressman Duval himself. But the right way was to go through Stone because Stone could open this thing up in ways that Duval could not. Duval could use the information, but it would be tricky; the Agency had many ways of protecting itself and Duval might get lost in the process. Willey was thinking about this as he closed the front door of his new condo and walked into the living room.

Instantly he knew — someone had been here. He felt it. Uneasy, he checked the bathroom, then the closets. He went into the guest room.

Nothing.

"Just my imagination," he thought. "Goddamn imagination!" No! The odor. That was it. There was an odor! Something different. Willey stayed alert. He trusted his instincts.

He checked to make sure he had locked the front door and went through the kitchen to assure himself that he had locked the back door as well. He grabbed a chair by the dining room table and sat down. His heart was pounding. No one was inside now, but someone had been. It must be the odor; something had triggered his reaction.

Pulling himself together, he slapped the table and stood up. Time to unpack the car; then he would call Stone's Portland office.

He went out to the car looking carefully around the area as he did, and after several trips he had brought in the four large suitcases which he set in a line along the hallway, the two large boxes which included books he was currently reading as well as a favorite coffee pot he wanted handy, and the small TV he planned to set up in the bedroom. He had left nearly everything packed in the car overnight with the exception of the three manila envelopes which he had brought in and placed in his briefcase.

He returned to the car once more and brought in the odds and ends which he had thrown in the car at the last minute. As he stood in the living room surveying his work he decided that things were now pretty much where he knew where they were. He proceeded to partially unpack so as to be able to get at the few things he would need right away.

He took his favorite coffee pot and went into the kitchen, measured out the right amount of coffee and water, and put it on the stove. Next he got the yogurt from the refrigerator and put it on the table and waited, hands on hips, for the coffee to perk. While he waited, he connected the TV to the cable, and turned it on. It worked perfectly.

He didn't really need the food or the coffee, he thought to himself, as he poured the dark coffee from the glass carafe. Kleinerman's bagels were still with him, and he suspected the coffee would give him a sour stomach. But he had wanted to make the coffee, wanted to have the heady odor of, in Kleinerman's words, "the good coffee," permeating the apartment. He ate the yogurt and drank the coffee while watching three young women on a television show prance around in the cause of weight reduction. With skin tight spandex and the blue ocean in the background it didn't appear to Willey that any of the performers needed to lose weight.

He sat back in the chair resting easier, the nervousness he had felt earlier now mostly forgotten.

He'd delayed long enough, it was time to call Stone's office. He rummaged around in his briefcase and found the phone number. He paused. It would be a lot easier to call from this phone, but earlier he had decided he would do it from a phone booth or a gas station downtown. If they were on to him at all, the first thing they would do would be to tap his phone.

The call would be safer, and he needed the exercise anyway, he mused, smiling to himself as he thought once again of the beautiful people exercising on television and getting paid for it. Maybe he'd wear spandex now that he was retired!

He started for the door, briefcase in hand.

Lawson Nabors had been in charge of the accounting section in Special Documents Division of the Agency for twelve years. In Washington that morning when he read the paper he knew he needed to speak to Ben Willey right away. Willey needed to know what had happened.

Nabors worked out of a wheelchair. Many years before when the chief accounting position had opened up he had been one of many candidates. Ben Willey knew of Nabors's work having watched him since he was first hired by the Agency. He was a hard worker, smart as hell, and thoroughly reliable.

There are always lots of excuses, if not real reasons, for not giving someone in a wheel chair the top job. Willey heard all these reasons. But it only made him more determined and he fought like the devil with personnel to get Nabors promoted. When Nabors finally did get the job, Willey had a friend for life.

Nabors tried to phone Willey several times that Tuesday morning to no avail. After a quick cafeteria lunch he tried once again, this time calling from the public phone outside the dining room.

The perceptive Nabors knew Willey was deeply concerned about some of the things that were going on in the Agency. Although Willey had never said so directly, Nabors picked it up in the kind of questions Willey asked, and was sure it was why he had taken retirement. Now he had some news that he was sure would further shake up his former boss.

The phone rang for the first time in Willey's Brunswick condo just as he was leaving to make his call to Senator Stone. He dropped his briefcase, and picked up the phone, "Hello."

"Ben, this is Lawson."

"What's up?" replied Willey quickly. Almost too quickly.

"I hate to bother you, Ben, but you know Charlie Gleason, the guy who did most of your contract work? His shop was ransacked yesterday afternoon. Ruined the whole place, and Ben — they killed Gleason."

"Oh shit ... old Charlie ..."

"The police so far think it was a drug deal gone bad," explained Nabors.

"Drugs? — I kept a close eye on Charlie — he never got close to drugs. He was no dealer ... not these days."

"The police don't know he was a contractor of ours."

"And they'll never find out, unless I tell them," Willey replied, feeling both frustration and a hint of despair.

"What good would that do Ben?"

"No good ... at least right now. I don't know enough about ... Damn, damn those bastards." Willey paused a moment and continued, "Lawson, thank you for calling. I know I've never said much about what's going on, but it's probably better that you don't know the details. In fact stay away from this; don't get involved any further. And for God's sake don't tell anyone — Agency or otherwise — that you talked with me."

"Ben, I just ride around in this chair and crunch numbers in my computer all day, but my head works all right. I'd be glad to help. I can call from public phones or from home."

Willey thought a moment. Nabors was the most trustworthy contact he had at the Agency, but he hated to involve him, or anyone for that matter. He knew though, could hear it in his friend's voice, that Nabors thought he was being protected because of his disability. And Willey also knew a friend at the Agency might be worth his weight in gold as things went along. "Lawson, do this: I can't tell you more, but keep an eye on the director's office — especially Edgar Steele, Richards's special assistant ... just watch, don't do anything. I'll call you at home within a few days. Remember, don't trust anyone." Then pausing for a moment thinking how hard it is to say thank you when it really matters, he said finally, "I really appreciate this, Lawson, ... I ... thank you."

He hung up, his hand remaining on the phone as he reflected on the tragedy he had brought upon Charlie Gleason — a strange friend maybe, but a friend nonetheless. He prayed silently that the same fate would not befall Lawson Nabors.

Nabors's call had brought him more than just the news of Gleason's death. It was a real wake up-call; they were on to him already. It was only a matter of time before they'd try something else. He had to get to see

Senator Stone. Once Stone had the information Willey had prepared for him, they would have no reason to threaten him, physically at least. If they had made the hit on Charlie Gleason yesterday, there was little doubt but that they now had him in their sights.

Willey sat for a moment, his hand resting on the briefcase containing the two remaining envelopes. He felt responsible for Gleason. By concentrating on his own retirement and preparing to expose what Edgar Steele and the others were up to, he hadn't thought enough about what his leaving meant to Gleason.

Gleason had asked him several times who would take over when he left. He hadn't taken the time to give Charlie a good answer. As soon as I left, Willey thought to himself, old Charlie probably worried himself near to death over the weekend, got half drunk, then called the only other person at the Agency he really knew, Edgar Steele. Yes, that was it. Charlie should have known better, but once given an opening Steele could con Charlie in no time. Willey cursed himself for his carelessness. He hadn't expected to fool them for long, but he could have bought a little time if he'd just paid more attention to what Gleason needed.

More than that, the killing confirmed the seriousness of Steele's involvement in the election shenanigans. Willey hadn't a doubt — it was Steele who destroyed the shop and killed Charlie, or hired someone to do it. After thirty years with the Agency you forget about coincidences; they don't exist.

Leaning slightly forward in his chair, chin in hand, he went over his plan once again. It was a good plan, but nevertheless they would be coming to get him very soon. Could he defend himself? He had never owned a weapon. He looked around, opened the kitchen drawer and grabbed a shiny steak knife and slipped it into his briefcase.

Once again he headed out the door to find an outside pay phone to call the chairman of the Senate Intelligence Committee.

Chapter Eight

Willey flipped the lock, pulled the door closed, and skipped down the steps.

The man was about seventy-five feet back, walking toward him from the end of the lot; he would pass just a few feet away from him. He showed no interest in Willey, who had stopped on the bottom step, and was now standing alert, watching ...

Was this a new tenant perhaps? Where was his car?

Cautiously, Willey shifted the briefcase under his arm and walked toward the Lincoln. The man continued on as though unaware of Willey's presence. They were now about twenty feet apart.

Abruptly the man turned to face Willey, his sharp, pale features apparent in the afternoon sun, a knife glinting in his right hand. Willey stepped back from his car and with a high-pitched scream he charged directly at the man covering the distance between them in an instant. He lunged at his would-be attacker, bringing his knee viciously into the man's groin.

Brill felt the terrible pain and the sickness wash over him. Caught off guard, he had no reason to expect such a reaction from his older, presumably, unsuspecting quarry. But as he doubled over he slashed out at Willey, his knife finding its mark below the rib cage.

Willey felt the blade scraping bone; panicked for a moment he twisted away and ran to the Lincoln holding his side, desperately clinging to his briefcase. He jumped in and quickly started the car. The tires on the big Lincoln squealed as he wheeled the car out of the lot and onto the street. Without thinking, he turned right and found himself speeding toward Cooks Corner on the outskirts of Brunswick.

Willey kept his right hand on the knife wound; it was wet to the touch, but so far there was little pain. He looked down and could see the blood oozing through his shirt. He felt okay, for now. No sign of shock. Yet.

Arriving at Cooks Corner he turned left at the light, speeding over the railroad tracks which challenged the car's soft suspension causing it to bounce and lurch dangerously out of control. He was heading north on Route 1. Checking the mirror, he noted that so far he had no pursuer. Still he couldn't know for sure since he had no idea what kind of car to look for. Ben Willey just wanted to get away. Fast.

The Police Station! Damn! thought Willey, I should have headed to the Police Station, not run away from town. But then he wasn't sure where the station was located. Maybe, he should stop and call the police now. He checked the mirror again. There was no phone available on this road anyway. And if there was what could he say that anyone would believe? No, in his haste he'd probably done the right thing, distancing himself from the man with the knife as fast as possible.

As the rush of adrenaline began to wear off he began to feel a little woozy, either from that or from the loss of blood he could see oozing through his shirt. Trying to focus Willey knew he had to call Senator Stone's office. He should have done it sooner. If he could get that call made, he could just hide out for a while. The road and the cars up ahead became wavy and swam before his eyes for a moment — then cleared. Thank God he'd given Kleinerman one of the envelopes. If all else failed at least one of the envelopes would be delivered to Congressman Duval in Vermont.

He was traveling close to seventy-five miles an hour, passing car after car. As he overtook one after another, he kept an eye on the rearview mirror still warily searching for pursuers. He didn't worry about being stopped by the police; at this point he would welcome them!

Another thought hit him! What if Steele knew of his friendship with Kleinerman? Damn! It hadn't taken them long to get Charlie Gleason. They'd find his connection to Kleinerman sooner or later. He had to get away, that was all. Then he'd call Kleinerman. Again he checked the mirror.

He was approaching the city of Bath. Before he crossed the Kennebec River heading north, he spotted the sign to Fort Popham. With a complicated maneuver involving a series of turns he was sure would gain him time, he was on Route 209 heading toward the ocean. Willey knew the area, and had been out to Popham Beach many times. He checked the mirror again. Still no company. Feeling ever weaker he knew he needed to stop for a few minutes.

He was having trouble holding the car steady on the narrow paved road. He knew he was driving too fast. He had to stop ... had to rest. Soon.

Willey jammed on the brakes and with a quick glance behind him yanked the Lincoln hard to the left. The rear end fishtailed, but the exhausted Willey, driving by memory now, turned out of the skid and the big sedan righted itself.

He'd almost missed the turn onto the narrow dirt road which headed toward the edge of the river. Flanked on both sides by short, scrubby trees and blueberry bushes, he eased the car slowly down the single lane road. Less than a half a mile in, he came to an open area, used for picnics by day and by lovers at night. The road seemed to peter out at this point so he swung the car wide to turn around. Too wide — the rear wheels spun out in the loose sand and the rear end hung up in a sandy washout.

Cursing his luck, Willey stepped on the gas, trying to move the car forward. No luck. Then he shifted to reverse with the same result. He tried rocking it as if to free himself from a snowbank, but the big Lincoln just slid further to the right and became completely caught up underneath. With the car still idling he opened the door and felt the blast of the afternoon heat. Perspiring heavily, he turned the air-conditioning on high and directed the vents directly onto his body. He turned the radio up; he hadn't been aware that it was playing.

Willey was wearing an open-collared cotton shirt with a T-shirt underneath. He loosened the belt on his khaki slacks. Carefully he pulled his T-shirt and the outer shirt up and out of the oozing mess of blood. The ugly wound was still bleeding freely. He had to stanch the flow. As soon as possible he would need to get it cleaned and find some antibiotics. He took out his handkerchief and and pressed it over the gash. Leaving the shirt hanging outside his trousers, he fastened his belt to keep the handkerchief in place.

Ben Willey put his head back to rest for a moment. At least he had eluded his pursuer. A wave of nausea swept over him. "I can't go into shock," he mumbled aloud to himself. "I can't ..."

He got out of the car and leaned against the left fender, feeling light-headed now, but strangely content. He could feel a cool sea breeze carrying the aroma of decaying seaweed in the air. He loved the sea air, the mix of sharp odors and the sounds of the sea; it was for these things that he always returned to Maine. He lifted his shirt to feel the soft wind against his hot skin.

Augie Brill didn't make many mistakes, at least not since he stopped using the white powder. In his business one couldn't afford mistakes. But he knew this time he had underestimated the man he was stalking. It had gone so easily for him yesterday with Gleason that he had not been prepared for Willey's assault.

Upon arriving at Portland International Airport Tuesday morning, Brill rented a Ford Taurus, insisting on Maine plates, and drove to Brunswick. His morning flight had been uneventful. He didn't like to fly, but he now had twenty-five thousand dollars in hand, with a promise of more to come. He staked out Willey's apartment with the idea that when Willey left the premises he would enter and take the envelopes. Simple. Although Brill wasn't sure at first, Willey had already left the apartment by the time he had arrived at the complex.

Brill had entered the apartment through an unlocked back window after checking it out from a distance and determining to his satisfaction that the premises were unoccupied. Once inside, he'd searched without success for the envelopes.

Brill had been breaking and entering for years and prided himself on being able to uncover things meant to be hidden. But after a thorough search of the few things Willey had brought in, he found no sign of the manila envelopes that Steele had described to him. From the way the car was packed with boxes, clothes and other assorted items, he knew that most of Willey's things were still inside the car, or perhaps the trunk. Not discouraged, he left the condo through the window he had entered earlier, congratulating himself that his temporary visit would go unnoticed. That left the car to be searched next. But he decided against breaking into the car in broad daylight because of the likelihood that people might be entering or exiting the parking lot. Instead he would wait.

Brill retreated to the shadows of the wooded area at the end of the parking lot, correctly assuming that Willey would soon reappear.

His patience was rewarded when shortly after noon he spotted Ben Willey returning from his visit to Kleinerman — carrying a briefcase.

Augie Brill smiled to himself. Of course, in the briefcase. He had found the envelopes.

At first he thought he would surprise Willey and take the envelopes by force. But to avoid attracting attention, he decided to wait in the hope that the next time Willey left the condo, it would be without the briefcase and he could enter and retrieve the envelopes.

Steele had told him to avoid violence but to get the envelopes at any cost. Brill recognized the contradiction, but with the money Steele paid him Brill could live with contradictions.

He had his "tools," an attache case which contained all sorts of listening devices, gadgets for breaking and entering, tapping phones, and a tracking device. Brill always carried a knife, and almost never used a gun. He didn't trust guns, didn't like them, having decided long ago they were more incriminating than useful.

Earlier, after his search of the apartment, Brill had taken a moment to attach a signal-emitting bug to the underside of Willey's car as a means of tracking the Lincoln if need be. Wherever the car went the signal given off by the bug would register at the base station that remained in his case.

He'd been told the effective range of the bug was at least twenty-five miles. He'd never tested it, but that seemed reasonable.

Safely back in the car he had looked around warily, but as far as he could tell, the struggle in the parking lot had gone unnoticed. He opened his attache' case and attached the base unit of the tracking device to a large battery he carried separately. Within moments he was picking up the signal emanating from the tiny transmitter. The little bug he had hidden on the Lincoln was doing its job.

Following the attack on Willey in the parking lot, Brill disappeared as quickly as possible, passing through the woods where he had hidden earlier and exiting onto a street where he parked the rented Taurus.

With a quick look at the map and the base unit signal Brill determined that Willey was traveling north, probably on Route 1. Studying the map a moment longer he started his car and pulled out, heading toward Route 1.

Brill maintained his speed just below the limit, staying with the flow of traffic. Just as Willey had done he traveled to Cooks Corner and from there north. When he arrived in Bath he drove on past the turn Willey had taken onto Route 209. A few minutes later as he crossed the Kennebec River, he noticed the intensity of the signal to his base unit had begun to diminish. Realizing he'd missed a turn somewhere, he quickly reversed direction, and headed south. Moments later he spotted the sign for Route 209 and after quickly checking his map, and hesitating only a second, he turned, and was now on the road Willey had followed earlier.

The narrow winding road tested the Taurus's handling ability; the well designed Ford met the challenge. The base unit signal began to strengthen and Brill smiled to himself knowing he was again on the right track.

Five or six miles down the road, the tracking signal reached maximum intensity on the indicator. Brill now knew Willey was somewhere within a half a mile. Still, he saw nothing. He wondered in what condition he would find Willey. He knew his quarry was wounded; he knew he had cut him. But how badly?

He spotted the turnoff.

He slowed, noting the fresh tire tracks.

He turned left off the highway, and drove about a hundred and fifty yards down the narrow dirt road. He stopped, shut off the engine, opened the windows, and listened. He heard music.

Checking to see that his knife was still strapped to his leg, he advanced, listening carefully as he went. He followed the fresh tire tracks on foot toward the river. The music was louder now — classical, highbrow stuff.

Up ahead, Ben Willey had returned to the front seat of the car to avoid the sun. He was perspiring freely, and hoped it was the heat and not his wound. The bleeding had let up. The steady, cool breeze emanating from the Lincoln's air-conditioning helped. Maine Public Radio had an all-Mozart program playing. "Must be my lucky week," he mused, "Lots of Mozart." His eyes were half closed, sleep was seconds away.

Then something — a sixth sense we all know we have but can never identify — alerted him, and he opened his eyes.

Brill was twenty-five yards away. When he was sure that Willey had seen him he began to run directly toward the car.

Willey grabbed the briefcase, opened the door scrambled out and running as fast as he could away from the charging Brill toward the steep bank bordering the river. At the top of the bank he stubbed his toe on a rock and fell, rolling over a couple of times but still hanging on to the briefcase.

Brill was on him. They grappled.

Willey broke loose again, and still holding the briefcase he started to run along the edge of the river — dangerously close to the water.

His knife in hand, ready to throw, Brill hollered, "Drop the case!"

The exhausted Ben Willey paused a moment, and looked back. He turned away and still holding his side, tried to continue running. He could barely make his right leg work; he staggered.

Instead of throwing the knife, Brill ran and easily caught up with Willey, tackling him, with his knife still in his hand. Surprising even himself, Willey swung at Brill catching him in the nose with the heel of his hand. The blood spurted. Furious, Brill slashed out with his knife. Willey dodged to the side. Brill slashed down again at Willey who was on the ground now. The knife caught the back of Willey's right hand, pinning it to the ground. He screamed in pain.

The briefcase lay unattended at his side.

Brill pulled the knife back to slash again but Willey rolled out of the way and struggled to his feet.

Everything was a blur to Ben Willey — the pain in his hand was searing, as though fire itself was consuming it. Blood covered the right side of his khakis and his shirt. He staggered a few feet further, wondering whether he had won or lost, as he thought fleetingly of his friend Kleinerman.

Then everything went black and he fell once again. As it had for centuries, the mighty Kennebec River rolled by a few short feet away.

Brill picked up the briefcase and looked at Ben Willey lying beside the water. Held there for a moment by the gory scene, Brill decided that he had in hand what he had come for. The afternoon tide would soon arrive and wash over the area where Ben Willey lay.

Augie Brill was suddenly aware of how exposed he was, standing there by Willey's body. He looked around nervously, but all was quiet; gulls soaring high in the sky were turning in wide circles, white clouds billowed but failed to block the sun, and the river lapped gently along the shore with comforting repetitiveness beside Ben Willey's still form. Brill trotted back toward his rental car, Willey's briefcase in hand.

As he passed the Lincoln the car stereo was still playing, but Brill barely noticed.

Ben Willey would have noticed. Less than two hundred feet from where Ben Willey lay without moving, Mozart's Horn Concerto no.1 was playing. Willey would have liked that.

It was one of his favorites.

Chapter Nine

"Two envelopes! What do you mean two? Three, Goddammit. Three envelopes!" Edgar Steele was beside himself. Moments before when Brill's call came in, he felt the problem was solved and now he found that Brill had retrieved only two of the envelopes. There was one more. Somewhere. Willey had hidden one of the envelopes, or .... God forbid, or already mailed it! But when? "Did you check the car?" he demanded.

"No," Brill replied, controlling his anger.

"Well go back and check the car — or maybe he taped it to his body."

"I am very exposed there — it's dangerous ...," he snapped.

Sensing Brill's rising anger, Steele regained control and said, "I know it's risky, but it's riskier not to go back. Are the envelopes addressed?"

"Yes.

"Well, what are the addresses on the outside of the two envelopes you have?"

Removing the two envelopes from the case, Brill replied, "One is addressed to Willey's post office box here in Brunswick, the other is addressed to Senator Everett Stone ..."

"Stone! Well that's good news." He couldn't have talked to Stone yet. But the third envelope wasn't there. Where the devil was it? Had he mailed it already? Steele's mind was working quickly now, "Augie, go back and be sure the other envelope isn't anywhere around his person or the car. And get rid of the body. I know I didn't tell you to terminate him, but it's just as well, he could be a nuisance alive ... then stand by. I may still need you. Let me know right away, Augie my boy — by the way you've earned the other twenty-five thou already."

That was the part Brill wanted to hear. Easy to put up with Steele's shit, or anybody's, if the money was there.

"And Augie, I want you to burn those envelopes. Make sure they're completely destroyed."

"I'll burn 'em off the road somewhere away from here. I'll make sure, I'll add a little gasoline before I torch 'em."

Brill had driven back down to Cooks Corner on the outskirts of Brunswick before phoning Steele. He put the two envelopes back in the briefcase and left the phone booth, hopped in the Taurus and headed north once more.

More cautious this time, he drove on past the unmarked turn which led to the area where he had assaulted Willey. Everything seemed normal, so after turning around, he entered as he had before driving all the way in to the open area where Willey's Lincoln was parked. About thirty yards from the Lincoln Brill carefully turned the rental car around to face out in case he needed to leave in hurry.

He approached the Lincoln. Then stopped, abruptly. Something was different. He could no longer hear the stereo. Had the wind shifted? He could feel the ocean air; high tide was approaching. The car was no longer running; the door which had been open was now closed.

He stood for a moment along the edge of the road partially obscured by the scrub growth along the edge of the road. Still he saw nothing. Heard nothing.

He walked over to the car. It was unlocked, but the keys had been removed from the ignition. He ran over to the bank of the river where he had struggled with Willey.

From the top of the bank he looked down to where he had last seen Willey — lying on the edge of the Kennebec with the salty waters reaching for his body.

Nothing. High tide now had brought the level of the river to well above where the body had lain.

Brill stared for a long moment.

Increasingly cautious, he went back to check the Lincoln again, looking for the third envelope. Before entering the car or forcing the trunk open, he looked in all directions, then up at the sky. He was terribly exposed and knew it. There was just the one exit and he was here in a wide open area. An airplane passing several miles to the south increased his nervousness. If a helicopter came by ...

He opened the door of the Lincoln from the driver's side, and slid in. The heat was stifling. He opened the glove box, and rifled it. An owner's manual, a bill of sale for the car, some fuses, antacids, a small screw driver — nothing. Under the seat he pulled out an umbrella and a misplaced placed audio tape. Over the visor on the passenger side, nothing. Then on the driver's side, from over the visor he pulled out ... a leather like wallet ... no, an address book. He flipped the pages and started to toss it, then paused and tucked it inside his shirt pocket crushing his cigarettes in the process.

He glanced around the inside of the car looking for anything else he might have missed.

Outside now, a light breeze offset the blazing sun. He used a long screwdriver he carried in his case to spring the trunk open. He felt around. Nothing, as he expected. But the carpet lining in the trunk had been pulled up in one place. The envelopes could have been hidden underneath originally, but none remained.

The third envelope was not there.

Brill was ready to leave; he wanted to get away. More than ready. The river must have claimed Willey. It was a deep cut; he had lost a lot of blood. Willey sure as hell didn't walk out of there. But who turned off the ignition and shut the driver's side door? Looking around quickly one last time, Brill ran to the rented Taurus and jumped in. He gunned the car swerving first left and then right before straightening his direction, and finally headed back along the narrow road to the highway.

This time to avoid establishing any kind of pattern he drove north a few miles and pulled into an information booth on the highway off Route 1, and got on the phone to Steele.

"I covered the car, inside and out — "

"Damn — nothing, huh, absolutely nothing? Did you look where they mount the spare?"

"I can search a car — like I said, no envelope, but I found a small address book over the visor," he said, pulling the address book from his shirt pocket.

"An address book? Open it — what's in it?" Steele inquired impatiently.

Brill said nothing, as he methodically turned the first two or three pages. "Not many names in here — wait a minute ..." he bent down to pick up a small piece of note paper that slipped out of the back of the address book.. "A slip of paper just fell out — "

"Oh?"

"It says on the top, 'Mailing addresses.' It's got that Senator Stone's address on it — the same address that was on the envelope I just got. It's got Willey's address too, same as it was on the envelope ..."

"Yes, yes, any more, Augie?" Steele interrupted impatiently.

"The last one is to a Congressman Alan Duval in Burlington, Vermont."

"That's the one, good work! You're on your way to Vermont!"

Chapter Ten

"It's the director of the CIA, William Richards, Congressman, on line one." Shirley Hogan was often the first voice you heard when you called Congressman Alan Duval's Vermont office.

Picking up the phone from where he was sitting on the corner of Jack Marston's desk, the congressman replied, "Alan Duval speaking." Duval had been talking quietly with the man responsible for his Vermont operation, having arrived from the airport within the hour.

"Alan, I'm glad I got a hold of you. How are you doing?"

"Bill, I'm in beautiful Vermont; I'm going to become a United States Senator in a few months ... I'm just fine!" replied Duval while winking at Jack Marston who was seated before him slowly shaking his head.

"Beltway bullshit," is how Marston described banter of this sort. The false enthusiasm in personal exchanges among "Washington types" reminded him why he avoided the District like the plague, and preferred to work in Vermont.

Bill Richards belonged to the other party, but he and Duval had become friends while serving together in the House.

"What have you got going today that you would need to call an unimportant congressman from Vermont — and no, I won't go back to South America for you," he continued jokingly.

Duval had been referring to a favor Richards had asked of him three summers before while he was attending a conference in Brazil on the future of the tropical rain forests. Richards had prevailed upon Duval to leave the conference for a couple of days and fly to Colombia to help the administration. Extracting a promise of no publicity concerning the request, Richards asked Duval to fly to Bogata, and from there travel by helicopter in land to a remote and beautiful region where the farms of Arturo Tomarra were located. The administration had been trying to make a deal with Tomarra whose extensive holdings in the tropical rain forests and throughout South America were legend. Duval's assignment was to show bi-partisan support for an aid proposal which would require Tomarra's cooperation in order to be successful. Duval, who supported the administration's initiatives in South America agreed to help, and went along with the request.

Bill Richards laughed and said, "No, not South America this time. You don't have to go that far — have you ever stayed at the Mount Washington Hotel in New Hampshire?"

"Sure, in Bretton Woods — the 1944 International Monetary Conference was held there, prior to the end of World War II. The Conference set the rules for international currency exchange for years to come. There's your history lesson, Bill, what else do you want to know?"

Ignoring the banter, Richards pressed on. "Ed Searly and I have called a hurry-up meeting of Great Britain and representatives of the Common Market countries. We've got some new stuff on terrorism we want to lay out, and in keeping with the way I've been trying to extend cooperation to anti-terrorist units everywhere whenever possible — and legal of course — we're trying to get extensive congressional representation — and you're my favorite member of the loyal opposition!"

Ed Searly was director of the FBI, and had responsibility for combatting domestic terrorism. Because of potential overlapping responsibilities, Searly and Richards — unlike their predecessors — had buried the hatchet and were working closely together on the problems of both domestic and international terrorism.

"Yeah, bullshit," replied Duval. "It seems to me you just don't want me campaigning here in Vermont because you know I'll whip that nineteenth century fascist you guys have running against me!"

Richards feigning hurt replied, " Alan, Alan, how could you?"

"Never mind that, when is it?" Duval inquired, purposely not looking at Jack Marston who was holding his forehead with the fingers of both hands, shaking his head and mouthing the word "no" in a stage whisper.

"End of next week, Thursday and Friday."

"Well ... I'm making a note. Get somebody to call my appointments secretary in Washington with the details, and I'll get back to you. Bill, I can probably do it," Duval continued, turning his back on Marston who had slumped in his chair, his head back and his arms spread as if invoking Deity.

"Alan, that's great!"

"By the way Bill — one other thing — have you got a minute?"

"Sure, go ahead!"

"I've picked up some peculiar information from a couple of sources — nothing very solid — it has to do with somebody screwing around with my campaign. Sounds like dirty tricks. It may involve faked photos or other documents. I don't want to say anymore over the phone, but the rumor I have is that there could be a couple of other senatorial campaigns involved. Any ideas?"

"Yeah, it sounds like dirty tricks — that's nothing new, really — say, I've got somebody going up your way Monday to do some advance work for the conference. I'll get him to fly through Burlington and he can meet with you or whomever you designate on this. Then I can get somebody looking at this, informally, of course."

"That sounds great. Thanks, Bill."

"Well, this works for me too. The man I'm sending up is not familiar with northern New England. He needs to be well briefed on the northern-tier states by someone who really knows the territory so he can answer all the questions our European visitors may have. We're trying to make it a nice trip for the spouses who come along. Know anybody that can help? A contact?"

"Sure," Duval smiled, looking at Marston for the first time since the conversation began. "Just have him call Jack Marston. He runs my Vermont operation and knows northern New England as well as anyone I know. He's the one your man should talk to on the dirty tricks business as well, because I won't be around on Monday."

"Come to think of it, Alan, you know the guy I'm sending — he arranged everything for you on that side junket I set you up with in South America. You remember Edgar Steele?"

Marston was alone in his office a few moments later when Shirley Hogan buzzed him and announced, "It's a Lila Maret, Jack, calling from Mt. Desert Island, Maine. She says she's a cousin of a man named Ben Willey. Does that mean anything to you?"

"Sure does." Marston pushed the line that was blinking and picked up the phone, "Jack Marston."

"Mr. Marston, my name is Lila Maret. I'm Ben Willey's cousin — I need — may I come to see you?" Without pausing she continued, "I know you don't know me, but as you may or may not know, Ben has taken early retirement from the CIA, and ... he's been acting, well ... I guess, strangely is the only word. I know this is confusing, but I have reason to think he may try to contact you and I'm about the only family he has left in New England. He could be getting himself in terrible trouble."

"Trouble?" Marston replied scowling and wondering what this was all about.

"He took some materials from the Agency when he left ..."

Until five years ago Marston hadn't seen Ben Willey since they graduated together from the University of Vermont. They met for the first time since graduation at a twenty-fifth class reunion, the first such affair either of them had attended. Marston heard nothing more until a couple of months ago when Willey phoned to say that he was retiring and would be in Burlington for a visit. He wondered if Marston would help him make some business contacts in northern New England.

Marston had gladly agreed. He knew the North Country well, having covered the territory as a road man for Chrysler Corporation years ago; before that he'd played baseball, fished and vacationed all over the northern three New England states.

Lila Maret continued, "Can we meet — I'm calling from Maine, but I'll be in Burlington on Friday?"

Marston, still trying to figure what was going on, said," Sure, but where's Ben right now?"

"We — I don't know!"

"Well, I hope I can help. Come by around eleven on Friday."

Lila Maret — travel writer, photographer, travel guide inspector, and manuscript editor was finishing up a stay at Bay View Landings, a resort hotel located just outside Southwest Harbor, a small village on the end of Mt. Desert Island, Maine. Mt. Desert Island was settled in the seventeenth century and it became home to both fishermen and farmer. Unlike the southern coast of Maine with its expanse of flat, sandy beaches, the rocky shoreline that encircles the island is broken up by small bays and ribbons of ocean that intrude upon the land, weaving in and out.

Lila had been commissioned to do an article about the island by one of the major travel magazines. Wanting to give the piece a different twist, she had chosen to avoid Bar Harbor, the center of tourist activity, and seek out less familiar but no less charming locations on the island.

She found Southwest Harbor and the charming inn, Bay View Landings. It was different, a bit old world, secluded, quiet, and steeped in nineteenth century charm. Bay View Landings overlooks a bay which opens to the broad ocean. For the second time in as many days Lila watched the whales out beyond the bay leaping and neatly folding back into the churning sea, disappearing below only to reappear again a few moments later.

It was an angry, cold June day which had brought rain, a brief clearing, then rain again. The chill winds whipped at the pines outside her corner window.

After hanging up from her call to Vermont she looked away from the window, and back into the quiet of the room. She found comfort and peace in her immediate surroundings, the century old-four poster bed, the saucy Chippendale table, and the antique gold-framed oil painting of a fisherman returning home to his family. The wallpaper was an old print, familiar, but where she had seen it Lila couldn't recall.

Standing only five feet two inches, Lila Maret was smart, independent, attractive, and an excellent writer. She generated a reasonable income out of her writing and editing which was supplemented by the interest on a lump-sum settlement she received from her wealthy, Iranian ex-husband who's attitude toward the independence of women, which he'd claimed to admire, disappeared soon after he and Lila were married.

Many of her friends and even her mother had urged her not to wed the handsome Middle East suitor. But she had felt courageous in defying that advice, and knew now that had been part of the appeal. From the experience she learned that defiance too often masquerades as courage when wisdom is what is needed.

When she wasn't traveling the globe, Lila made her home in a mountain-side condominium she owned at Jay Peak, Vermont's northern-most ski area. It was during her time at Jay that she would take on the occasional editing jobs for which she was much in demand. Jay Peak also afforded a close proximity to both Montreal, Canada, and Burlington, Vermont, and their international airports. The location also provided the solitude she desired.

Shivering slightly from the cool Maine air pouring off the window, Lila's thoughts returned to the task at hand. Grabbing the phone on the small table, frowning, she dialed. The operator answering asked her to stand by her party would be returning the call. Moments later her phone rang.

She answered.

After a pause, she replied, "Yes, Edgar, I'm meeting him Friday, in two days. I'll call you after."

She listened a few moments longer and said, "Yes, okay," and hung up. Still frowning, she paused, and stared momentarily at the phone, her hand still on the receiver.

She turned away and went to the window, her attention once again drawn to the ocean raging beyond.

She could no longer see the whales.

In Washington, Edgar Steele had been working feverishly throughout the week preparing for the conference in New Hampshire at the Mount Washington Hotel. With the information gleaned from Willey's address book, Steele was now convinced that Willey had mailed the third envelope to Congressman Duval's Vermont office and all he had to do was head it off. Duval was the immediate target, and Willey knew that. Logically, he would have sent one copy to Senator Stone and the other to Duval, holding on to the third one for himself. Augie Brill had intercepted the one intended for Stone along with the copy he planned to retain.

Willey was probably dead, the river must have risen with the tide and floated him off the ledge to a watery grave. The business with the ignition having been shut off, the keys missing and the car door being closed nagged at him, but even if Willey wasn't dead, Steele had talked to enough people about Willey's peculiar behavior over the last few months so it was already understood among upper echelon staff that Willey was suffering from delusions.

It was easy to start such a story in the highly compartmentalized world of the CIA, and especially from Steele's position in the director's office. The story about Willey's "problem" was beginning to come back to Steele from sources in the Agency who had no idea where it had started. In each case Steele would emphasize his concern for Willey's mental health and ask for understanding. The story was so widespread by now that even if Willey resurfaced it would be impossible for him to reestablish credibility or get anyone to listen to anything he might say about the Agency. Key people in the press had been provided enough information to prevent their being duped by Willey. As was so often the case the press had been "had" and they didn't even know it. Whatever Willey said, his words would be treated as the ravings of a madman — and surely never see print.

Using as an excuse his concern for Willey's mental health, Steele was able, as a result of the special relationships of the CIA to state and local police sources as well as the FBI, to set in motion a large scale investigation on the possible whereabouts of the missing Ben Willey. The Maine State Police had impounded the Lincoln; the Coast Guard had put extra patrols on the river to search for the body.

The phone buzzed. Steele listened.

"The director would like to see you — can you come up now?" Bill Richards's secretary inquired.

"On my way," Steele replied scooping up two file folders which held the planning materials for the Mount Washington Conference.

As Steele walked into the director's office after being announced, Richards's eyes flicked toward the clock. He smiled to himself. Steele somehow always managed to get to his office faster than any of his other immediate staff. "How are we doing on the conference, Ed?"

"Everything's on track — the good news is that the FBI is cooperating in a way no one would believe. J. Edgar must be spinning in his grave. The bad news is that nearly all our European visitors need their own travel agent. Almost all of them have made plans to vacation after the conference, but they're going in different directions and to different resorts! Some down to the Cape, others up to the Balsams, a few to Stowe, Killington, Sugarbush in Vermont — you name it!"

Steele shifted gears and became more serious. Opening the first of the two folders, he said, "The planning team's work on this has been first class." He went on to describe how the conference design met the goals that had been established through an extensive number of international phone calls. Richards interrupted occasionally with questions which Steele handled with deft and admirable professionalism.

When Richards was made director of the CIA after resigning his seat in Congress, it would seem from press accounts that he didn't have an enemy in the world. The reality was that a number of people in the White House — faceless yet powerful people — deeply resented the role Richards had played in the South American intelligence leak known as the Everson Episode. The price of peace, or at least a cease-fire, required placing some former White House staffers from the previous administration in some of the key positions in the Agency. Richards had been around Washington long enough to realize that the price was not unreasonable. He had accepted "advice" from top assistants to the President on who should fill certain vacancies. A former secretary of state, called to second Steele's appointment.

Steele had worked for the man in the previous administration after finishing his graduate work at Johns Hopkins. Steele had never held a responsible line position, and at first Richards was at a loss over what to do with him. Then he got the idea of making Steele a staff assistant to himself as director. In doing this, he left the job responsibilities purposely vague, hoping to use Steele to prod the bureaucracy when he wanted to get things moving on one front or the other. He had never been sorry. Steele, he knew, had a little of the hustler in him, tried a little harder, perhaps was a bit of a gamesman. But if at times he seemed to have his own agenda, he was nonetheless smart as hell, and very effective.

"... so I'll be flying up Sunday night," continued Steele.

"Are you flying into Portland?"

"I think so ..."

"Could you go through Burlington, Vermont instead, I've got something I'd like you to handle?"

"Yes, Burlington would be okay ...", Steele hesitated, "I don't know what the flights are. I figured Portland was a little closer, and probably had a better choice of flights."

"I need you to go through Burlington and meet somebody at Congressman Duval's office on Monday morning. You should still be able to get to Mt. Washington by late-afternoon — possible?"

Steele's eyes barely flickered when he heard Duval's name; the irony of visiting that office was not lost on him. He replied simply, "No problem — what have you got going there?"

"You remember Duval — you set up that special side trip he took in South America to go and meet with Arturo Tomarra. Duval is a friend, you know. Anyway, he thinks somebody's mucking around in his campaign; sounds like dirty tricks. I don't know if there's anything to it, but I promised you'd meet with his guy in Vermont and talk it through with him — I know he should go to the FBI, but you know how they are in the other party, they don't trust the Bureau."

Steele, at first stunned then amused at the suggestion, maintained his outward calm.

Richards continued, "I told Duval that you were looking for somebody who really knew the north country so we'd have all the answers for our foreign visitors. He said Jack Marston, the guy you worked with on the South American side trip, has lots of experience and knowledge about northern New England."

"I'll be glad to meet Mr. Marston; I only dealt with him over the phone before. It'll be good to see him in person."

Chapter Eleven

Lila Maret arose Thursday morning to the same mix of cold and rain that she had found when she arrived, a few days earlier. It was time to leave; she'd had enough. She'd rented the ocean front room to be able to watch the sun rise over the water in the morning, and to see and feel it bursting through the trees filling her room. The explosion of sun on summer mornings in Maine was part of the appeal that drew her back time and again. But Maine failed her this time, first with the rain, then the fog, and now the cold.

She packed her two bags, stuffing in the five rolls of exposed film. She closed up her computer and put it in its carrying case, slung her purse over her right shoulder and took one last look at the comfortable room. It would take her two trips to carry everything to the car. When she returned to the room for the rest of her things, she stopped, and took one last look out at the ocean. Then she turned quickly about and walked briskly down the wide stairs to the front desk.

She had to remind the desk clerk of the professional discount they had agreed upon, but with that problem resolved she was soon behind the wheel of her Subaru on the first leg of her seven-hour trip across northern New England.

As she settled in for the drive, her mind drifted to the assignment she had accepted from Edgar Steele. Lila had worked for him before. Because of the nature of her work and the large volume of necessary related travel, she supposed she was a natural for the simple assignments he had given her. This was her third such assignment. The two other times he had engaged her help she had been traveling outside the country, once in Israel, and another time in France. On these trips, she had acted simply as an observer, reporting back to Steele whatever she picked up. It hadn't been much. In Israel he had asked her to attend a cocktail party and talk with certain people to determine their attitudes on recent American changes in Middle Eastern policy. Another time, while she was in France attending a film festival, he had asked her to report on anything she could uncover on a couple of Algerian film-makers' murky background. In neither case did she feel she accomplished anything.

Steele had phoned her at her Jay Peak condo yesterday, and she returned his call after calling her answering machine for messages. She'd been surprised at the request. Though she said nothing she knew the CIA had responsibilities for matters beyond the borders of the USA.

Anticipating her concerns about this, Steele explained that this was a special case. He said that an Agency employee had retired and was acting strangely, probably suffering a breakdown. The man, Ben Willey, was a considerable risk to the Agency and even more to himself. Willey, he said, had taken classified material and might be sending it to a congressman in Vermont named Alan Duval.

Steele cautioned that even if it were being sent to a congressman, Willey could be charged with a breach of national security. Steele was trying to protect the guy, to keep him out of trouble, and he needed Lila's help.

Each time she worked for Steele he paid her well, and included a liberal expense allowance in the payment. Nonetheless, this time she was uneasy. She would have to misrepresent herself. Somehow it didn't feel quite right, but she hadn't felt as though she could turn it down. "Trade offs," she mused. "Trade offs."

After about three hours in the car and while crossing the border from Maine into New Hampshire she began to smell the odor of sulfur generated by the paper mills in Berlin, New Hampshire. Later when she arrived in Gorham, New Hampshire, fifteen miles south of Berlin, she spotted a motel in the center of town where she had stayed once before. Impulsively she swung in the drive; the rest of the trip could wait until morning. She parked and checked in.

She rose the next morning to a bright June day. Looking out the window of her motel room, she found the weather system which had persisted throughout her stay in Maine had lifted. Droplets of rain on her window were burning away from the heat of the early morning sun. She felt a sense of anticipation inspired by the beauty of the New England summer morning. Sensitive to color from the time she was very young, she had noticed each year how the buddings on the trees were a unique light green during June; when another month passed, and the leaves filled out the colors would become full and darken slightly, bringing the lush north country to summer's full bloom.

Lila Maret had traveled the world looking for beauty and excitement to write about and to photograph. But she knew that for her there was no greater beauty than that offered by northern New England in the summer.

◆ ◆ ◆ ◆ ◆ ◆ ◆

Back in Brunswick, Maine, Herbert Kleinerman again dialed Ben Willey's town house. Still no answer. He hadn't heard from Willey since Tuesday. It was now Friday. On Thursday evening, Kleinerman had driven over to

Willey's condo, but found the doors locked and no one answered when he rapped on the door and rang the bell.

Kleinerman was traveling to Toronto, Canada for a long weekend, a fact he simply forgot to mention to Ben Willey when he last saw him. Kleinerman had been engaged as tournament director for one of the major chess tournaments held in Canada, the Eastern-Canadian Swiss Open. It was to begin this evening and run through Sunday.

Willey's envelope was lying in the drawer with the Kleinerman's airline tickets. When he put the phone down he looked again at the padded envelope. The arrangement was to mail it if there was a lapse of seventy-two hours. But this bothered him, since it meant something might have happened to his friend. Kleinerman drummed his fingers, and stared straight ahead. He then busied himself with the few things he had to do before he left.

Later, when it was time to go, he picked up the envelope and slipped it into the zippered section of one of his bags. Greta was coming down the stairs as he locked the front door. They exited out the back door; Kleinerman put the bags in the trunk. With the plane scheduled to take off at eleven o'clock they had plenty of time to stop at the Post Office on the way to the airport.

Kleinerman backed out of the garage still concerned for the whereabouts of his friend Ben Willey.

◆ ◆ ◆ ◆ ◆ ◆ ◆

"I'm Lila Maret, I have an eleven o'clock appointment with Mr. Marston," Lila introduced herself to the receptionist.

"Oh, yes. Good morning, Ms. Maret. Have a chair won't you?" replied Shirley Hogan, who got up from behind her desk and rather than using the intercom walked down the hall to Jack Marston's office to let him know his visitor had arrived.

As was his custom, Marston walked out to the reception area and approached Lila Maret with his hand extended. "Nice to meet you, Ms. Maret. Let's go down and use the boss's office where we can be comfortable," he said, glancing over at her and flashing a conspiratorial smile to accompany his suggestion.

Marston sized up his visitor. A small woman, yet striking; someone you would never miss, never ignore. She walked with a strength in her step, poised, perhaps a bit aloof. He ushered her into the comfortable, attractively furnished office of Congressman Alan Duval which was located at the end of the hall.

"You came all the way from Mt. Desert Island this morning?" inquired Marston, as he gestured toward the sofa and chose the high wing chair for himself. Lila Maret made herself comfortable at the end of the sofa. She smiled, crossed her legs, and sat back. She appeared completely at ease.

Marston continued, "My wife and I used to spend time there but I haven't been up there for ... maybe ten years. Great area. Beautiful."

When Marston first greeted people he often talked along like this, not waiting for answers but using the time to watch people, to observe their reactions. He was scarcely aware that he did it. It was his way of getting to know them.

Answering Marston's first question, Lila smiled and replied, "I drove as far as Gorham, New Hampshire and stayed in a motel, then came on early this morning. I've been writing an article on Mt. Desert Island ..."

"Gorham, oh yes," Marston remembered playing ball in Gorham almost forty years ago on a blazing hot day, at a ballpark located in the center of town. He started to tell his visitor of this, then thought better of it and said simply, "I hear it's been rainy up there."

"Yes, this is my first visit where the weather really spoiled the time."

"Oh, you don't live there?" Marston inquired.

"Oh no, Mr. Marston, I'm a Vermonter, I live up in Jay — right at Jay Peak, I have a condo there."

"I see," replied Marston. To Marston, Lila Maret seemed self-assured, in control, in her mid-thirties or maybe less; perhaps fifteen or twenty years younger than himself. He continued, "Ben Willey came from Maine, I just assumed ..."

"Yes, he did," Lila replied, relieved that Marston had been the first to raise the subject. She paused a moment, "This may sound a little strange — I don't quite know where to begin."

Marston smiled. "Plenty of time," he said, "just take it from the top." He leaned back in the chair continuing to admire his attractive visitor. She was slim; her skin creamy smooth. The near perfect pale complexion was set off by jet black hair and dark eyes. These were eyes, he knew intuitively, that could flash with joy, or anger, or could suddenly soften in a way that would take a man's breath away — or at least his, Marston thought to himself smiling inwardly.

Her hands folded in her lap, Lila went on: "Mr. Marston, as you know, Ben Willey worked for the CIA. He retired as of last Friday, and left for Brunswick, Maine where he leased a condominium. People from the CIA have called me ...." She looked down at her hands which she had unconsciously been rubbing together, "They said he has been acting peculiarly lately, and apparently they have been watching him. They believe he left the Agency Friday with classified information, then copied it and distributed it around for some unknown reason. Mentally he's just not right, they told me."

Marston left his chair and walked to the window. The fifth floor offices of Congressman Alan Duval offered a magnificent view of Lake Champlain now sparkling in the distance. Turning from the window and the view, Marston looked at Lila Maret and said, "He was here a few months ago. He seemed fine ..." As he trailed off, he thought back trying to recall his last conversation with Ben Willey.

"Did he say anything?"

Marston glanced at Lila Maret, and said, "What do you mean? Say anything about what?"

Lila tensed, "Oh, I don't know ... I'm just ..."

"Just trying to figure it out," said Marston completing her thought and relieving the tension that momentarily flared.

"I guess that's it," she continued. "Did he send you anything in the mail? The people who contacted me seem to think you were on the list — or at least that the congressman was." She stopped, paused, then continued decisively, "Can I ask you to contact me if you get anything in the mail from him," she hesitated, "... and not open the package? They told me they're trying to protect him, but if that material gets out they'll have to prosecute. I'm the only relative left in this part of the country. However if you prefer not to give me the material he sends, then the CIA has provided me with a contact for you." She spoke rapidly, virtually blurting out the last of it, belying for a moment her poise and seemingly calm demeanor.

"If anything comes here it will probably be addressed to Duval, although Ben might send it to me," Marston said buying time. "Where's Ben now?" he inquired

"That's just it, we're not sure."

"Who's we?"

Lila's face darkened. When she replied her eyes were looking past Marston, "Just me and the man who called from the CIA."

Marston hadn't been trying to throw his visitor off; on the contrary he had gone out of his way to put her at ease, but he sensed a strange inconsistency like she somehow wasn't telling it all. Instinctively Marston wanted to help. He found himself looking at his visitor in a way he hadn't looked at a woman for quite a while. Perhaps that was it; maybe her charms made him unusually attentive to what she was saying.

Jack Marston had been widowed for well over a year. After Ann died he was surprised at the extra attention he was given, especially by women.

He was a problem to be solved, or so they made him feel. And there were some women for whom his single status was of immediate interest. But he had finessed all of it.

But Lila Maret intrigued him. She was so terribly controlled, poised, and yet she signaled vulnerability. Marston saw it in her eyes or thought he did. Perhaps it was the small nervous gestures or the worried frown that flashed across her brow for just a moment before it disappeared.

Not long after Ann's death, friends urged him to meet women who might be available for dating. He couldn't imagine what that would be like. But Marston enjoyed concerts, movies, and didn't like attending them alone so after a few months he finally took his friends' advice and invited a woman who taught at the university and whom he had known for some time to go to dinner and to the theater.

At the end of the evening he left his friend Martha Livingstone with a friendly kiss on the cheek, and mumbled something about making future plans. He enjoyed the evening. But he never got around to asking her or anyone else out again.

Before going out he spent hours worrying about the date. It had been too long. With Martha he spent time determining how he should act; how to relate to a young (Martha was seven years younger) woman in the 1990s. His last date had been in the 1960s!

He wondered what she would expect. Could he keep it casual? He worried about any sense of intimacy. How would that feel after so long? And he didn't want to insult or embarrass Martha. His worries, albeit in a slightly different way, were the same worries he experienced over forty years ago on the occasion of his eighth grade graduation dance.

While the evening with Martha had been pleasant, even fun in some ways, he knew she was a friend and would always be a friend; but only a friend. He couldn't imagine more than that.

He decided the romantic part of his life was over. He thought he'd adjusted to Ann's death fairly well. But his doctor, a friend for many years, laid it on the line during his last physical, and told Jack he was fooling himself if he thought he was reconciled to the loss. "Doc" Phelan said, "Dammit Jack, your frame of mind is no different than it was two days after Ann died. You're experiencing some kind of low grade depression and you're doing nothing to get out of it."

"What do you want me to do? Should I take ..."

"You can use pills if you want — plenty of doctors will prescribe them for you, but not me, not now. More often than not with this kind of thing it just postpones the fact that you have to face the world alone — and in a different way." Doc Phelan paused, and concluded more sympathetically, "Just reach out a little Jack, and call me if your problem with insomnia gets any worse or you experience any other of the symptoms we talked about. Okay?"

Most of the time Jack Marston kept busy with his work. He had friends to play tennis with once a week; he ran five miles once or twice a week. He read voraciously. But he knew underneath that all was not well. At two different times, for no reason he could identify, he experienced half-hour crying jags at home early in the evening. He told no one. Unfortunately for Jack Marston life had become a matter of avoiding unhappiness; he could barely remember experiencing joy.

These thoughts raced through his mind as he reached the end of his discussion with Lila Maret. He really didn't want the conversation to end, but there wasn't much more to say. He agreed to help her get the envelope when it arrived and before it was opened, to protect Ben Willey from charges of violating national security. It seemed kind of strange the way the Agency was going about it, enlisting an outsider — albeit a relative — but it was probably some guy down the line who was an old friend of Ben's trying to shortcut the system a little to protect him. Marston could understand that; he would do the same. Too many people around government these days took themselves and the government too seriously. Long ago, Marston vowed not to be one of them.

Lila Maret and Jack Marston walked together slowly down the hall. Lila was talking about her book, a different kind of travel guide that included within it historical, social and economic vignettes about New England. Such a guide she hoped would greatly broaden the perspective of the traveler who was using it. Lila was discussing with Marston some of her research findings.

"You're enthusiasm for your research is contagious," Marston said, "And you have other projects under way as well?"

Lila laughed, "If I get bogged down with the book, I can rest a while and work on an article. I like to keep a lot on my plate."

Once in the outer office Marston stopped to introduce Lila to Shirley Hogan, and continued, "... and Shirley, we may get a package in the mail with Ben Willey's return address. Under no circumstances should that package be opened. Make sure everyone in the office knows that."

"The mail always comes to me, so there won't be any problem."

"Thanks, Shirley, it's a confusing situation that I won't go into, but the important thing to know is that the material in the envelope is classified. If it were opened it might get my old friend Ben Willey in trouble, and we can't have that," he said flashing a smile at Shirley Hogan and holding it for a moment longer as he turned again toward Lila Maret.

Lila, standing quietly, reached out her hand to Marston and said, "Thank you so much. I'm relieved. I really dreaded asking you," Lila said, feeling honest and straightforward for the first time.

Marston shook her right hand, then, not letting go, he brought his left hand on top so he was holding her hand with both of his and said, "Just stay in touch — we'll help in every way we can." He wanted to say more.

When she was gone, Marston walked back to the other end of the open reception area where Shirley Hogan's desk was located. He stood at the window looking out on the city, the lake, and the mountains beyond. He wanted to tell someone how he felt.

Shirley watched for a moment and said, "Well, wasn't she a charmer!"

Marston turned on his heel and snapped, "She's just a kid!"

Shirley Hogan stared after Marston as he walked back toward his office, her momentarily puzzled expression changing to a knowing smile as she reached to answer the phone.

Marston had sent everyone home shortly before five, the phone buzzed. "Congressman Duval's office," he answered.

"Mr. Marston, Lila Maret. I'm sorry to bother you again. I believe I left my sunglasses there — probably in the office where we met."

Marston's pulse jumped, "Just a minute — Lila," he replied, using her name for the first time.

He found her glasses on the small stand at the end of the sofa, in Duval's office. Picking up the phone beside the sofa he said, "Right here waiting for you."

"Oh, good, I thought they must have been there. Will you be there a while? I don't want to inconvenience you. I'm at the university library, and I can get down the hill in fifteen minutes ..."

"No problem, I'll be here until six ..., or can I meet you up there somewhere and then you won't have to come down in traffic."

Lila paused, "Do you come out this way? I'm overnight at the Holiday Inn since I need to get back to the library in the morning."

Marston's spirits rose; he would see her again. He replied, "I'll be in the lobby of the Holiday Inn at ten after six."

"See you then," Lila said softly, gently replacing the receiver.

Lila Maret had been sitting off to the side of the lobby when Marston came through the door. She stood and greeted him in the middle of the lobby.

"Thanks so much. I hope this wasn't too far out of your way," she said taking the sunglasses he held out to her.

"No problem at all," he replied, turning away awkwardly, as though to leave, yet looking for a reason not to. "Say, have you got time for a drink?"

"I sure do," Lila replied.

Moments later they were comfortably situated in the bar off the main lobby. They chatted amiably for a while when Marston interjected, "Say, I've got an idea. "I have to be at the Radisson for a special dinner honoring Congressman Duval in about an hour, would you like to be my guest? I'll introduce you to the congressman — and to all of Vermont's 'four hundred' who'll be there — if there are four hundred!" he quipped.

"An hour? I'd have to get ready?" She thought a moment, looked up at Marston, smiled, and said, "Sure, I'd love to."

Lila went to her room to change. Marston waited in the bar, sipping on his beer and wondering if the composer of the weird-sounding music playing on the juke box was mentally deranged. Certifiable, he decided, after a while.

In her motel room getting ready, Lila Maret was having second thoughts. It had been too easy to say yes to Marston's invitation. She hadn't bargained for this.

Back in Washington, the traffic was beginning to clear. After six o'clock on a Friday in the District, only a few dedicated workaholics can be found still pushing papers. Elected officials and staffers head to their home districts while many of the vast army of government workers are on their way to the Maryland shore and relief from the heat. Mostly it was the poor who remained.

And Edgar Steele.

Steele dialed the Holiday Inn in Burlington. Earlier there had been no answer when the desk rang Lila's room.

"Yes?" she said as she picked up the phone on the first ring.

"Edgar here. I've been trying to get you," he said trying to mask his irritation. "What can you tell me?"

"Mr. Marston's agreed to give us ... me, the envelope when it comes. I explained ..."

"We can't find Willey," Steele interrupted — "the man is truly unbalanced and I'm worried about him. I need that envelope. I don't want him hurt anymore. Find a way ... Can you find a way to stay close to this Marston until we're successful? Stay right in town if you want. Haunt this Marston, use your charms."

"Hey, wait a minute!"

"I didn't mean ... it's just that we need to get that damned envelope, and if Marston doesn't give it to you, I'll have to send someone in to take it!" Steele said more than he intended.

"You mean you'd take it by force — steal it?" Lila asked incredulously.

"I have to have it ..."

"Edgar, My God, I'm in over my head here!" Lila was thinking of the evening ahead and the friendly hospitality Marston had offered and she had so easily accepted. She was glad she hadn't told Steele she was going out with Marston. His approval would have devastated her.

Hoping to placate matters, Steele tried charm. "Hey pal, I'm sorry, just stay close to him and let me know what's going on, okay?"

For a few moments Lila didn't answer. Then she said in a subdued tone, "I'll call you tomorrow, when I can." She hung up.

For a few moments longer Lila stood motionless, her hand still resting on the receiver. Marston expected her to be ready in a few minutes, but she needed time to think. She began pacing, and wondered fleetingly why she had ever quit smoking. She stopped to turn on the FM radio built into the television set opposite the bed. As she fumbled with the dial she was shaking her head, her mind alive and angry. Moments later later she turned off the radio, walked to the window, and after fiddling with the venetian blinds sat down in the corner chair.

Moments later she had gotten up, took out her valet bag and prepared to dress for the dinner.

When she first spoke with Steele about the assignment, he faxed her a scratchy picture of Willey along with some limited background information. She figured at the time that she would have the one meeting with Marston and be on her way. But now she had agreed to go out with him, all the time masquerading as Willey's cousin. It didn't feel right.

She liked Jack Marston. She tried to convince herself that what she was doing wasn't really dishonest, but now that she had met Marston for a drink and he had invited her out to the awards dinner, her conscience was bothering her.

At their initial meeting he had quickly put her at ease. When a few minutes earlier he offered his spur of the moment invitation to the awards dinner, she had quickly agreed. She thought her reasons were that the dinner might open up some professional opportunities, but during the ride downtown in Marston's car, she realized it was not professional curiosity alone that had lured her to attend the dinner at all.

He was easy to be with. There was no overly clever conversation, no attempts to impress. There was a hint of weariness about him — or was it sadness? He gave her the feeling that she had all the room in the world — but that she didn't need that room. She was drawn to him, yet it wasn't sexual. Or maybe only a little. She had made those mistakes before. No, Jack Marston was going to be a good friend and Edgar Steele and Ben Willey be damned!

◆ ◆ ◆ ◆ ◆ ◆ ◆

If ever anyone was born to live and work in Washington, D.C. it was Edgar Steele. The man looked and walked like he was always in a hurry, leaning forward, almost as though advertising his need to be first. He combed his hair straight back, ignoring the way it emphasized his receding hairline. Steele, whose IQ level was in the genius range, had established a brilliant record in a small high school outside of Chicago. He attended George Washington where he graduated with top honors. School officials had identified early that Edgar Steele was different. If he was occasionally anti-social, or if his temper flared in a way that caused problems with other students, school officials wrote it off to his background. Difficult, but brilliant they said.

As he watched out the window, traffic was still exiting. The lights of some of the cars were turned on and flickered like dutiful fireflies; in his mind he once more went over the problem created by Ben Willey, a not insignificant matter. Still Steele was not overly concerned, as he was confident that he had gotten on top of it fast enough to prevent Willey's involvement from having any effect.

Augie Brill had also complicated things. It wasn't like Augie to screw up, but by physically attacking and maybe killing Willey, he created another set of problems that Steele would have preferred to avoid.

After Brill had taken the envelopes from Ben Willey, and left him for dead, Steele decided it would be best to get Brill out of Maine. He would need somebody in Vermont anyway, the way he had it figured, so who better than Brill? In Vermont Brill would be out of the way of any investigation into Willey's death if a body showed up. If not, he could back up Lila, if her efforts were unsuccessful. Despite the overzealous attack on Willey, Steele still considered Brill a good operative: unafraid, patient and capable of breaking into Fort Knox if necessary.

Steele now needed to know if Willey was dead or alive. It nagged at him. He had been quietly planting doubts about Willey's mental stability for some time. Willey was now so generally discredited that even if he reappeared, no one would believe him unless he had solid evidence.

Still, the critical factor for Steele was that he get his hands on the third envelope before it was opened. Everything would have to remain on hold until the envelope was in his possession. For the two days following Brill's assault on Willey, Steele failed to find a trace of evidence concerning the missing man's whereabouts. Using the far-flung resources of the Agency, Steele found that that no one matching that description had been admitted to any of the area hospitals. Willey's Lincoln remained unclaimed behind a chain link fence at a yard near the county sheriff's office.

Steele loved the game. He was a complex, brilliant man and when his plans were upset as they had been by Ben Willey, Steele felt a rush from the challenge. He loved money; and he also loved pleasing his idol and mentor, Alex Konig, a man whom, when he pictured him in his mind, he often confused with another man, a man called "Dutch." Steele interned with Konig one summer while in college. Konig had taken an interest and they had remained in contact over the years. Dutch was one of many men who came and stayed with his mother for a time when Steele was a young boy. Dutch had left like the others, but not before bestowing a few acts of kindness on the lonely, impressionable ten-year-old. Memories from that time were sad or painful, faces of most people only a blur. The few good memories were of his mother and Dutch. The dark side of his past was shaped by the uncertainty born of the drugs and alcohol from which his mother was never totally free. Fear and terror had been an early and constant companion; escape his only hope.

His intellect freed him from this past, but at a price.

Edgar Steele had worked feverishly since seven thirty that morning on structuring the international anti-terrorism conference to be held at the Mount Washington Hotel. For years international cooperation in combating terrorism had been given only lip service, with little action taken. But now, by agreeing to attend the New Hampshire conference, the western industrialized nations had finally recognized the importance of finding mechanisms and procedures by which they could jointly respond to acts of terrorism. Breakthroughs were already occurring in the sharing of information, and the upcoming conference at Bretton Woods offered the possibility that unified strategies and policies were within reach. Steele had drafted a series of agreements for the conferees to act upon, and provided case study material to illustrate the significance of each agreement. This level of specificity was unheard of at most international conferences, the result being that agreements often fell apart shortly after the meetings ended. Steele worked hard to make sure this conference would produce results, for if success were achieved, the quiet hero would be the talented, complex, Edgar Steele.

Chapter Twelve

The Radisson Hotel faces west, overlooking the widest part of Lake Champlain, with the Adirondack Mountains of New York State standing tall in the background. Marston drove to the underground garage and within minutes he and Lila were standing outside the large banquet room where a mix of environmentalists, politicians, Chittenden County do-gooders, and a few that could be described by all of these terms were gathered. Milling around, glasses in hand, the guests dabbled in polite conversation regarding the upcoming performance of *La Traviata* coming to the Flynn Theater the next evening, a major gift bestowed upon the university, and in quieter asides there were whispered words about a major official in the Department of Public Safety who had been caught in flagrante delicto with the wife of the Attorney General at an out-of-state conference.

Marston and Lila arrived a bit late, but found the bar still serving. Marston noted with amusement the double take of his friends when they saw him accompanied by an attractive younger woman. Lila was wearing a simple black dress with silver earrings and a delicate silver necklace. Understated, but just right. Accompanying Marston as she was, Lila was provoking curiosity among the invitees.

Lila was something new!

"You've got the natives buzzing," Marston whispered in her ear, smiling inwardly with a hint of pride.

"Oh, I hope not," she replied self-consciously, looking away.

Marston had spotted Duval across the hall and watched a moment while the congressman talked easily with one person after another. At dinners of this sort, it was good politics to let Duval work the room on his own. Still, Marston believed that Duval should never be without staff around him. If he became isolated Marston would be at his side in moments. There would be no problem this evening, however, Duval was the guest of honor and there was little chance he would be left alone.

The cocktail hour ended and it was time to find a table. Marston spotted some friends from the university, and joined them at one of the large round tables to the left of the head table. Completing the group was the head of one of the new local software companies and her spouse, the senior public relations officer from IBM, and a couple of state senators, all people Marston knew and liked,

It was like a thousand banquets he had been to throughout the years.

The head table faced the door from the back of the room and flower arrangements brightened each table. Attractive young waitresses from the university dressed alike in some sort of Swiss motif. The young waiters bustling about taking drink orders looked ill at ease in stark white shirts, black ties and black pants. Their outfits were ill-matched with the rundown brown shoes or sneakers they wore, something the headwaiter, to his chagrin, had overlooked when outlining the dress code. The wait-crew worked feverishly delivering the skimpy salads to each guest.

"How much is your boss going to win by, Jack?" boomed State Senator Ed Wescott, a member of the other party, but tacitly a strong supporter of Alan Duval.

Sitting comfortably at the table now, Marston replied, "Ed, I know you won't believe me, but this thing isn't in the bag by a long shot. Meacham," Marston continued referring to Duval's main opponent, "has proven that he can raise money; he's got the national committee's attention. They think he's got a chance. And the mood is souring out there — it's a bad year for anyone connected to Washington."

"You believe that Jack? Come on, you just want to pick my pocket again," said Wescott who had already made a sizeable contribution to the Duval campaign. "The polls show your boss ahead by ..."

"What they show is that Meacham has gained ten points in the last three weeks, and he hasn't even started with TV commercials!"

"Christ, you really *are* nervous. Meacham's gained ten points because he started at zero! How about Duval's TV — you haven't started yet, have you?"

"No, and I don't know exactly when we will start — usually it's earlier than this — the campaign staff are all young people you know, novices — they make me nervous; they're barely old enough to vote." Marston was sending a subtle message that complacency would be dangerous; he fully expected Wescott to pass that message along to his friends.

While Marston finished sparring with Wescott, Lila Maret was comparing notes on travel experiences in France with Edna Baxter, an economist with special expertise in the European Common Market who had been traveling in France and Belgium for the past six weeks. Marston, his conversation over for the moment, turned his attention to Lila Maret. Animated as she spoke, her gestures seemed fresh and exciting to him. From this Marston derived a momentary sense of sadness, of nostalgia, for what he saw was something he could remember and understand, but was unsure that he could ever know and feel again.

Following the salad came the inevitable chicken. Lila asked, "How many of these dinners have you attended since you entered politics?"

He laughed, "Enough so I haven't ordered chicken in a restaurant for twenty years!"

Pulling her chair closer Lila said, "Thank you for asking me — this is pretty much a new experience for me — at least in Vermont. I attended a few events like this in Washington some years ago, and I ..."

"Excuse me, Lila," Marston interrupted rising to his feet. Lila's eyes followed Marston who was looking toward the door where someone was signaling wildly for him to come over. "I'll be right back."

Marston moved hurriedly to the back of the hall. Lila cast a glance at Congressman Duval sitting at the head table. Duval's attention was also on Marston's visitor at the door.

"Yes, Peter, what do you need?" Marston's calm voice belied an uneasy feeling that came over him the minute he had spotted the young campaign aid at the door. Peter Bryann handed Marston a copy of a newspaper clipping, explaining, "This was in the *Washington Tell-Tale*. It says there's a big story, a scandal that's going to break about Duval's campaign — the bastards don't say a damn thing about what it is — can you believe someone printing this crap?

"Calm down Peter," Marston said, "You'll give the congressman a heart attack," he said, glancing out of the corner of his eye at Duval who remained attentive to what Marston and his young visitor were up to.

"John Godine says to bring Duval back to your office after dinner and he'll meet you there. Okay? Can I tell him you'll be there?" The young volunteer shifted nervously on his feet, waiting for Marston's reply.

"Tell John I'll be there — and I'll get Duval if he'll come," he said, and then with a smile concluded, "He's the boss you know!"

Bryann grinned back. It was all new to him, and exciting as hell. Marston hoped Duval had seen this last relaxed exchange, the smiles, and the pat on the back he had given Bryann just as they parted. Still, it wouldn't do much good. Duval was a hard man to fool.

As he sat back down at the table he took a small pad from his pocket and quickly scribbled a note.

"Trouble?" Lila asked curiously.

"Yes — I'll be right back." Marston rose and walked as unobtrusively as possible around the back of the head table until he was standing directly behind Alan Duval. He whispered in the congressman's ear and handed him the note. With that he backed off and waited near the end of the table in case Duval wanted to scribble an answer.

Duval looked up and merely nodded.

Marston worked his way back to his seat and leaned over to whisper an apology to Lila Maret.

Between courses the master of ceremonies introduced various VIPs in the audience including the mayor, a former governor, a famous aging movie star who resided in northern Vermont, and Vermont's own Olympic medal winner in cross country skiing, Wendy Pepin.

At the head table, Gordon Vanderhoof — the man many people credited as the father of the environmental movement in Vermont — was introduced. The venerable octogenarian was much loved and respected throughout Vermont, and thus the obvious choice to present the award to Duval. It was Vanderhoof who had provided the original inspiration and much of the start-up money for the "Vermont Way" program. The Vermont Way was a multi-purpose organization with a major emphasis on environmental education for young Vermonters. The program had expanded and now dealt with the education of the general public as well. As the program grew and prospered over the years, it became the symbol of Vermont's national leadership in environmental conservation.

Vanderhoof briefly discussed the origins of the Vermont Way and then described in glowing terms the role Alan Duval had played. "Congressman Duval has made enormous contributions to Vermont, New England, and even beyond the political boundaries of man ... he has touched this world, and his hands have bestowed and nurtured life out beyond our time ..."

After the fifteen minute introduction, he concluded, saying, "It is now my honor to present Congressman Duval with a token of our esteem that can only symbolize in a small way the respect, admiration, and love we feel for him."

Vanderhoof picked up the box laying next to him on the table, removed the cover and took out the gift wrapped in white tissue. Before handing it to Duval, he unveiled a plaque with a brass plate inset into a lightly-stained piece of Vermont rock maple. The words honoring Duval were inscribed in golden raised letters with the outline of Camel's Hump, Vermont's most distinctive mountain, as backdrop.

The crowd rose as one, and the applause filled the room.

Marston watched the congressman and felt a surge of genuine affection for the man. He was close to Alan Duval, and knew the innermost family secrets. Six years earlier when Duval had decided to run for office Marston had signed on early. Within a short time Duval had come to rely heavily on Marston. Jack Marston had been the one Duval called when his mother died while he was traveling on official business outside the country. When Duval's only son had been missing for over ten days while hiking in the wild Basque country in Spain, it was Marston who kept after the State Department to force inquiries, while at the same time providing moral support until the boy turned up safe. And when Duval's wife Ellie was charged with drunken driving following an automobile accident, it was Jack Marston who talked long and hard with Ellie and Alan, leading Ellie to finally face the fact that her presumed psychiatric problem was in reality, alcoholism, and to finally confront her long-standing problem with pills and booze.

Ellie had checked into "Lindy's Place" an alcohol/drug treatment center on the Maryland shore. Since then she had stayed dry, become active in AA, and in the last two or three years was finding life worth living.

Marston's thoughts drifted further back to when he first met Duval. Already a veteran of Vermont political wars, Marston retained few illusions about politics or politicians. Duval had won him over easily, quickly; Marston never understood why or how. Mostly he decided there was a human dimension, a fundamental decency to Duval that could survive the best or worst that Washington could offer. And he'd been right.

Born in St. Albans Vermont, a railroad town in the northwestern part of the state, Duval had been a hockey star in a town that loved its hockey. His father was born in St. Albans and worked for the railroad all his life. His mother had moved down from Montreal as a young girl and worked for over thirty years in a small downtown department store. After high school Duval enrolled at Boston College on a hockey scholarship where he compiled an enviable record on the ice, as well as in class. Following his four years at Boston College, he enrolled at Rensselaer Polytechnic Institute and obtained an advanced degree in environmental engineering.

Duval had met his wife-to-be, Ellen Smyth, in his last year at Boston College. Ellen, was an undergraduate at Boston University with a major in music. Ellen's father was president of a small bank in western Massachusetts. Her father, while not possessing great wealth, held a position of substantial respect in the community, and was active in countless social endeavors. The Smyth family welcomed young Duval, a roman catholic, into their circle despite differences in religion and social background. The Smyths were staunch congregationalists. As Alan Duval remembered it, he loved Ellen from the day they first met.

For Ellie's part — Ellie was the nickname bestowed by Alan — she found Duval handsome, exciting, unpredictable, and was flattered that he chose her. Ellen Smyth never quite overcame her insecurities and as one result was never truly conscious of her own breathtaking beauty. She supported Alan's political career without ever having understood why he would want to be a part of that rough and tumble world. They had one son, Alan Jr. now in his early twenties.

Following graduate school Alan returned to Vermont. Environmental issues had yet to appear in a major way on the political scene. Duval often told his close friends that in the old days the only Vermonters interested in the environment were a few "country club liberals" who were either retired wealthy "transplants" or as in the case of the younger ones, "trust fund transients." Nonetheless Duval courted this small constituency despite their mixed political loyalties.

Over the next few years Duval had made a name for himself with his fledgling consulting firm. As environmental issues emerged on the front pages of Vermont's newspapers, Duval emerged as a spokesman and a leader on the issue for the concerns of Vermonters across the political spectrum. As it developed whenever debate arose on an issue affecting the environment, Duval was usually questioned by the Vermont press. Curiously, while other Vermont environmentalists were often chided for their elitist approach, this was never a problem for the self-effacing former high school hockey player.

As time passed, his ability to move with equal ease among old friends and new gave evidence of an emerging political talent. He announced for Vermont's House seat when it became vacant and when he was easily elected to Congress it was clear the state had a new kind of politician on hand.

When Alan was first elected to his House seat they purchased a home in Bethesda, Maryland, and Ellie adjusted to life in the District although neither she nor Alan ever became prominent players on the social scene. When she and Alan had lived there less than a year, both of Ellen's parents were killed in an automobile accident while traveling to Florida. The loss devastated her, and she had great difficulty adjusting to it. It was at this time that her alcohol and pill problem surfaced. For a while it had been rough going for both she and Alan, and it was unclear to Jack Marston among others whether the marriage would survive. But at least in part due to Marston's intervention, Ellie was able to get her life back on track. For the first time in years she now took an interest once again in music and became active in a variety of community activities.

Marston thoughts were brought back to the present as Duval stepped to the podium to speak.

His remarks were tight and well organized. He traced the history of the environmental landmarks in Vermont from the original planning legislation in the 1960s, to Act 250, which put the brakes on runaway vacation home development then threatening southern Vermont. He described other federal and state initiatives that had been enacted or were pending. He gave generous credit to The Vermont Way and to individuals in both political parties who played major roles in the success story.

He concluded, "We stand at the vanguard of a new era. Our state — small as it is in a nation of larger and wealthier states — has always been willing to lead. We have proven that our concern for our future will guarantee our future. This then is Vermont's mission. We have provided a vision for all to see, a lesson that all of America has begun to hear and embrace."

As he concluded, the room which had become silent burst into enthusiastic applause. Even among an audience that had sat through many such speeches, it would be difficult to find anyone who had not been touched by Duval's words. When Duval was "on," and he'd been "on" this evening, it was hard not to be a believer in Vermont's only congressman.

People were moving toward the head table seeking to shake the hand of the guest of honor. Others, after waiting a while to try to get to Duval, gave up and moved toward the open doors at the opposite end of the hall.

Lila said to Marston, "I enjoyed this. This is very different from State Department and embassy dinners, at least the ones I've attended, more intimate somehow."

"Most of the people have known each other for a long time," Marston replied, "and it makes for easy relaxed conversation."

Her eyes shifted from Marston to Duval then back to her escort. She sensed a loyalty — a bond of some sort between Marston and Duval. Marston himself seemed unlike other politicians she had met. The drive and intensity found in political types was missing. Still sitting at the table waiting for the crowd to clear, she made this observation to Marston.

He smiled, and replied, "That's probably why I'll never run for office. Most politicians are different than I am. They live for the big moment, the big victory, the big story, and of course, most of all, for the love of the crowd. I am different I guess," he said, looking directly at Lila for a moment as though he he had never seen her before. He looked down and quickly continued, "For me it's the small triumphs, the moments when you know something is better than it was —not just because the press says so. You just know it. I'm afraid those occasions are rare these days in American politics. It's sad, but in politics today, it's the illusions that matter. We've lost our sense of proportion and with it our commitment to substance."

"But Vermont is different than Washington, D.C., or even the large states, wouldn't you say?"

"Vermont has no problems it can't solve if it wants to badly enough. The press has a lot of influence, but Vermont is small enough that people are able to tell when they are being had by the politicians *or* the press. Part of the attraction here is that everything is human scale. Everybody can be part of the action if they want to. I believe Vermont is a better example of our system of government than some — although, believe me, Vermont has a long way to go." He paused, thinking a moment before continuing, then concluded, "It's just that here in the green mountain state everything is possible."

Ignoring the last, Lila persisted, "But why do people like Duval, the decent ones, why do they want to expose themselves to the critics, the press — and risk losing all their privacy? They never get rich, at least not without skirting the rules or waiting till they leave office. Why do they run?"

"You're right, it isn't money. And believe it or not the politicians I know are generally more thin-skinned than average. For a lot of them I think it's a matter of testing themselves — going to do battle. They take it hard, terribly hard, when they think they're criticized unfairly — and they nearly always feel that criticism is unfair!"

The bulk of the crowd had left the hall and Marston and Lila Maret were walking slowly toward the door. Marston nodded, smiled and shook hands with people as he moved along, introducing Lila when possible. He turned to Lila and said, "I'll take you to meet Alan when things are more relaxed. The information I got from the kid at the back of the hall and the note I brought up to Duval was to let him know we had to reconvene back at the office tonight, or at least as soon as Alan can get loose from the crowd. I'll drive you up the hill and drop you off at your motel — I'm sorry I'd really hoped to stop for a drink and hear more about your travels."

"No need to drive me up the hill, I'll get a cab ... or ... or could I just wait for you?" Lila replied, hesitatingly.

Marston stopped; he had hoped to spend time with Lila over a drink. He said, "The meeting won't last too long — Alan hates long meetings. That is — if you don't mind waiting?"

"I'll be fine, I really do want to talk with you," she said, only partially successful in deluding herself that her interest in Marston was merely that of a journalist.

They drove the short distance to Duval's office, parked in the basement garage and entered the elevator. Inserting his key to unlock the elevator Marston shrugged and said with a frown, "That's funny, the elevator is unlocked — I can't believe Alan got here before we did — and the campaign staff doesn't have keys."

As the elevator began to climb, a bell-like tone signaled softly as they passed each floor. Lila broke the silence, "I think Vermont elevators travel slower than those in the city."

Marston laughed, "By God, I think you're right!"

As the bell sounded to signal their arrival on the fifth floor, the empty quiet of the building was interrupted ... a woman's voice cried out. A door slammed. Again the woman shouted — discernable this time saying, "Hey — stop!"

The sound of someone running echoed through the building and another door banged shut.

Then it was quiet.

The elevator holding Lila and Marston had stopped. The two passengers froze for a moment. Their eyes met. Automatically the elevator door opened. Marston signaled for Lila to wait, and he flipped the switch to lock the elevator on the floor. He looked out, glancing in both directions, then walked rapidly down the hall, looking about as he went. Lila hesitated, then followed. Suddenly they heard a new noise; someone was running down the central stairwell.

They stood still for a moment in the hall, close together, almost touching, listening. Neither spoke. Then everything was quiet again. When their eyes met once more, they both smiled, moving apart slightly, self-conscious from intimacy born of fear.

Marston spoke first trying to be casual said, "When they forget to lock the elevator, kids get in here sometimes and raise hell — especially on the weekend." He wondered as he said it if he believed that explanation.

As he approached the office door, key in hand, someone behind him said, "Hold it right there!"

They both turned.

"Oh, I'm sorry Mr. Marston. Someone got up here and broke into your office — I can't imagine how!" Millie Stevens one of the building's security officers had confronted them. When she first approached them she stood braced, nervously holding her flashlight away from her side, her only weapon.

Millie was gutsy; Marston wondered how management got away paying security people like her only five or six bucks an hour. He said, "Someone must have left the elevator unlocked, Millie."

"Oh no, I locked the elevator myself like I always do when I make the rounds — someone was already here," Millie Stevens replied.

"Already here?" Marston said as though to himself. He frowned and turned to unlock the door of his office, then turned to Millie again and said, "You say you think they got in here?"

""He was in there all right," Millie replied decisively.

"Congressman Duval and a couple other people will be right along Millie, so leave the elevator unlocked. Okay?"

"No problem," Millie replied, more relaxed now.

Once inside Duval's office complex Marston wandered through the several individual cubicles and offices to discover if anything was missing. The two valuable hand-sculpted urns that Duval kept in his personal office had not been touched. Everything in his own office was where it belonged as far as he could see. Nor was anything thing else in any significant disarray. Checking Shirley Hogan's office, he came upon a filing cabinet that had been forced but nothing seemed to be missing. He stood staring at the files and said, "Well, if we've been robbed I better let the police look around before I go any further."

As he was taking stock of things, Congressman Duval entered accompanied by Bill Camilli and John Godine. Millie Stevens stood in the background.

Marston quickly briefed Duval on the break in. Puzzled, Duval didn't seem overly concerned. Marston showed him the file that had been forced, to which Duval advised, "Let's keep the feds out of this Jack, just call the locals. No sense having friends in high places if you can't use them!" he said, kiddingly referring to Marston's friendship with the chief of detectives in the Burlington Police Department.

"I'll notify Carl tonight, and he and Shirley can inventory that file in the morning — although I'm damn sure there's nothing in there that amounts to ..."

Lila Maret was standing quietly to the side when Marston and Duval realized simultaneously that she had not been introduced.

"Congressman, this is Lila Maret, a friend of mine. Lila is a writer, and she lives up in your old stomping grounds, at Jay Peak," said Marston.

Duval, taking her hand, smiled warmly and replied, "You're a lucky woman — I learned to ski there. That area has great skiing and yet still has the feel of the 'old Vermont'"

"Thank you. I'm pleased to meet you, honored really — but I think I'm in the wrong place now," Lila said, feeling awkward, but all the while maintaining her poise.

"Nonsense," Duval replied, "You make yourself at home."

Marston showed Lila to a comfortable chair in the waiting area, found some magazines and placed them on the end table next to her, then followed Duval and the others down the hall.

Godine and Camilli were waiting in Duval's office. Godine sat in one of the wing-back chairs, while young Camilli paced nervously stopping only for a moment to look out toward the lake.

"Let's get comfortable," Duval said looking pointedly at Camilli who abruptly stopped pacing and balanced himself against the window sill. Marston grabbed a side chair, and Duval pulled out the swivel chair from behind his desk.

Godine quickly outlined the story carried in the *Washington Tell-Tale*. "It doesn't really say a Goddamn thing; I'm surprised that even that rag used it. It's a story about what's coming, but so far it's a non-story."

"You could insinuate a story like that about anybody," Camilli inserted, trying unsuccessfully to remain silent.

The room was quiet for a moment. Duval looked at Marston inquiringly.

"Jack?"

Marston rubbed his chin and replied, "Here's how it looks to me. First, if they haven't got anything better than that, they wouldn't have run the story in the first place. So there's more to come. They'll probably run what they have as kind of a series. Secondly, to get a paper — even a bad paper — to run a series of crap like this, in the way they are doing it, means that somebody on that paper is taking outside direction — somebody's pulling the strings."

Camilli, in frustration, moved away from the window to the center of the room and interrupted, "We've got to find out what they've got, or think they've got!"

Again the room fell quiet. Duval looked at each man in turn, got up and walked over to the window to look out over the city, and at the moving lights flickering from the small boats on the lake. Turning from the window he blustered, "Goddamn it — let's get it on the table! You owe me your best guess on this even if it embarrasses you — or me!" The three men looked at Duval. The rare use of profanity got their attention, and made the point.

Duval continued, "We need to find out what this is. We need to talk about what it could be. I told you before, I'm clean — that's not bullshit, I'm clean!" A trace of anger flared in Duval's eyes, then disappeared as he went on, "Stories like this are always about money, sex, or the misuse of influence. I haven't taken any dirty money; I haven't got a girlfriend or even a one-night-stand they can hang on me, and, "shaking his head with a wry smile he concluded, "I don't have enough influence to misuse if I wanted to!"

Godine spoke up, "Look, somebody's got something and they're twisting it. If we could just figure what they had, we could get out ahead of it. As it is, it's nothing but smoke and mirrors! "

Bill Camilli still looking anxious said, "One other possibility — remember the guy who wouldn't run for president last time? The skeleton wasn't in his closet, it was one of his kids."

"I know where you're going with that Bill," Duval snapped, "but Ellie's been clean for over three years," he said referring to his wife, "no booze, no drugs — if it's something before that ... we handle it ... whatever it is."

Sensing Duval's fatigue, John Godine leaned forward in the chair and said, "We can't do much until we know more. I'm going to reduce the number of ads we're running this summer to guarantee that we'll have money if we need a last minute ad blitz to offset this ... and, I hate to Alan," he said looking at the young congressman, "but I'm going to book more out-of-state fundraisers for the same reason. We've got to do it; TV's the only way to answer unexpected attacks and the only way to get to a broad audience fast enough. I intend to have that money on hand."

Chapter Thirteen

Brill waited. The smoke from the ever-present cigarette held between his lips climbed in an agonizing, almost sensuous pattern upward toward the ceiling. No hint of a draft disturbed the smoke which, when it reached the ceiling flattened out and disappeared, the chemicals in the smoke joining the residue already darkening the overhead paneling.

Brill's eyes had become accustomed to the dark, as he stood motionless watching from across the street. Assisted by a full moon, he had no problem seeing who entered and exited the parking garage at the rear of the building which housed Duval's Burlington, Vermont office complex. He had hastened back to this vantage point after his foiled break-in.

Brill had arrived in Vermont late Wednesday night and checked in at one of the larger motels on the east side of the city near the airport. From this location he was able to come and go easily without attracting attention. He had tried to get a direct flight from Portland to Burlington, but frustrated by the limited service, he ended up renting a car and driving the two hundred miles.

He went out the first thing Thursday morning and visited the post office to try and determine that *if* an envelope had been mailed from Maine on Tuesday when it would be likely to arrive. Almost all east to west mail took a minimum of two days, often three days, depending on the volume of mail. It was unlikely that Willey could have mailed the envelope on Monday, since he hadn't arrived in Brunswick until after the post offices would have closed. Brill estimated that it would arrive in Burlington, Thursday at the earliest. It was possible he'd given the envelope to someone else to mail which could further cloud the time of arrival. By asking a few simple questions of the clerk, he was further able to determine the frequency and timing of deliveries made to Duval's office.

Of course the really gnawing question was, if Willey mailed the envelope to Duval, why had he retained the other two. He could think of reasons, but they were not totally convincing.

After visiting the post office, Brill proceeded to familiarize himself with the Burlington area, first purchasing a city map, identifying major landmarks, checking on the location of Duval's office, and plotting the easiest ways out of town should he need to leave in a hurry. Augie Brill knew the importance of knowing the territory he was operating in and how to vacate that territory in a hurry. This he had learned from the days when he'd been involved in moving large supplies of drugs to and from major cities throughout the world.

Earlier in the day he made inquires at a nearby gas station about the building he was now in, and discovered that it was not only empty but that its location was perfect for his purposes. The entire second floor was vacant. He didn't even have to rent it.

Late in the afternoon he entered the building, climbed the stairs, and deftly forced the lock on one of the office doors. Inside, he reset the lock and went to the window. Across the street, three floors above, he could see into offices of Congressman Alan Duval.

Augie Brill had patiently observed the building for the balance of the day on Thursday. Friday, when he assumed his post overlooking Duval's offices once again, he found that things remained quiet. When the congressman's office closed for the weekend, Brill waited until it was nearly dark, and when there was still no indication of any activity around the office, he decided to go over and take a look. He felt assured no one was in Duval's office, so he made his decision. He wanted to get into the office to be sure the envelope he was after hadn't arrived and simply been set aside, and to pick up any other information that he could. By the time the security guard Millie Stevens surprised him in Duval's office he'd already determined that the envelope was not there. He found nothing else of particular interest and had been preparing to leave. Getting caught was just bad luck.

He figured now that when the envelope did arrive, he would have a good chance of intercepting it. When he broke into Duval's office he hadn't worried about building security. Experience had taught him that in small towns, security — where it existed — was untrained, unarmed, and underpaid. When the female guard had happened upon him earlier, the only risk was that she might get a good look at him. But Brill had pushed out of the office with his arm covering his face; and he knew the guard couldn't have seen his face clearly enough to identify him.

He had been watching the office now for almost an hour. After the incident with the security guard Brill waited a short while intending then to retire to his motel. But just as he was about to leave he saw the lights blink on in Duval's office. People were entering the office. Patiently Augie Brill reestablished himself in his vantage point. He couldn't identify the individuals that passed back and forth in front of the windows. The only ones he would know on sight would be Congressman Duval and Marston. As he watched, it appeared there were three or four people meeting in the corner office which most likely belonged to the congressman himself.

He was trying to identify Jack Marston who, as Steele had pointed out to him, was the man responsible for Duval's operation and the one most likely to take responsibility for the envelope when it arrived in the mail. Earlier Steele had faxed Brill a picture of Jack Marston, along with a fact sheet including his address, phone numbers, make of car, and the number of his license plate. But from where Brill was watching he still couldn't identify any particular individuals.

Over an hour had passed before the lights finally went out once again in the office across the way. Brill maintained his watch, hoping to see if any cars left the garage underneath the building. At that moment two cars headed down the outside ramp of the garage and onto the street.

Brill left the vacant office, flipped the lock on the door and raced down stairs in time to see the two cars heading up the street.

Marston's was the second car.

Augie Brill hurried over to the small vacant lot where he had parked his rental car, a Honda this time. Wasting no time he jumped in, started up, and exited the vacant lot. Within moments he was less that a hundred yards behind Marston's car which was heading east, up Main Street; a woman sat in the car next to Marston.

Minutes later, still about a hundred yards ahead, Marston's crossed into South Burlington and his left turn signal began to blink as he approached the Holiday Inn. He turned into the motel parking lot and pulled to a stop. Moments later Brill entered the same lot just as Lila Maret and Jack Marston were walking toward the door to the lobby of the motel. He drove past where Marston had parked his car and took the Honda to the far end of the lot where he turned into a parking space, stopped and killed the engine.

From there he watched Marston and the young woman enter the lobby. Brill felt a flash of envy. Where could he find a woman in a town like this? He sat back, lit another cigarette.

And waited.

It was around ten-thirty when Marston drove Lila back to the Holiday Inn with Augie Brill following behind.

As he got out and walked with here to the lobby, he'd asked, "Would you like a nightcap?"

She hesitated only a moment, and replied, "That would be nice."

For Lila, this man Jack Marston was a new experience. Comfortable. "What you see is what you get," she thought to herself. He was neither reticent about his opinions nor insistent upon them, and she noted in him a shyness, a reserve. It seemed to match her own, and with him she found she could risk a little — even talk about herself. That he had recently lost his wife didn't surprise her, but neither of them pursued the subject.

Watching him at Duval's awards dinner, she was amazed at the number of people with whom he was acquainted. He would greet people, then turn and introduce her easily and naturally. It was all done smoothly. He was always in control, waving now and again across the crowded room, never missing anyone seeking his eye. As he chatted briefly with the guests, he spoke the sometimes mysterious language of politics; understanding was possible only if you knew the code words and shared the history. Lila enjoyed her escort's insights on Duval and other Vermont political figures, who up until now had been only names.

As she looked back on when their first meeting that afternoon at his office, she recalled that while he appeared detached, not really interested in what she was saying about Ben Willey, the apparent detachment was not disinterest but more a matter of style. He had waited for her to tell her story and she had done so. And at the dinner she was able to see his personality unfold — one exuding warmth, humor, and charm.

Inside the cocktail lounge at the Holiday Inn, they talked quietly, relaxed and comfortable, sipping their drinks slowly. Marston had been speaking of the history of the Jay Peak ski area and telling Lila how the development had gotten its start. Almost before she realized it and deciding quickly to limit the time she would spend the next morning at the library, she had responded by inviting him the next day to watch the installation of the towers for a new chair lift that was being constructed.

"They're transporting steel towers in one piece from somewhere in Canada all the way to Jay Peak."

"That must be something to see," Marston replied, imagining the scene.

"Come up tomorrow," she offered, "You can see the helicopters swoop right up the valley from the deck of my condo — better still, we can drive or climb right up close to where they're working — I'll cook dinner after." She stopped.

He started to draw back, but then looked at Lila who had surprised herself with her invitation. He replied, "I'd like that. I've got a political fundraiser to attend with Duval at eight o'clock in the morning, but I can get out of town by eleven — get there no later than twelve-thirty?"

The date was set.

Chapter Fourteen

After leaving Lila at the Holiday Inn, Marston headed out Route 15, to his home in Underhill.

The moon shone bright, and Marston could see Mt. Mansfield clearly outlined against the purple sky. This evening the countryside was bathed in soft light; the lofty mountain stood as sentinel and friend to those traveling east. The idea of living under the mountain had appealed to both he and Ann when they bought the bungalow. They fantasized themselves becoming experts on the mountain's secrets, and unearthing some of the long forgotten but legendary smuggled goods which were hidden in the notch, "A fantasy, yes," Ann had said, "but fantasies and myths are part of the equation we call truth."

Marston found some cassette tapes under the seat that he hadn't played for months. Inserting Schubert's 9th Symphony, *The Great,* into the tape deck, he turned up the volume and, as always with Schubert playing, wondered how anyone could achieve such greatness in a life that spanned but a short thirty-one years. He hadn't used the tape deck in the car for a while; he wondered why, but the music began overtaking the introspective moment. Hearing the music now reaffirmed his love for the magic of Franz Schubert.

Reflecting on Lila Maret's invitation to visit the next day, Marston found he was looking forward to it with real anticipation. Unexpected as it was, he was surprised at how fast he had accepted her invitation.

In the morning he would stop at the office for a look at the mail. After that he would meet Duval at the Sheraton for a session with the "Regulars." An unusual Saturday fund-raiser was scheduled for later in the morning, also at the Sheraton. After that it was on to Jay Peak. Spending the day with Lila was something to look forward to — and he did.

It was midnight. He pulled his car alongside the small bungalow and realized then that he had been so immersed in his thoughts he scarcely noticed the journey. He sat for a few moments in the car with the engine running, listening to the final strains of Schubert's finest work and wondering for the umpteenth time where such genius came from.

When he got out of the car and headed up the walk he noticed once again the plants and shrubbery along the edges of the house, and knew that he could no longer postpone trimming. This time he resolved to actually do something about it. Progress? He chuckled to himself, and, assisted by the light from the moon, he bent over and pulled a handful of weeds from among the flowers. "One of these days ...," he said aloud and went inside.

Augie Brill rose early Saturday morning and brought a take out breakfast and extra coffee to his second-floor perch across from Duval's office. At six-thirty in the morning there were few people to attract Brill's attention. He finished the food and started on his second large cup of coffee.

Just before quarter of eight, Brill spotted Jack Marston's car. Marston drove up and stopped in the "No Parking" area across the way by the front entrance of the building, apparently choosing not to bother with the underground garage at that early hour. Marston left the car and promptly disappeared into the building.

Brill watched. He lit a cigarette from the one he was smoking, then threw the inch-long stub on the floor and was stepping on it just as the lights appeared in Duval's office.

Moments later, a young man on a bicycle wearing black lycra shorts and a white helmet pulled up and parked by the front entrance of the building, just a few feet from Marston's car. The young messenger hopped off the bike, set the kickstand in a practiced way, and retrieved a large envelope from one of the saddle bags flanking the rear wheel.

Brill froze in the act of removing the cigarette from his lips; his right hand poised, still holding the cigarette inches from his mouth. The young man with the envelope headed toward the main entrance.

Stepping on the freshly lit cigarette, Brill hurried for the door. He had little doubt where the messenger was heading with that envelope. He flipped the lock on the door and raced down the stairs, out of the nearly vacant building. On the street now he stopped. Marston was coming out the front door along with the messenger whom he had apparently met in the lobby. The messenger handed him the envelope. Marston gestured his thanks, got back into his car and pulled out.

Brill hurried to the side lot where he had left the Honda. He had his sights on the envelope and he planned to stay close to Marston until he could get his hands on it.

Marston had a head start, and Brill was afraid at first that he would lose him. But he soon spotted Marston's Dodge stopped at a red light half way up the hill on Main Street. Brill hung back about four car lengths.

Marston passed the university campus and as he approached the South Burlington line moved into the left-turn lane at the light in front of the

Sheraton and stopped, waiting for the green arrow to appear. Brill remained well back, but was glad to see the turn signal when it came on.

Marston pulled into the Sheraton and parked near the front entrance. Brill followed and drove past the spot where Marston was parked. He watched through the rearview mirror as Marston got out of his car and entered the hotel. Marston's hands were empty; the envelope undoubtedly still in the car.

Marston had parked in a highly visible spot near the front door. It would be impossible for Brill to get near the car and jimmy the lock unobserved. If the car was unlocked, Brill figured he might be able to open the door and grab the envelope quickly enough to avoid attracting attention. He left his car and walked back past Marston's, looking casually through the side window. The envelope was in plain sight on the back seat. Brill turned as though he had forgotten something, and grabbed the back door to open it.

Locked!

"You want something?"

A man was approaching, a slight frown on his face.

"No ... No, I just remembered another errand," replied Brill, hoping the security man hadn't seen him try the handle on the back door of Marston's car.

The plainclothes guard said nothing, but continued to eye Marston's car and Brill suspiciously. Brill returned to his own car, got in and drove out of the lot and down Williston Road toward the airport. He traveled a couple of miles before turning around and heading back to the Sheraton. This time when he drove in, he stayed well clear of the front entrance and parked where he would be unobserved, but where he could still keep an eye on Marston's car. He didn't dare try for the envelope again; there were too many people around.

Brill lit a cigarette, and waited.

The "Regulars" were a group of mostly men, all early supporters of Duval. They had provided advice, money, and encouragement to Duval years before when he had first given indication that he might run for office. They were party standbys; elder statesmen who held things together through good times and bad. Duval had been an attractive candidate from the start, and the Regulars moved quickly — not wanting him to be spoiled by special-interest groups. Most of the members were conservative by Duval's standards, but despite some differences, he had grown genuinely fond of them and listened to their advice even if he didn't always follow it.

Marston had once said to Chuck Coddling, one of the members now arriving at the meeting, "You guys hold it all together so the 'yahoos' can do their thing every four years, and then they disappear into the sunset never to be seen again, until or unless some 'epic' cause catches their fancy and spawns their return."

"Yeah, that single issue bullshit is going to destroy the party before they're done," Coddling had rejoined.

Duval's campaign staff had rented a medium-sized room for the meeting and the fund-raiser to follow. The crowd filled the room comfortably. Coffee and danish were set out on a table along the back wall; people were helping themselves. Several men were gathered together talking with Duval who had arrived early with John Godine. So far, no women had shown up, although Marston had insisted that Godine try to get some women to attend.

"The problem, Jack," Godine said, "is that the activist women don't really like these guys, and that's probably not going to change."

Marston spotted Benny McLain, the contractor, who was talking with Buster Chapin, past president of the Vermont Labor Council and T. "Sonny" Smith, president of the Champlain Bank. "Buster, thanks! We appreciate it!" Marston waved as he acknowledged a campaign contribution Chapin had made.

Chapin walked over and said, "Okay, kid." He called virtually everyone "kid." "You know I would have done something for your buddy too, but he just don't get it!" Chapin was referring to a contribution he might have arranged for Tad Stephanson, who was running for governor on the party ticket. He continued, "On Memorial Day our candidate for governor — Stephanson — is in the parade in Barre, you know, and he's driving a friggin' Jap car! A Nissan, for Christ sakes!"

The granite industry in Barre had a strong labor tradition and was itself suffering from competition from imported products from Europe, India and Asia. Buster was strongly "Buy American."

"Come on Buster, they make those Nissans right here in the USA — Tennessee, I think," Marston said with a smile.

"Yeah, I suppose they made those Goddamn Zeroes — the airplane, you know — I suppose if they made those here it'd be okay they strafed the fucking air fields at Pearl Harbor and Bataan. Anyway," he said, having vented his anger and now speaking more calmly, "it'll be a cold day in hell before I support that ..."

Duval had moved to the front and was trying to get people's attention, "Grab a chair — I want to talk with you — hear what's going on out there."

Some overstuffed chairs were pulled in beside the straight chairs which were being set up in a semicircle several rows deep.

"Who's got anything on their mind? Tell me what I need to hear!" Duval inquired over the noise in the room, interrupting a half dozen or more unfinished conversations.

No one spoke for a few moments, then Benny McLain said, "Alan, I don't think it's serious right now, but you ought to know Meacham's got some of his supporters coming home, you know, the ones who jumped ship and supported you both times before."

McLain always spoke first, it was an unwritten rule that others would defer to him. It had always worked that way. Neither Marston nor Duval had any idea why.

"Thanks, yes, we know there's some slippage there — but we don't see it as serious yet. There are so many independents now that even if we lose all the crossovers from the last time, we'd still win."

"... If you don't lose the independents too!" someone said.

"Right," Duval grinned. "Yeah, that's right — but we're close to where we were last time with the independents, and they were a big bonus on election day.

"Are you getting down south at all, Alan? — I was at a banker's convention in Rutland, and everybody south of Rutland feels neglected — like no one ever gets down there," inquired Chuck Coddling.

John Godine interrupted: "If you want, I can show you; Alan's been down there more than any other major candidate. But I'm glad you asked, 'cause what we're starting to do with these southern 'hits' is advance Alan with staff people in the communities — we've found that you get more than double benefit by a good strong advance effort — then pretty soon they're saying 'he's always down here!'"

"You'll never fool 'em in Bennington," Buster Chapin bellowed out. The group laughed.

Duval shot a mildly reproving glance at Godine and said, "Whatever the truth is, the fact of the matter requires that whoever is campaigning statewide in Vermont has to get down south; and to make sure the people down there know you've been down, you have to get the press to cover your visit. Who said, 'If it isn't in the paper, it didn't happen?'"

The questions from Duval's Regulars were easy, their concerns mild, expressed this morning as a small gesture of independence but without rancor or anger. Duval knew that what was important was that he meet with this group from time to time, provide these old friends a special kind of access, a sign. Any gesture to let them know that he hadn't forgotten or didn't appreciate them. These were the little things, the symbols that kept the process alive. The Regulars were unconcerned, the election was in the bag. Or so it seemed on this June day.

Marston, who had been listening quietly off to the side, got up and left the room. After visiting the men's room, he poured more coffee and looked for the campaign staff working on the fund-raiser to follow shortly. Godine caught up with him in the lobby.

"There'll be about sixty, I think," said Godine, referring to the fund-raiser. "A lot of the people attending will be new; they've never met Duval. Some of them don't have a hell of a lot of money, but there's a few with some potential. I always like to see new faces."

"Where'd you get the list, Volvo owners?" Marston needled Godine, who constantly worried that Duval catered too much to elitist intellectuals and overlooked "lunch pail" Vermonters.

Godine cringed, and gestured a swing on Marston who feigned getting out of the way. Neither gave any evidence that they were worried about the election. They'd been through tough ones before. They figured this one was in the bag.

Lila Maret arrived at the Bailey-Howe Library at the University of Vermont before eight AM. She had gotten up early, grabbed a quick orange juice and coffee, and was out the door. She continued her search the next two hours for background material for her book. Today it wasn't working. Most writers have days like this whether editing, writing or doing research. She sat back looked at her watch and said aloud, "To hell with it, I give up."

Closing the books on the table, she grabbed her notebooks and put them in her briefcase, checked to make sure she had everything, and within three minutes was speeding north on I-89 toward Jay Peak.

As so often when she was returning home after being away for awhile, she had that singular nervousness she could never explain, a sense that she should hurry; that she was returning to where she belonged and ought never to have left.

On Route 105 now, Lila — like so many others who traveled this road — took time to reflect on the open land and the working farms along the way. They reminded her once again that the Vermont of legend and storybooks was a real place ... and still a special place.

The Missisquoi valley is one of the most beautiful in the state. Farming here is still central, and the chaos of development has not yet corrupted this part of Vermont. The fields were plowed and planted and the new green of summer was reaching toward the heavens once more. The Missisquoi River followed the road Lila was traveling like a friend encouraging her home; the mixture of odors in the air stirred wistful childhood memories. And now she could see Jay Peak, Lila's mountain, beckoning in the distance.

And she was having a visitor: Jack Marston. Lila said his name aloud. She liked the sound, she also liked the man. He was hard to get to know maybe, but kind. Perhaps too shy for the political world he found himself in, but how well he handled it, Lila decided as she thought back on the previous evening at the Radisson.

She hadn't accomplished much that morning at the library and grudgingly admitted to herself that Jack Marston might be intruding on her well-organized world.

She increased her speed as she neared home.

Chapter Fifteen

Jack Marston left the fund-raiser when it was nearly over and headed north on the interstate, following the route Lila Maret had taken earlier. Beside him on the seat of the car was a small bag carrying clothes more suitable for a day on the mountain.

Two miles from the St. Albans exit Marston checked his rearview mirror and once again spotted the Honda. From even a half a mile away, Marston could tell it was the same car. He was surprised — when he had left I-89 at the Georgia exit to buy gasoline, the Honda had done the same. Now the car followed him back onto the interstate. Coincidence?

He dismissed it; he was still thinking about the meeting with the Regulars. Both the meeting and the fund-raiser that followed had gone well. Feedback from the new supporters was positive. They asked tough questions, some of which indicated that this audience knew something about what went on in Washington. Duval was an insider now, and had to defend the current scene. Being an incumbent was no longer an advantage. Funny how politics changed. But insider or challenger, Marston reflected, if you can somehow convince people that you'll do what you think is the right thing, they'll support you even if they don't agree with you on many of the issues. The voter wants honesty and integrity. Too often people running for office — pandering to one group or the other — missed that point.

The trip went quickly. When Marston drove into Montgomery Center, he abruptly forgot politics and found himself anticipating the day ahead with the attractive lady he was about to visit. Young lady, he reminded himself. To his friends, Marston had explained the lack of women in his life by pleading shyness. Strange how this small, black-haired women had broken through that ploy. And at least for today he was glad of it. Hard to explain but ... yes .... glad of it.

The Jay Peak ski area has two entrances: the main entrance, and, just to the south of it, the state side entrance. To reach Lila's condominium, Marston had to turn off within two or three miles of the latter entrance. She had given him directions, but to make sure he had it correctly in mind, he pulled the Dodge off to the side of the road and let the car idle while he checked the directions once again.

Satisfied he was on the right track, he glanced in his rearview mirror before pulling back on the road. Odd, he thought, the Honda had reappeared. It was still a half mile back. He shrugged his shoulders and pulled onto the road.

Following Lila's directions, he correctly turned off the main road and was soon alongside her mountainside condominium. She had parked her Subaru beside her condo as she said she would. Pulling to a stop alongside her car, he spotted Lila on the second floor deck waving at him. Marston hopped out of the car, grabbed the small bag in which he had packed clothes, set the power lock on the car, shut the door, and breathed deeply of the mountain air.

Marston was familiar with Jay Peak, but only as a skier many years earlier. The mountain's summer personality was new to him.

"Great timing," Lila hollered down, "I think you're early."

"Yeah, I got away early. You look — ready to go." Marston stumbled on the words as he gazed on his hostess, who was neatly attired in light blue jeans and a white polo shirt; casual clothes that to Marston made Lila appear softer, even younger.

"Come on up," she said. "They're bringing in some of the towers today for sure. One of the helicopters has gone over already!"

Marston trotted up the stairs and caught his toe on the top step. He stumbled for a moment. He stopped and looked up at Lila. She was waiting with a broad smile at the top of the stairs. When she placed her hand on his arm to steady him, Marston picked up the scent of dusting powder, worn after her shower. The scent, light as it was, filled the air and provoked in him a stab of desire.

Her hand remained on his arm as she smiled and said slowly, "Take your time, we've got all day."

It seemed to Marston as though it were all happening in slow motion. For a moment he wasn't sure of what words to use to fill the awkward moment. "Thanks for asking me, this should ... I'm going to enjoy it." Changing the subject, he pointed to the small bag he was carrying and explained with a sheepish grin, "I'd like to get out of my 'uniform.'" Then almost formally he asked, "Where would you like me to change? So I'll look as ready to face the mountain as you do?" He said it awkwardly, like lines spoken for the first time in a play.

Lila smiled to herself as she directed him to the spare room. The distance between them had, for a moment, narrowed.

Marston changed quickly into jeans and a short sleeve casual shirt, and slipped into an old pair of running shoes.

"Ready?" Lila asked when he emerged.

"Ready!" he replied.

Lila picked up the small knapsack from the kitchen table. "Lunch," she explained, in response to his inquiring look. "Let's go!"

Once in Marston's car, they drove past the condominium, pulled out onto the main road and headed toward the ski area. After entering the area, and passing by the large parking lot, with Lila showing the way, Marston managed to drive part of the way up the mountain on a service road used primarily by the heavy equipment brought in to work on the construction of the new lift. Finally, after some heavy going which prompted Lila to suggest they would have been better off in the Subaru, they were stopped and waived off toward a temporary parking area.

They locked up the car and began to climb on foot at a brisk pace, not straight up, but at a slight angle to the mountain. They could see a wide swath of trees that had been cleared for the new chair lift. It ran from below the highest point visible on this side of the mountain down to the ski area parking lot below.

"The line of the lift up the mountain is at a slight angle to perpendicular; did you notice?" Marston inquired.

"They do that to diminish the effect of the wind as much as possible — at least that's what one of the workers told me," Lila replied.

"Makes sense; the winds can be brutal on this mountain."

They continued their brisk pace for a quarter of a mile before they came upon a small group of people already assembled and waiting for helicopters. Spectators outnumbered the construction workers who were trying to contain the visitors a safe distance from where the towers would be brought in.

The exertion from the climb was welcome. It felt good, Marston decided. It had been getting pretty warm in Burlington earlier in the day, but here there was relief for both of them in the steady cool breeze wafting off the mountain.

As they neared their destination, Marston paused a moment to scan the area, trying to identify the ski trails that had challenged his considerable talent years ago. "If I'm not mistaken, I used to spend most of my time over there," he said, gesturing to his left. "The area to the right doesn't seem familiar at all," he frowned.

"That area you remember is the first trail they developed on this mountain. It's tough skiing; not for the fainthearted!"

"I remember," he smiled in reply. "I wonder what it would be like to do that again — especially the 'black diamond' trails, after all these years?"

"You would do fine, I have no doubts," she replied. Marston caught sight of Lila's eyes sparkling in the sun.

"It's like a bicycle, you know. You never forget ..."

"No, but you do lose your nerve," he observed, still staring at the mountain.

Lila laughed broadly at Marston's comment. "Nerve is no longer the issue, or shouldn't be. You must satisfy who you are today, not appease what you remember you once were!" After a short pause, she continued. "When you stopped skiing, did you decide never to try it again?"

"No, I don't think so ...," he chuckled, "I guess if a person isn't careful, events begin to dictate your life — I simply had a bad knee for a while. Attempts to ski the same way again were too much of a challenge."

"But Jack, nobody is keeping track of how well you're skiing; there's no particular standard to achieve. I love the Japanese word 'aikido' — I'm probably misusing the word, but to me it means to work off the strength of others — go with the flow."

For a brief time nothing was said, each of them alone with their thoughts.

When they came upon a good place to rest and watch the construction, Lila took out a blanket and spread it on the ground. They were located a short distance from the small crowd, which was maintaining a nervous buzz of anticipation as they all awaited the approach of the next helicopter.

Jack's thoughts were still on what had seemed to him to be a double-edged conversation, when from above he heard the distinctive THUMP-THUMP-THUMP of an approaching helicopter. As though sketched in for a scene in a movie, the great steel bird came abruptly into sight. The dark spider-like object moved methodically through the air, the tower suspended beneath it seemed an out-of-place tentacle, stark against the blue sky. The machine approached fearlessly as though programmed to challenge both the timeless history as well as the beauty of the ancient mountain.

Lila and Jack stood up now, watching in silence as the aircraft slowly descended. It carefully positioned itself to maneuver the tower which was swaying slightly beneath into place. Its noise shattered the mountain air.

"Symbolic of our time, isn't it?" Lila whispered to her companion. "How long has the mountain been here? Eons I guess, just existing. Then that thing — spewing gasses, made of steel taken from the bowels of earth — is to be erected as a monument to man's need to dominate the mountain ...," Lila spoke seriously and with passion, as much to herself it seemed to Marston, as to him.

"Hey," he interrupted, trying to reestablish the lighter mood, "I need to get you with Duval. That's his line!"

"No, no, don't misunderstand. I'm not criticizing. I believe in using the mountain, I like to ski — I even ride the lifts, but watching those things being set up — the new lifts, the towers ..." Lila shook her head, "it just seems so presumptuous, like ... shouldn't someone ask the mountain?"

Marston laughed and placed his arm around Lila's shoulder. Unconsciously she moved closer.

After about twenty minutes, the tower — one of over twenty-four needed for the new lift — was set in place; the helicopter swirled around a couple of times as though showing off for a film crew, and created a breeze that could be felt as far away as where Jack and Lila were standing. The machine then rose in the sky, plunging vigorously to the west as though straining at an imaginary tether.

It was quiet now. They sat back down and Lila reached for the thermos of iced tea and the paper bag containing bread, cheese and thinly sliced salami. The other spectators began to move back down the mountain, and Marston and Lila ate quietly.

"Delicious!" Marston commented.

"Mountain air will make you hungry. Food's best for you when you're hungry. Have more salami," she offered.

Marston wondered aloud about this woman who just before was speaking wistfully of the timelessness of nature, and now was playing grandmother — encouraging him to finish what there was to eat.

She laughed, "I admired my grandmother — but there are new questions for each generation. The questions for ours seem very tough. We're abandoning a lot of our myths, but we don't have substitutes — our time is taken up by playing with things made of steel and plastic, or with watching numbers scurry maddeningly through our computers. Numbers dominate us. Silly number games are determining winners and losers."

"Is that what your book is about?" Marston asked.

"Oh, no; I'll tell you about the book when we get back to the condo. Maybe you'll have some ideas. I try never to talk about the book without having a pad and pencil in hand! At the rate I'm going with it, I shouldn't talk about it at all." With this she stood up, repacked the remainder of the lunch and returned the thermos to her knapsack. She began to fold the blanket and Marston pitched in to help.

As they started back down the mountain, Jack reached out his hand. Lila took it in hers. Not saying much as they descended, they remained hand-in-hand until they reached Marston's car which they left parked among the others at the bottom of the mountain.

The lot was a busy spot since it was the only place to park for those working on the mountain as well as those such as Lila and Jack who had come to watch the helicopters.

They traveled the short way to Lila's condominium in silence. Marston pulled in alongside Lila's car and shut off the engine. They sat without moving. Jack looked at Lila, put his hand over hers and said, "Thank you, I..."

"Shush," she said, tilting her head and giving Marston a strange pensive look out of the corner of her eyes. "Come on in."

Marston got out of the car, locked the doors and followed her up the stairs.

In the kitchen now, Lila put the thermos and the leftover food away while Jack stood by awkwardly.

She walked over to him. Standing very close she looked up and said "You don't have to say anything," she kissed him gently on the cheek and continued, "or do anything."

He replied hoarsely, "I know," and placed his hand gently under her elbow.

When her lips touched his cheek it had been like an electric shock, and the tension for Marston was nearly unbearable. Standing this way, he touched her cheek with the back of his fingers and then pushed aside an imaginary lock of hair. She stood perfectly still, looking up at him. He started to kiss her and felt her body tense, even tremble a little. He stopped. She reached for him and he wrapped his arms around her and they kissed. They stood for a few moments and kissed again, exploring ever so little, ever so slightly. Marston slipped his hand under the back of Lila's shirt and felt warm bare skin. Lila took a short breath and shivered.

He started to back away. "No ... it's all right, Jack." She said, again pulling him closer.

Both of his hands were now on the warm soft skin of her back. Moving his head away from another kiss, as though to see her better, Marston asked, "Is this ... okay?"

"Very okay," she replied. She grasped his hand and urged him along with a simple, "Come."

She led him into her bedroom. Again they kissed. Lila touched his face and said, "Give me a minute ..."

Marston sat on the edge of the bed, confused for the moment, his heart racing. But he wanted her; God, how he wanted her. He removed his shirt, uncertain. He went to the window and closed the blinds. The sun had gone behind the mountain, and the light in the room was dim. The mountain was quiet. Lila returned wearing a rose satin robe and went over to where he was sitting on the bed. She bent over, placing her hand on his cheek, and kissed him. At the same time, she pushed gently against his chest until he found himself on his back. She lay beside him, still touching his face.

They lay this way for what seemed a long while, then Lila gave a shiver from the cool evening air coming through the window. "Jack," she said, "let's get into bed."

Marston undressed deftly as Lila pulled the covers back. He got under the sheets and turned his face up at Lila. She stood for a moment looking down into his eyes. Then she removed the satin robe and stood there for a moment in the evening light. To Marston it seemed like perfection in miniature. He knew he would remember the image of her standing there outlined against the fading light for as long as he had time on earth.

And then she was warm against him in the bed. Again a long moment just lying together without words. And then urgently — as though there would never be time enough — they became entwined.

At last there was for each of them a warm place. Their hands began to explore. They touched ... giving ... taking ... loving, not demanding. Now there was no hurry; they knew there was time, because for now time was their own. And finally, as they began to move together, Marston knew calmness, knew himself again, and all the questions in his mind disappeared.

For Lila this man was different. She gave without fear. Too often hurt ... it had been so long. She felt the warmth, the rising tension — and still she gave. Then the gates opened, "Ah ... God ..." she cried and her body reached ever higher. Then they were there, together, for a magic moment.

Lila fell back sobbing. She tried to turn away, but Marston pulled her to him. "Lila, stay — you're wonderful that way ... stay."

They lay together for a long time. They slept for a little while, then they made love again. Easily, still gently. More familiar now, but still with magic.

Once more they slept. The shadows outside deepened. Marston looked at his watch. It was eight PM. He lay back. Lila felt him move and, knowing he was awake, she said with a smile, "Tell me the story of your life."

Chapter Sixteen

The noise would have gone unnoticed except for the pervasive silence of the quiet mountain setting. Marston stopped talking and listened. He sat up. It was not yet completely dark, but the shadows had lengthened and the air was now much cooler.

The strange noise they both heard was an unwelcome intruder.

They had been talking quietly of things often left unsaid between lovers; times of joy and moments of anguish. They shared these things — at first tentatively, but with the sharing came a trust, something too long absent from their lives. The closeness each felt grew stronger in the dimly lit room, and neither Lila or Jack wanted to destroy that sense of intimacy by leaving the rumpled bed. And so they remained there, passions quieted, softly holding hands. Lila talked about her marriage and the sense of failure she had had when she could no longer play the role her Svengali-inspired husband demanded. Marston spoke of his twenty-five years with Ann, and the emptiness that seemed to grow, not diminish as time passed and her death grew more distant.

For each of them there were some tears; but they knew for these moments at least they had let go of that other time.

They made plans for the rest of the weekend. Marston had intended to return to Underhill and work on revisions of Duval's speeches. Copies dating back several years lay in the manila envelope on the back seat of his car. Lila mentally canceled her plans to rework the outline of her book. She had promised Marston dinner, but the steaks remained in the refrigerator.

Then they heard a noise again, a different noise.

Marston jumped from the bed and ran to the window.

"Sounds like someone's fooling with the car! Hey ...! What are you doing?!" He grabbed his jeans from the floor, pulled them on, buttoned the top button and zipped. Retrieving his shoes from under the bed, he ran out of the room down the stairs and through the patio area. In the shadowy light he had seen a man take something from the back seat of his car and then run off.

When he and Lila reached the car, he could see the man about a hundred yards ahead, running down the drive toward the main road. His features were clearly illuminated by the flood light located halfway down the drive.

Marston ran after him.

He could see the man was carrying something. Marston ran harder, thinking he was closing the gap and forgetting to worry whether he could overpower the burglar when he did catch him.

Then it happened — Marston stepped in a hole. His right foot turned underneath his weight and he fell face down on the tarred drive.

Marston had not been wearing a shirt, and the fall had skinned his right arm and the right side of his chest and stomach. Lila helped him up and together they walked back to the condo. She filled the sink in the bathroom with soap and water and helped Marston wash the dirt and tar from his wounds. She found an elastic bandage which Marston wrapped around his ankle after resisting Lila's suggestions for icing it.

With things quiet now Marston said, "About the only thing in the car was the packet of old speeches. I don't understand why in God's name anyone would want to steal five years worth of Duval's speeches — or anyone's speeches for that matter." He stood up, shaking his head and gingerly taking a few steps to test his ankle.

"Could you identify him?" Lila asked.

"Probably. He had thinning hair, a round ugly face like a thug in a James Bond movie. Heavy-set, but he was light on his feet and could run like the wind.

"He must have been in that damned car that was following me the whole way up here. I wish I'd paid more attention to it ... This is an odd one — what could he possibly want from me — or Duval for that matter? He must have gone after the wrong person."

Marston again sat down, shaking his head from time to time as though that would make things clearer.

They settled for a light supper of soup and sandwiches. Donning light sweaters, they carried the food to the deck where they could look out on the mountain as it cast its deep blue outline against the darkening sky. By the time they finished eating the sky was dark, but the first hint of an emerging moon was already beginning to soften the black of the night.

They brought their dishes in, cleaned them off stacking them in the dishwasher. Lila went over to Marston, and said awkwardly, "Will you still be able to stay tonight?"

Marston paused only a moment and replied with uncustomary seriousness, "Yes, I'd like to very much." Then looking down at her he smiled.

"Why not?" He said, thinking of the file now missing from the back seat of the car, "The dog ate my homework!"

Chapter Seventeen

On Monday morning the *Burlington News* carried the story as a side bar on the front page:

Body Discovered
State Department Official
Dead in Maine
UVM Grad

"The body of Benton Willey, who retired
only a few days ago from the State
Department, was found washed ashore on
the banks of the Kennebec River in
Maine, one mile south of where his
abandoned car had been discovered a few
days before. Willey, who on retiring
had planned to live in the Brunswick
area, had been listed as missing.
According to police investigators, an
autopsy will be performed to determine
the cause of death. They refused to
speculate and said they have ruled out
neither suicide nor homicide."

It was a story Marston might have overlooked in the past.

He arrived at the office as usual at seven fifteen on Monday morning. Over the last couple of years, he had gotten in the habit of picking up the morning paper and a take-out breakfast which he ate at the office before the others arrived.

It was the reference to UVM that caught his attention. Marston sat back in his chair, placing his feet on his desk and turning in such a way as to look out on Lake Champlain as it swept out of sight to the south. His mind was on his old friend Ben Willey.

Marston was feeling pangs of conscience, regretting that he hadn't picked up on the depression Willey must have been experiencing. Desperation. Willey had been desperate. Marston took a deep breath, angry at himself.

And this morning he was also thinking of Lila Maret. She hadn't said a lot about Willey; Marston wasn't sure what the relationship really was, or how close they were. Earlier, he had wondered whether he would call Lila this morning, but he knew now he must call her. He glanced at his watch and decided to wait until eight o'clock.

Marston turned on his computer and checked the electronic mailbox for any messages from the Washington staff. Human relations problems had greatly diminished since the computers had been installed. Somebody must have once thought that nothing could ever improve on the telephone, but now this, Marston reflected. Anger and frustration caused by delays due to "telephone tag" now disappeared. Marston quickly disposed of a couple of simple interoffice memos, finished several letters left over from Friday, and opened his appointment book.

CIA Director Bill Richards's special assistant Edgar Steele was due in the office around ten, something Marston had momentarily forgotten. From what Steele had told Shirley Hogan when he called to set up the appointment, he needed information on vacation spots in northern New England. The information was needed for those attending the international conference at the Mount Washington Hotel at Bretton Woods, and who planned to stay on and enjoy part of the summer season in the north country.

Duval had asked Marston to bring Steele up-to-date on the rumors of the "dirty tricks" to which the *Washington Tell-Tale* had referred. Duval hoped that Richards, with whom he had served in Congress, could help. Marston had said nothing but doubted that Steele would pay much attention to concerns as vague and undocumented as these rumors were. But Richards and Duval had talked about it so Marston would follow through.

Marston had worked with Steele before. They had talked several times over the phone and at great length when Duval had traveled to Brazil and then taken a hush-hush side trip into Colombia as a favor to Richards and the administration. Marston had found Steele to be efficient, personable, and someone who followed through. He had rather liked Steele — at least over the phone — despite a slightly "too smooth" style. His manner reminded him of an insurance salesman he once knew who skyrocketed to prominence in his company, only to be discovered as a complete fraud a year later. Marston wrote off his uneasiness on this score as a symptom of his own disdain for the necessary but phony collegiality so often exercised in Washington. He rummaged around in his desk and bookcase for the materials on northern New England he planned to give to Steele when he arrived.

It was eight AM; time to call Lila. Before dialing, he read once more the short but prominently front page story describing the death of Ben Willey.

He stared at the phone a moment, and with a sigh full of angst, he grabbed the receiver and dialed her number.

"Hello?" she said softly.

"Good morning, Lila," he replied in an almost formal manner. He paused, the sound of her voice had elicited an almost electric reaction from his body. "How are you?"

"Oh, hi. Fine."

"Expecting someone else?" Marston said lamely, still trying to strike a light tone.

"I — my agent was supposed to call — on my book, you know ..."

Marston paused again, feeling the distance in her voice. During the time they spent together on Sunday, Lila had periods where she became distant — her mind elsewhere. Throughout the day she had seemed strangely quiet. On his trip home that evening, he searched without success for what he might have said or done that had changed the mood.

Unsure of finding the right way to tell her, he plunged ahead. "Lila, I need to tell you something ... There's a story in the paper — Ben Willey is dead. His body was found along the Kennebec River up in Maine. They aren't sure, but they ... it may be suicide or ... there's not much else in the story."

There was a pause, then, "Oh, my God!"

"Lila, come on into town; we'll talk. You were trying to do what you could. He apparently just lost the handle on life. Some people do ..."

"I'll be down ... late morning," Lila replied softly, so softly Marston could barely hear.

She stood without moving, staring at the phone in her right hand, poised as though waiting to learn more, something to make sense of the crazy situation in which she found herself. She had once confided to a friend in Washington who worked on the hill that she occasionally took on short assignments from the CIA. Her friend, an older woman who had been around the State Department for years before moving into the legislative branch had looked at her and said, "Be careful, those people play hardball, and not with just the bad guys ... you may find a time that you wish that you'd never gotten involved."

When Lila had first become involved with the CIA, what she was asked to do had seemed simple and the expense money was enormously helpful in supporting the travel necessary for the articles she wanted to write. So she had chosen to ignore the older woman's advice.

The kettle on the stove began whistling. Lila removed it from the burner but decided against drinking any more coffee. She wanted to get on the road to Burlington as quickly as possible. She had told Marston she was planning to spend days this week doing research for her book at the university library. He suggested they meet for lunch on Monday since Duval would be campaigning in Rutland that day and giving an early evening speech on the campus of Middlebury College.

Lila thought back on Saturday night. Following supper, she and Jack had sat on opposite ends of the love seat talking quietly but not quite touching as music played softly in the background. The sexual tension felt earlier was quieted, but their desire for each other remained just below the surface, poised to flare again. Jack had gotten up from the love seat several times as the evening progressed, walking the length of the room to test his ankle.

Lila watched him, her head resting on the back of the love seat, relaxed and comfortable. This was the first man she had felt anything for in a long time. He was different. Since her marriage, most of the men she met socially would immediately invoke in her a defensive reaction, but not this man. Somehow Jack Marston had disarmed her. And, she decided, she was glad he had.

They remained this way for a while, slightly domestic but mainly just comfortable with one another. Later on, when it was time to go to sleep, Lila walked to the end of the love seat and leaned over to grasp Jack's hands in her own. With a smile he rose and, still holding hands, they walked into the bedroom.

A few minutes later Marston was lying in bed with his hands behind his head, speculating aloud why anyone would want to break into his car. Lila was in the bathroom, the door ajar. He said, "He must have been looking for drugs — or — I wonder ...? That car that I saw on the way up this morning — I suppose he must have followed me. I can't understand why. When that guy broke into the car, he ignored my briefcase — which at least looked important, and then for some reason he grabbed that padded manila envelope, the kind you get at the post office ... and all it contained was a bunch of Duval's old speeches."

Lila froze in route from the bathroom. She had been only half listening. Standing in the doorway bedroom now, she felt the rush of adrenaline as Jack said the words "padded manila envelope" for the first time. Stunned, she wondered whether he'd said it before and she missed it. "Padded manila envelope" were the exact words Edgar Steele used to her over the phone when he called asking for her help.

Now she knew.

Without a doubt, this envelope was a look-a-like for the envelope that Willey was to have mailed to Marston and that she was supposed to intercept. It was obvious: Somebody else was after the envelope Willey had mailed. They must have seen Jack Marston carrying this one and thought it was the one they wanted ... and gone after it.

But who? Had Edgar Steele put someone else on this? As she thought about it she began to wonder whether Steele would have assigned someone to steal it after hiring her. If so, why? Was it that big a deal — a burglary?

Or maybe someone else was after it. But who? Foreign interests? Too far-fetched. Or was it?

She stood motionless in the doorway as these thoughts surged through her mind.

Woodenly, she began to walk toward the bed. Marston raised his arms to receive her. Clumsily she said, I'm sorry Jack, I ... I need a few minutes. She left the bedroom and returned to the darkened living room where she sat down once again on the love seat.

As she thought over what happened during the day, Lila realized that she had scarcely thought of Steele or the assignment he'd given her. It had never seemed like a big deal in the first place. After all, helping the CIA intercept materials to protect against security leaks while at the same time aiding a man who was obviously suffering from a mental illness was, as Steele had said, "Just a plain decent thing to do." It wasn't as though she was playing around with any heavy-duty stuff like Middle East peace plans or new developments in the bomb. The assignment had seemed a snap at first. When she had first met him, Marston had unnerved her — but that had more to do with the chemistry between them than the assignment from Steele.

Up until now it had been a perfect day. She hadn't climbed the mountain in a long time, and spending time outdoors with someone she cared about had been an unusual and welcome treat. She knew he felt as she did that the time on the mountain was an adventure to be savored. Something they would always remember. Like the late afternoon lovemaking ...

But after the burglary of Jack's car, she knew she was into something she didn't understand. And worst of all, she couldn't explain it to Marston or he'd think that all of this ... she blushed ... all of this had been simply an attempt to get in his good graces and retrieve the envelope. Christ! She hoped Steele was happy. She felt like a ... she felt unclean.

Still on the love seat, her thoughts turned to the man she would soon join in her bed. She was attracted to this quiet gentle man from the outset, surprising even herself. He was a politician, and she had known plenty of politicians when she lived in Washington. She was not impressed with the breed. Once, while writing an article on the area, Lila had coined a phrase which she now used often to describe many of those she met in D.C.: "Myopic egomania; an illness that afflicts at least half of those representing us in the hallowed halls." The staff hired by the politicos were no help either, and seemed more dedicated to maintaining the charade than contributing in any discernible way to the public good. Washington had not impressed Lila Maret.

But this guy Jack Marston: A politician, yes, but more. A philosopher. She had surprised herself when she asked him to come spend the day with her. Surprised too, when he eagerly accepted. For the most part, Lila lived her life in Jay isolated and away from people, content with her work and the heady Vermont mountain air.

Marston changed that.

When they returned to her condo from their day on the mountain, and she found herself in his arms, there was no fear or pulling back; the late afternoon lovemaking had been natural, relaxed. But the burglary changed everything. If Jack ever found out she had been hired by Steele to con him, he would certainly think it had all been an act. Just thinking about it hurt.

She remained alone in the semi-darkness for a long time, then finally went back into the bedroom, hoping fervently that Marston had gone to asleep.

He hadn't.

He watched her quizzically as she got into bed but he said nothing, waiting for her to explain. She sat upright, the light still on, and said "I'm sorry, Jack, I'm tired — I need to sleep. Good night." She squeezed his arm, put out the light and turned her back."

These thoughts all returned to her again moments before when Jack called with the news about Ben Willey. When she finished talking with him, she stood perfectly still, the phone remaining in her hand. Again she relived the terrible conflict that raged in her mind as she had stood in the doorway of the bedroom wishing she could disappear. Lila shuddered as she remembered turning her back after getting into bed.

In the dim light she had stared at the wall feeling unworthy of the relief tears might bring. Wide awake for hours into the night, time and again she cursed herself as a fool ...

Jack Marston hung up, turned in his chair and gazed once more out the window.

But he never really saw the travel-book view before him: the sparkling blue waters of the lake; the tiny boats speeding frantically about like dolphins at play; the scattered white clouds; or Whiteface Mountain in the distance. They might as well not have been there.

He was thinking about the phone call. He hadn't realized what a shock Willey's death would be to Lila. And then he recalled perhaps for the hundredth time the bewildering events of the weekend: the time Lila and he had spent on the mountain and later the excitement and warmth of her bed, then a quiet peaceful time interrupted by the strange assault on his car and the chase that followed. But then after supper, when she had come to bed, he reached for her and she had turned away.

In the middle of the night he heard her sobbing. He touched her shoulder. "Lila?" Without answering, she turned and reached for him. They made love. This time with a fierceness, Marston remembered, with an intensity not present earlier and that he did not understand. She clung to him and it seemed she wanted to envelope him so that he could never leave. When it was over she turned away, and wept.

Marston lay back wide awake, for the first time in a long time remembering the pleasure a cigarette would provide.

Later, much later, he slept.

Chapter Eighteen

"Well, that's really helpful," Edgar Steele said, flashing a warm smile as he glanced toward the door as though preparing to leave.

"Look over that material. It may generate more questions," Marston said. He and Steele had been talking for a half an hour.

Seeing Steele for the first time in person, Marston felt he had sized him up correctly. Just as he had seemed while speaking on the phone about the South American trip, Steele was smooth, decisive, and, Marston admitted to himself grudgingly, likable. And he was a good listener, no doubt about it. Everybody loves a good listener, and Steele was a master.

But there was something about him that bothered Marston. The man was just too smooth for his taste. Marston smiled at his cynicism. He knew he was overly critical of Washington operatives, even those on Duval's own D.C. staff. In his own mind, the beltway — I-495 — was a man-made barrier between contemporary government and the reality of life as most Americans lived it.

Marston shared with Steele a lot of information on the various vacation opportunities in the north country available for the Mount Washington conference visitors. There was little Marston didn't know about New England, and Steele absorbed the information, taking notes as Marston talked.

When they were finished and Steele had given indications of leaving, it was Marston who said, "The director and Congressman Duval talked about one other thing ..." he paused for a moment. Marston had unconsciously called Richards "the director" and used Duval's official title to underscore the more formal and serious dimension to their next topic.

Continuing, he said, "Director Richards suggested that we provide you with some of the specifics of what appears to be dirty tricks showing up in the campaign. He said you might have some ideas on this." Marston showed Steele the stories that had run in the *Washington Tell-Tale* and told him about the conversation that had been overheard at the Georgetown party and relayed to Duval by Bill Camilli.

Steele listened quietly, his hands still and relaxed, resting in his lap. "Interesting," he said, looking directly at Marston, "We haven't picked up any indications that anything like this is going on in a widely organized way. But we do have 'listeners' placed throughout the country so that if we find that sort of thing is showing up we can alert the FBI — it's their jurisdiction you know — we would call them in and they'd stop this stuff in its tracks." Then, continuing a bit smugly, he concluded: "It's not like it used to be, you know; both services work pretty well together."

"Congressman Duval really appreciates his friendship with your boss and his offer to help," Marston replied. He realized somehow that the man sitting across from him had little interest in any problems emerging in Duval's campaign, and decided that reminding Steele of Duval's friendship with Richards was about all he could do. Steele's self-congratulatory comment earlier about how well the services worked together had irritated Marston, who abhorred self-serving plaudits. Understatement was part of the Vermont tradition. But "belt-way bullshit" was part of Washington, and effected even the good guys, Marston decided long ago.

Steele, sensing then that he had irritated Marston, spent a few more minutes assuring him that the Agency would look into Duval's concerns. Steele couldn't know this, but when Jack Marston's antennae went up, it would take a lot more than the lathering of words to put things straight.

Meanwhile, out in the front office, Shirley Hogan was greeting a visitor. Lila Maret had arrived in the office. "Welcome again," Shirley said lightly.

"Oh, thank you ... I ..."

"Jack's tied up with somebody, but it won't be much longer and he said to make yourself at home. Would you like a paper? We have the *Burlington News*. Is that okay?"

"Yes, fine, thank you," Lila smiled at Shirley, took a seat and turned her attention to the paper.

"Oh, by the way, I have something here for you;" Shirley called out, "Jack told me you were looking for this envelope on Friday.

"The post office put it in the box we use for the campaign letters. They do that sometimes. I called the campaign office and sure enough they had it. It had just arrived. He said to give it to you when you came in."

With that, Shirley casually handed Lila a large padded manila envelope, and as she did so she noticed the slight tremor in the hands reaching to accept it.

Lila smiled nervously and said, "Thank you, thank you so much." She opened the burgundy-colored attaché case resting beside her on the floor, placed the envelope inside and closed the case.

"Coffee?" Shirley offered.

"Yes ... fine."

The attention Marston had earlier lavished on the petite brunette had not been lost on Shirley Hogan. If Marston thought this pretty lady deserved special consideration, then Shirley would provide some of the same!

Marston and Shirley Hogan had been together for a long time and a bond of mutual trust and loyalty had been forged and nurtured. Shirley's intuition was also at work and while she had no idea Jack and Lila had been together over the weekend, she found herself curious about her boss's new friend.

Lila had replied absently to the offer of coffee, her mind racing as she tried to digest the fact that she had finally recovered the envelope. As she reached again for the newspaper, she was startled by a familiar voice.

"Lila Maret, how are you?" A smiling Edgar Steele walked toward her, his right hand outstretched.

Lila felt the blood rush from her face, but she stood and held out her hand.

"I'm ... fine, Mr. Steele," she replied.

Jack Marston was walking behind Steele and he called out, "That proves it, everybody in Washington knows everyone else, it *is* a small town!"

"Washington parties, you know," replied Steele, "not political ones. We met in Georgetown, an embassy party I think, isn't that right?" he said pointedly.

"You have a good memory, Mr. Steele," Lila replied, helplessly going along with the charade.

It had been necessary to say something, but Steele had overdone it. Lila felt vulnerable and angry. Her mind flashed to the envelope sitting in her attaché case. Giving it to Steele would have to wait she decided, reveling for the moment in her chance to get even.

After Steele and Marston had shaken hands for the last time, Steele winked at Shirley Hogan, waved to the others in the room, and was on his way.

With Steele gone, Marston walked over to Lila and standing close to her said, "Come on down to my office," He shot a quick look at Shirley Hogan, who was taking it all in, and explained, "where we can talk."

Once in the office with the door shut, Lila took the single overstuffed chair; Marston sat on the corner of the love seat. He felt awkward; as though the right words must exist, but he didn't know them.

"I hated calling you this morning ... with the news about Ben. "

Lila looked down at her hands and replied, "Jack, it's okay; we ... we weren't really close. It was just a shock."

Taking her hand cautiously, Marston said, "Want a little lunch?"

When Lila smiled, her head tilted down and slightly to the side, and her eyes widened. Whenever Marston saw Lila do this he felt he had known her for a lifetime. He wanted to reach out and touch her but he held back, the uncertainties of Saturday night lingering in his mind.

"Of course," she said, moving to get up.

But Marston was still holding her hand.

"Lila, wait, I have to ask, are we ... okay ... us?" Before she could answer, he said searchingly, "Saturday was very important to me."

Lila wanted to reach out and put her arms around him, but she was afraid this would bring tears. Instead she looked at Marston, squeezed his hand and replied, "I can't explain right now but ... I apologize. It's my fault but — sometime I'll make it up to you."

Resigned that he would learn no more, Marston kissed her gently on the brow, then looked at her for a long moment.

"Come on," he urged, "lunch!"

Much of Church Street in downtown Burlington has been closed to automobile traffic, the successful result of a revitalization effort creating an attractive and busy pedestrian marketplace. Jack and Lila walked in the bright sun, up the center of the street. They headed toward a favorite restaurant of Jack's around the corner on Pearl Street, four or five blocks away. The food was fancy, expensive, the decor "19th century elegant;" but privacy was assured in the partially curtained booths, and lunch or dinner was always accompanied by classical music, usually Mozart, the owner's personal favorite. The restaurant was nearly always Jack's choice on special occasions.

The bright day, Jack Marston's light banter about the up-scale shops they passed on their walk, and his outrageous comments on some of Burlington's colorful political history had served to take Lila's mind off the conflict raging within.

They had progressed halfway up Church Street when Lila spotted the two men. They were talking to each other outside a bagel shop about a hundred feet away. One man, dark-haired and very pale complected, was gesturing with his hands as he was speaking. His companion — Edgar Steele — caught sight of Marston and Lila, and hastily grabbed the jabbering man by the arm, spun him around and in seconds the two disappeared inside the shop.

They were quick about it, but not quick enough to elude Lila's sharp eyes. She had no doubts about whom she had seen standing with Steele. She instantly recognized the pale man's features and pear shaped body as those she had seen illuminated by the flood light in her condominium parking lot two days before.

To Lila's relief, Marston failed to spot the two men. He continued to talk about the curious events leading up to the election of a Socialist mayor some years before.

"Everybody talked about the 'Democratic Machine,' but the machine had stopped doing much of anything. It ran on its reputation. Democrats mostly got re-elected by habit, not by any great organizational effort.

"So the Progressive who wanted to be mayor, acting like a veritable 'Pied Piper,' organized the younger generation who increasingly were living in the city, while the older more prosperous citizens moved into the suburbs and out in the country. The so-called machine was fast asleep, and when people woke up the day after the election, the paper announced that Burlington had elected a Socialist mayor! The insurgents won by ten votes!"

Marston stopped talking for a moment and looked quizzically at Lila. She was desperately trying to put the vision of the intruder she saw talking with Steele out of her mind.

Forcing herself to act normal, Lila asked, "What were the Republicans doing all this time?"

Marston laughed, "It was hard to tell who was more angry, the Republicans or the Democrats. Actually, I think the Republicans were really angry at the Democrats, since they didn't figure they could ever win in the city, and they thought the Dem's were demonstrating total irresponsibility by letting the election slip away to — heaven forbid — a Socialist!"

Marston had reached a point where he observed Vermont politics more as a game than a cause. This kind of detachment served him in good stead when passions surrounding an internal party issue became inflamed, or people started to believe that the future of the party and even civilization itself could hang on a single issue. That was when he would remain calm and often play the role of peacemaker. Party regulars, conservatives and liberals each insisted that he, Marston, was truly on their side.

"Actually, the Socialist was so old-fashioned in his Socialism that it was like a time warp."

Lila continued to try to listen and act normal. But a jumble of strangely connected events were running through her head; the break-in of Marston's car, Ben Willey's death, and now seeing Steele in downtown Burlington with the man whom she knew for sure was the burglar. It was too much.

How could Steele do this? What else wasn't he telling her, she wondered angrily? Thank God she hadn't handed him the envelope that Shirley Hogan had given her back at the office.

But what should she do now? She wasn't about to pretend that the break-in had never occurred, that she hadn't seen the man streaking down the parking lot with Marston right behind him. No way.

Should she confront Steele and ask him what was going on? Maybe, but, ... or perhaps she could talk to Marston, tell him everything, ask for his help. Sure, and have him walk out of her life? Or maybe she should just open the envelope and see what if anything it revealed.

Chapter Nineteen

The story broke that evening on the six o'clock news, the announcer speaking in ominous overtones.

"Congressman Alan Duval, on a recent trip to South America, ostensibly for the purpose of working on the preservation of Brazilian rain forests, is reported to have taken a clandestine side-trip. In a remote area of Colombia, Duval allegedly met with a well-known drug overlord; a man said to be one of a half dozen of the largest drug distributors in South America."

As the story flashed across the screen, Marston, while in his office alone had been casually monitoring the news coming over the local TV channel, jumped up and activated the VCR to record what he was watching. He stood staring at the screen without moving until the segment ended.

Stunned for a moment, his mind fueled with adrenaline, Marston ticked off what the story meant and the calls he needed to make to friends, supporters and others. He grabbed the phone and dialed Middlebury where Duval had left a number where he could be reached. The schedule called for Duval to rest prior to his speech at the college, but Marston knew rest would be elusive for Congressman Alan Duval on this Monday evening.

He listened impatiently to the phone ringing on the other end and as he did simultaneously two other lines lit up on his own phone. Marston ignored them, figuring it was Godine or Camilli, either of whom would be at the office in moments anyway, if he was any judge. Or maybe it was the press, looking for a reaction to the story on TV? He was glad to avoid talking to anyone from the media until he had at least spoken with Duval and Godine.

Everybody needed to be saying the same thing.

The anchorwoman on local TV had finished the story by self-righteously suggesting that the station would have ignored the story which broke that afternoon in the *Washington Tell-Tale*, but that they had been provided with enough evidence and a promise of photographs to follow, and decided they had a responsibility to the public to air the story.

What the anchorwoman didn't say, Marston reflected, was that the station had usually differed with Duval's positions on environmental and a host of other issues, and this was their chance to nail him.

Still waiting for someone to answer the phone in Middlebury, Marston was startled by pounding on the outside door leading into the office. Cradling the phone, he left his chair and went to the reception area to unlock the door.

"Who is it?" he barked.

"Jack, it's me. John Godine."

"You see the TV?" Marston asked as he unlocked the door and let Duval's campaign manager pass.

"Christ yes. What the fuck have they got?"

Godine's face was flushed, his tie askew, but Marston didn't smell booze which some years before had been the talented Godine's near undoing.

"It's that Goddamn South American trip — the rumor of mischief Camilli told us about — this is it."

"You knew where he went and what he did on that trip, didn't you? Weren't you supposed to go with him?"

"Yes, I was," Marston paused, thinking back for a moment, "but they said 'no staff.'"

"Who said 'no staff'?"

"State, as I remember it — the conference was in Brazil, that wasn't the problem. As it was presented to us the side trip was to try to influence Tomarro, and the State Department didn't want any staff on the side trip into Colombia."

"What? Colombia?" Godine was apoplectic.

"State kept it hush — didn't you know about it?"

"He took that trip before I signed on to the campaign. I was lawyering at the time. I didn't follow events that closely back then; no need to," Godine explained.

"At the request of Bill Richards — Alan served with him in the House you know — anyway, now that he's head of the CIA, he asks our man to take this side trip into Colombia to meet with Arturo Tomarra — this is before everybody knew how big a crook Tomarra is. His reputation as a drug baron only developed in the last year and a half. They set it up that Duval would visit the huge ranch Tomarra owns out in the wilds of Colombia.

"I worked with a guy at the CIA to work out arrangements, but they insisted we do it without press or staff. They told Duval that this could really help in reducing the destruction of the rain forests in Brazil, where Tomarra owns one hell of a lot of land, and where he has a lot of influence as well as a lot of friends. If Alan went along, it would show bipartisan support. Of course Alan would do anything to help with this cause — meet with the Devil himself."

"Sounds like that's who it was."

"But at the time no one knew how deep Tomarra was into the drug business," Marston interjected.

Godine finally sat in the chair Marston offered, paused a moment, and then asked with a frown, "Sounds to me like somebody knew what a bastard Tomarra was and either didn't want Duval to know what kind of a crook he had been asked to cosy up to, or," again he paused, "or pure and simple, they wanted to make our boy look bad. A set-up, in other words."

"The story they gave us back then was that the administration wanted to make some agreements with Tomarra before they passed the Rain Forest Protection Aid Program. Tomarra has holdings damn near the size of Texas and his cooperation at the time was critical. So Richards convinced Duval that by going to see Tomarra, he was showing bipartisan support," Marston said. Tomarro's drug dealings were unknown at the time..."

"Except, maybe, to the people who wanted to link Duval with him."

"Why was the CIA in on it and not just State?" Godine had spent five years with the State Department prior to returning to Vermont.

"I dunno, maybe they're working together on this one."

"Huh, I wonder ...," Godine replied, his disbelief apparent. He continued, "One thing new guys in Washington, like Duval, never get through their head is that you can't trust the fucking CIA — no one ever could, no one ever will be able to. Sure, they got a nice guy like Richards out front now, but do you think they let him know what's going on? Like hell!" Godine shifted in his chair, and glancing at the phone said, "You going to try Duval again?"

Marston dialed and waited; still no answer.

"Somebody will have told him by now," Marston said, glancing nervously at the clock on the bookcase; he went on, "You know the Washington game better than I do, do you think Richards will confirm that Duval went to Colombia at the request of the CIA?"

"You never know with that crowd."

"That's what I'm worried about," said Marston. "When I set this up, I was working with a guy named Edgar Steele, a special assistant to the director, Richards. He said we had to keep it very quiet — something about other countries down there wanting the same kind of special preference on things we offered Tomarra."

"Trust me Jack, it may have more to do with the CIA mucking around in State's business."

"But we need Richards to back our story. It's bad enough if he does, I mean, our boy looks like a real dunce getting in that thick with someone like Tomarra, whom he knew nothing about."

The phone buzzed.

"Congressman Duval's office," Marston said, answering it quickly. He leaned forward.

"Yes, Alan?"

He listened, then said, "We have it on the VCR. John's here. Anything you can tell me?" he asked pausing, then, "We'll have to get something out tonight." Again he listened.

"We can't leave it out there unchallenged or every paper in the state will ...," Marston left the sentence unfinished, his voice rising. He had intended to finish with "crucify you," but decided that alarming Duval more than he already was wouldn't be useful, and he left the thought incomplete.

He glanced up at Godine, whose discouragement was apparent, as Duval explained what he wanted.

"Okay Alan, as soon as you can. Stay with that, and thank God for a lazy Vermont press!"

He hung up and stared out the window for a moment. Godine waited. Marston shook his head as if to bring himself back to the present and flashed a wry smile at Godine.

"Sorry, John. The good news is that it looks like there's just a part timer, a stringer, covering the Middlebury speech — normally we'd howl at lousy coverage like that, but with luck, the person covering him won't be experienced enough to know the right questions.

"Duval's promised a statement for the eleven o'clock news. He wants us to work it up. He told the stringer, a young kid I guess, told him or her that he can't comment without seeing the story, and so far the kid believed him. That buys us a little time."

He paused, looking right at Godine and said, "The bad news is, I don't have a clue what to say about this trip, and *I set it up*! If Duval did screw up, a woman or something, over and above what they already have, I sure hope he levels with us — it's the only hope we've got on this kind of deal!"

Marston grabbed a yellow pad from the top shelf of the bookcase, picked up his pen from the desk and held them out toward John Godine saying, "These are the times we earn our money!"

◆◆◆◆◆◆◆

Duval exploded.

"The bastards are always available when they want you to do some — fucking — thing — Goddamn him!" The target of his anger, was no less than his friend Bill Richards.

Marston had never seen his boss so angry. Duval's language seldom strained beyond the occasional mild expletive.

After delivering his speech to the Middlebury College audience, Alan Duval left the hall and rushed back to his Burlington office. Sitting at his desk now in Burlington, with one hand on the phone, he'd been trying, to no avail, to reach Bill Richards at his office or at home. But the CIA chief was unavailable at either of two numbers. For the third time, Duval reviewed the one paragraph statement Marston and Godine had prepared. And for the third time, he tossed it back on the desk.

"It's no good if Richards won't verify it. He'll have to," he said mostly to himself.

For Jack Marston's part, politics had been his business long enough that he knew the dull humdrum of a politician's day could be changed instantly. Without notice, a candidate could be confronted with decisions affecting the rest of his or her political life. When so confronted, it was critical that a response come quickly, clearly and most importantly, accurately.

He knew too well that often times complicated ethical and political decisions had to be made in minutes or at best in a few hours. Not only did the correct response have to be found, but tactical and strategic choices had to be made, recognizing that the answers would be interpreted by a cynical and woefully uninformed press, too often in two or if you were lucky three sentences. Unforeseen challenges of this kind could spell life or death to a political career.

Duval, Marston and Godine, each of them knew without saying that this was such a time. Their political antennae came alive. Uncertainty fueled the tension in the air. They could feel it.

Marston remembered years before when his friend former Governor Dick Ashton decided he couldn't support the national ticket because of the war in Vietnam. The principled decision cost him a seat in the U.S. Senate a couple of years later. His political career suddenly at an abrupt end.

Marston thought back on the time when Ashton's successor, against the best advice of his advisors, had initiated the state sales tax in order to preserve the effective but controversial programs for the poor which were begun in the sixties. This act of courage was rewarded with a resounding re-election victory. The voters had surprisingly approved. Another turning point ...

Duval was experiencing a politician's worst nightmare; Marston watched him carefully. Pressure situations were part of the game, but scandals involving women, money, booze or drugs were messy, the worst kind. The way the media broke the story on Duval's sidetrip to Columbia hinted at all of these things, and they didn't have the whole story yet. They were obviously waiting for the next installment from whatever was their source. Thank God there were no pictures.

The three men knew that the press goes after such a story with a vengeance, and every aspect of a person's life is fair game. For Duval, this would be a test under fire; one he would have to pass to be elevated to the U.S. Senate.

For all the pressure on him, Duval appeared to be in control after his initial explosion at being unable to connect with Richards by phone. Marston reflecting for a moment, decided that to him Duval had always seemed ageless. Politicians, he decided, don't age like the rest of us. They look the same until they retire, or alas, they lose. Then it all happens at once, overnight, and like the life of "Dorian Gray," we suddenly see them: their vulnerability, the lines in their face, the graying hair ... They become like the rest of us: human.

John Godine broke the silence. "It's ten o'clock, Alan. Better we get this out, even if Richards denies it for whatever reason, we can't leave this unchallenged."

"Yeah, and if he doesn't confirm it then I've got the head of the CIA calling me a liar," Duval shook his head, "Go with it. Call the TV people first, then we'll try to get the wire service on it." In Vermont, the AP wire served most of the newspapers and all of the radio stations. Godine took the statement into the next office to start making calls.

"Want a drink Alan? Or would you like some coffee?"

"You bet I want a drink!" And then the magical Duval smile flashed across his face and once again he was young and invincible as he had been the first day he skated out on the hockey rink so many years before.

"But as you know, some wise man once said: 'Never take a drink when you really want one.' Let's have coffee."

With Godine down the hall making press calls to let them know he was faxing the prepared statement, Duval and Marston sat quietly drinking coffee and talking, for the moment ignoring the story of Duval's "secret trip to meet with the South American drug lord," as TV was characterizing it during program news breaks.

"Are we making tracking calls tonight?" Duval inquired, referring to the phone banks that had been set up to do persuasion calls nightly until the election.

"Yes — I think they'll give us some feel for the effect of this thing fairly shortly," Marston replied, glancing at the clock, "But we'll know more, of course, in a day or so down the road when a lot more people will have heard the story, and we can also factor in your reply."

Neither man said anything for a while. They sat in a silence born of trust from earlier trials they had faced together.

"This could be the end of it, couldn't it Jack?"

"Yes, Alan, it could," Marston replied quietly.

Marston got up to close a window that had been opened earlier in the day. He had to push it a couple of times to get it in a position where he could lock it. Instead of returning to sit with Duval, he stood some distance away, his back to the window.

"Alan, I've got to have it, all of it." Marston broke the silence with his forceful demand. "The statement gets us through until morning, but the 'Tell-Tale' is promising part two, with pictures," he added.

Duval sat motionless, hands in his lap, looking out the window. Finally he turned to Marston and said, "I'm honestly not sure what they have. I've been replaying this thing in my mind since I first heard it might be a problem. Over and over. I just don't know for sure. This so-called ranch I visited is out in the middle of nowhere. It exists like a small city. Hell, it *is* a small city.

"When I got to Tomarra's ranch there were a lot of people staying right at his place. It was like a regular hotel, with lots of guests, members of his family, and staff around. Everyone was very gracious. I'd never seen a layout like this.

"I'd had a rough trip on the helicopter and I was feeling kind of woozy. A doctor, he seemed legit, gave me something ... some pills, and told me to take a nap, which I did. I was out like a light for several hours."

"Did they drug you or ...?"

"I suppose, now that I think about it, maybe. The second day I went jogging and when I returned, I went to the basement area where they have a sauna and a whirlpool — restricted to men, I thought. I was just going to get into the whirlpool — I was naked.

"The whirlpool is located right off this fancy exercise room adjacent to the men's and women's locker rooms. All of a sudden, in walks a young lady — a beautiful young lady, believe me — unfortunately she was as naked as I was, and there we were," he paused. "But she just apologized and left. No big deal."

"Did you see her again?"

"Oh yes, she was a relative of Tomarra's — a cousin or something."

"You saw the girl at parties, at some of the social occasions?"

"Sure, there were events of some kind every evening. They have the entertainers flown in. One night they had an outdoor barbecue and dancing in the courtyard, real 'South of the Border' stuff."

"Did you dance with this woman?"

"Duval's face darkened and he said, "I know where you're going with this, Jack, but ..."

"Alan, damn it, level with me!"

"You think I was set up; you forget Richards is a friend of mine."

"You better find out pretty soon that Washington friendships are very different than the kind you learned about in St. Albans, Vermont! Anyway, Richards may not even be in on it. But I'll bet a grand against a dime the girl is." He persisted, "Then what happened — Alan, we're both big boys ... Did ...?"

"I didn't sleep with her ... and yes, I could have!" With that, Alan Duval angrily slammed the desk drawer, stood up and headed for the door. At the last minute he turned and said, "I'll be at the Sheraton tonight," and walked out.

Right at that moment, John Godine was coming down the hall. Duval stormed by without a word. Godine, who'd been around long enough to know when to say nothing, stared after Duval as he passed.

Returning his gaze toward Marston he inquired, "Trouble?"

"You know our boy, John. When the chips are down he has to be alone for a while to think. I had to ask some tough questions.

"Every politician I've ever known panics when you get too close — they let it happen for a few moments, then they get scared and run. They can make love to the crowd, but they can't hack it very well one on one! That's really what happened here."

"Did he tell you what happened in South America?"

"Partly, I think, though he hasn't really admitted what happened yet, even to himself — and of course he feels like a damn fool." Marston sighed.

"Well ...?"

"He was set up all right. There was a woman ..."

"There always is," interjected Godine.

"... maybe he slept with her maybe he didn't, you know the rule..."

"It ain't what it is, it's what it looks like!" Godine interjected, quoting Duval's press secretary who spent all his waking hours crafting the congressman's public persona, and exasperating the rest of the staff in the process.

"Doesn't matter, they say they have pictures that will prove it anyway."

"Sex and drugs. Two out of three so far. I hope they haven't got anything showing him taking a bribe."

"Doesn't matter; if the tabloids set their teeth on this one Duval will be history. John," he paused, then slowly in an even more ominous vein, "we are in very serious trouble. Even if Richards confirms he sent Alan on CIA business, at best the election becomes a long shot if they show pictures of him with a naked woman. Thank God TV has held back on the pictures so far! Without Richards confirming Alan's story, ... well ...?" Marston threw up his hands.

He grabbed his jacket, slipped it on and said, "Duval will want us here early. Let's get some sleep, we're going to need it."

Chapter Twenty

On the same evening that Burlington television broke the story on Congressman Duval's trip into Colombia, Lila Maret had returned to her Jay Peak condominium and was sitting outside on her deck gazing at the mountain, its majestic presence outlined against the darkening sky. Lila's briefcase containing the unopened envelope lay next to her on a small wicker table.

The phone rang.

She knew it would be Edgar Steele, and hated herself for her indecision, for her uncertainty about what to say to him. It rang again. Lila was at first tempted not to answer, but after the third ring, picked up.

"Edgar here ... Did you get the envelope?"

She hesitated.

"No, not yet," she answered with the lie.

"Did you ask?" His irritation was audible.

"Yes, ... I'm sure they'll give it to me when ..."

"What's the matter? You sound —"

"I'm sorry, I've been dozing." Another lie.

"I'll call tomorrow ... if I don't reach you, I'll leave a message. Set your answering machine." Then he added angrily, "The damned envelope should be showing up!" He hung up.

Lila had known Steele's call was coming and was upset at her indecision. It wasn't like her; out of character and she knew it. She thought of herself as a woman in control. In charge. And now all this. She needed to confront Steele or give him the envelope. She had done neither. Unable to sit quietly any longer, she left the deck and went inside.

She tried to put it out of her mind and spent the evening organizing her notes on the research she had done the last couple of visits to the library. Later, she went to clean up a few dishes. When she came into the kitchen she glanced at the clock and snapped on the small TV on the kitchen shelf figuring she was right on time for the eleven o'clock news,

Moments later the anchorman came on with the story of Alan Duval's secret trip to meet with the Colombian drug kingpin. As the story developed Lila froze, watched without moving, holding a glass plate aloft in one hand, a towel in the other. The water from the faucet ran endlessly, unnoticed in the background.

The impact of the story was not lost on Lila and she well understood what it meant and what it would mean to Jack Marston. When the anchorman finished she dropped the towel put the plate in the sink and dialed Marston's home number. No answer. Maybe the office. She tried that — still no answer. Lila began to pace.

At lunch that day Marston had maintained a light mood. He hadn't pushed her for answers on her curious behavior and sudden change of mood on Saturday night.

During the meal, Marston talked of his experiences in Vermont politics, and went into some detail about Duval's Senate campaign. She knew from what he said that there had been a hint of some dirty tricks. The story she just witnessed on TV had obviously been part of it. Duval's denial of any wrongdoing and his insistence that he had been asked to take the side-trip into Colombia by the CIA seemed straightforward, albeit a little bizarre.

Lila tried both numbers a few more times, then went to bed and planning on an early start in the morning, set the alarm for five-thirty.

◆ ◆ ◆ ◆ ◆ ◆ ◆

Shirley Hogan had been around politics long enough to know when trouble was in the air. And the story on Duval's trip to Colombia, which she had watched at home on the six o'clock news, was trouble in spades. She called Marston, offering to come in and help after the story broke. He thanked her but said simply, "Let's you and I get here a little early tomorrow, okay?"

Shirley arrived Tuesday morning at seven o'clock; Marston was already sitting in his office reading the *Burlington News*. The phones hadn't started ringing but they both knew that the lines would light up shortly. Shirley sat in the chair across the desk from Marston. For a while she said nothing.

After a while she asked quietly, "How bad is it Jack?"

Looking up at her he smiled, sadly, and said, "Bad Shirley, very bad."

She knew if he had more to say he would. That's the way he was. She'd wait it out, questioning him would accomplish nothing.

He put the paper down, folded it, and offered it to her. Shaking her head she said, "I've read it ... at the house."

It was only minutes past seven but already the sun's rays were bouncing and sparkling off the blue waters of the lake. The gentle coolness of the Vermont June morning was giving way to the warmth that summer promised. Small delivery trucks were stopping along the street, introducing the noises of a city coming to life. A disheveled woman of uncertain age, whom Marston recognized as a regular on the street, was sifting through a trash container searching for empty beer and soda bottles to be redeemed at a grocery store for five or ten cents. This kind of litter had become a cash crop for the poor and homeless.

Thinking aloud, Marston said "Did you ever believe that the most impressive result of urban renewal would be homelessness?"

Shirley didn't reply. She was used to Marston's trick of talking about one subject while thinking of another.

Barely pausing, Marston changed the subject, "This week will be a tough one ... be prepared. Alan will need all of us in one way or another."

Changing the subject again, he asked, "Did that envelope ever show up? You remember, the one Lila Maret wanted us to give her?"

"Yes ... it was in the campaign mailbox, addressed to the Congressman, and it had Ben Willey's return address on it. I picked it up yesterday morning and gave it to her when she came in at noon — you were in with that guy from the CIA."

"Edgar Steele," Marston said the words slowly, thoughtfully.

"Was that all right? You said to give it to her — I'm sorry I forgot to tell you."

"No, fine — that's what I said. Funny, Lila didn't mention it at lunch."

"Lila, huh?" Shirley interrupted, acting surprised at Marston's use of Lila's first name.

"I suppose she thought I knew," Marston continued, intentionally ignoring Shirley's comment, but the sly look he cast her way gave him away.

"Jack, I hate to change the subject but we all need to know — what's the story on this South American trip that was on the tube last night? Did Congressman Duval really go and see that drug dealer?"

"God, Shirley, I wish I could explain what is going on but I can't. At least I can't make any sense of it. Duval did go to see this Tomarra, and he did it at the request of the CIA, just as he said in his statement."

"So the CIA can clear it all up then?"

"They can, but will they? They may have a million reasons, including plain old politics that they'll drag up to keep from admitting they sent our man to see Tomarra. The worst of it is that there may be more dirt coming."

"More?" Shirley was shocked.

"Just hang in there, pal — you always do," Marston smiled sadly.

"Serious, huh?"

"Serious."

He rose from behind desk and said, "Coffee time, I'll get the water, you fix the pot."

❖ ❖ ❖ ❖ ❖ ❖ ❖

Congressman Duval called in before eight that morning and asked Marston to arrange a ten o'clock meeting in the office. In addition to Marston, Godine and Camilli, pollster Eddie Fine and long time loyalist Marlene Brownell were also to be called. Marlene had paid her dues and then some through years of service to the party and asked nothing in return. She was, operating pretty much on her own, the best political fund-raiser in the state. She not only could raise money but was a trusted confidant of party members from all shades of the spectrum.

Everyone arrived on time, and the group wasted no time in getting to work. Gathered in chairs around a coffee table in Duval's office they began assembling and analyzing information as it arrived. Tallies from the persuasion polls done the previous evening were brought in but revealed little. The story was too new. Many people contacted by the pollsters had not yet heard the TV allegations about Duval. Of those people that had heard about the breaking story, most wanted to hear more before commenting. The story was too new for polling to mean anything. Those who were already opposed to Duval were simply confirmed in their opinion. The *Burlington News* that morning ran the story in the second section, reflecting the conservative nature of their news coverage as well as reflecting disdain for a story which first broke on television.

The *Rutland Courier*, an aggressive down state paper covering most of southern Vermont, had an exclusive of its own. A front page story announced that Paul Wellington of Rutland was going to challenge Duval in the primary.

Bill Camilli was talking about this to the group, "... not only did they confirm that Wellington is going to run in the primary, but get this — he already has in hand half the money he'll need to mount a decent challenge! He has almost as much money in hand as you do Congressman, and you're a popular incumbent. Where the hell did he get that money?"

"How'd he raise it that fast?" inquired Marlene Brownell, frowning as she spoke.

"Big secret. You know that crowd, always unhappy ... can't stand to support a winner even in their own party," Camilli replied.

"I know, but they never raised any money before — something's strange," she said.

"The timing of this announcement and the charges against Alan are curious enough ... *and* when you add the questions about the source of his money, it looks like it was planned that Wellington and his crowd would benefit from the attack on the congressman. How could this have happened?"

Shirley Hogan knocked on the door which had been closed and entered without waiting for an answer, "Director William Richards of the CIA is returning your call Congressman," she announced.

As the group started to get up to provide privacy, Duval said, "No — No, stay here, I'll get it in the other room — Jack, Johnny G. you better come with me.'

Duval and the two men went into Marston's office; Duval picked up the phone. "Bill, thanks for calling, I ..," He listened for a few moments, his face tightening before he interrupted saying, "Hey Bill, I got a problem and I need your help. You know what it's like. You had a tough race your first time out, I only want ..."

Duval's face flushed with anger as he listened. Marston got up, and stood right in front of Duval and said in a stage whisper, "Don't piss him off ... you're seeing him Thursday."

Duval spun away from Marston displaying his back, "Bill, I can't accept this as your last word. I made that trip at your request ... I can't worry about the State Department or your concern about precedents ... that's bullshit; my career's on the line! My Senate race hangs on this!" He listened for only a moment more, then interrupted again: "Never mind — I expected more from you." He hung up.

Marston and Godine exchanged looks. They were silent. Unthinkable but true, the CIA chief would have no comment on the affair. Finally Duval said, "Come on, let's go back in the other room and tell the others."

When they returned to Duval's office the expression he wore told the worst. Duval was showing the strain of the last fifteen hours, but it was time for him to leave, and he said calmly, maintaining control, "Thanks for coming in. Today I've got stops at General Electric, lunch in the executive dining room at IBM, a meeting with the anti-development crowd in Williston and then on to good old Franklin county! Pray for me," he said kiddingly, flashing the famous Duval grin.

After the beleaguered candidate left the room, with John Godine trailing behind, Marston said to those still remaining, "Nobody should have to face what he's going to get today, he's falling like a stone in the polls, the CIA director won't back his story, then out of nowhere comes a well-financed ding-bat from his own party to challenge him in the primary. Anyone have any suggestions?" he asked.

The room remained silent.

◆ ◆ ◆ ◆ ◆ ◆ ◆

Perfect timing ... the Wellington challenge was a work of art ... The newspapers stressed the fact that he had already raised more than half of what he would need."

Steele listened to the praise over the phone, smiled and replied, "Thank you ... we're on track. I want to have the last envelope in my hands before we run the next story. The Tell-Tale will put out the best stuff as soon as I say — pictures and all. But nothing today: We'll just keep them sweating!" Again he listened, his face registering exquisite pleasure derived from the praise he thrived on. Then Steele said, "The congressman's top aide has promised to give it to my operative. He apparently swallowed the story completely. He doesn't have a clue that this has anything to do with the election. And I do have a back-up man on site if this doesn't work ... but it will ... We'll have it very soon, sir."

Edgar Steele hung up the phone in his room at the Mount Washington Hotel. Looking once more out the window at the formidable mountain, Steele decided that he had indeed picked the right spot for the terrorism conference. Here in the higher elevations, the late afternoon sun cast a reddish glow which reflected off small patches of snow still in evidence at higher elevations. The lower part of the mountain was bursting forth with a springtime rush of green. The air was clear and cool.

Steele had the one piece of business left: retrieving the last envelope. Lila should have it in hand it by now, but he knew the mail service could be slow and unpredictable. Still he wanted the loose ends tied up. With the newspaper report of Willey's death, the only unfinished business was the envelope.

As soon as he had it, the *Tell-Tale* would run part two of the story guaranteeing Duval's plunge into political oblivion.

Edgar Steele stared out the window, a thin smile on his face.

◆ ◆ ◆ ◆ ◆ ◆ ◆

Meanwhile back in Burlington while digging around in the Special Collections section of the university library, Lila Maret discovered some long-buried material that described in language of the mid to late nineteenth century the story of the development of "carriage trails." Carriage trails were winding roads suitable for horse-drawn carriages that carried vacationers to the summits of a number of mountains in Maine, New Hampshire, and Vermont. Prior to air-conditioning, mountaintop hotels were a cool respite for city dwellers. These resorts came into vogue in the middle of the nineteenth century, financed by the railroads seeking to increase railroad passenger traffic.

A few of the trails, such as the Toll Road on Mt. Mansfield in Vermont are still in use, others are long forgotten and overgrown. Mountaintop hotels are now almost nonexistent.

The material she had uncovered was just what Lila had been seeking to distinguish her north country travel guide from other similar if less ambitious travel guides written about the northern tier New England states.

Lila had called Marston early that morning at the office. Although he welcomed her call, he had assured her there was nothing she could do to help at the moment. Lunch would not be possible, but he invited her down in the late afternoon, and she agreed she would meet him there.

She worked through the noon hour. Warmer now, the library smelled of summer, a mix of floor cleaners, perspiration, cosmetics, and old books. Dust particles floated in the air carried by the sun's rays streaming through the windows. Hollow sounds echoed as people roamed through the stacks, or scraped their chairs when rising to stretch. Ensconced at carrels throughout the library, researchers were poring over materials or sitting back pensively, forming images for the mind.

The materials Lila had come upon that morning were restricted to in-house use, so she had spent a good part of her time photocopying and taking notes. It was the hard part of research: time consuming, plodding, unexciting, but as important as the writing itself.

It was almost noon when she came upon one of those moments familiar to many students and she found herself doubting the materials she had earlier uncovered. She wondered if the morning's find would seem as exciting when she sat down to put the book together as it had this morning. She found her pencil becoming "heavy." Low blood sugar she decided.

Glancing at her watch, she shoved her books and materials aside, stood up, and stretched. The sun streamed in; the bright summer day beckoned.

Lila left the library and stepped outside; she found the fresh air welcome, the sun high in the sky and almost too warm. She followed the winding walk across campus to the university cafeteria.

Lila wasn't really hungry, but she bought some yogurt and found an empty table in the corner of the dining room. From her seat at the table she watched the young students. Their rituals seemed distant to her, but still she remembered. She had been part of this only a few years ago. Now she could only observe. College-age men and women were talking and bantering at a large table nearby. The women seemed in control, sure of themselves despite dressing like poor imitations of Charlie Chaplin. To Lila, the young men seemed almost comical in their seriousness and yet so like sleek racehorses wanting — but embarrassed — to break free. Lila Maret was engulfed by a strange sadness triggered by memories which were near to the surface on this June day.

If she could only try again. It wasn't fair to have one chance with life and the decisions one made about that life. Choices were so irrevocable. We all should get a "Mulligan" on life, she mused. An idea for an article.

She laughed at herself to shake off the momentary depression. Lila got up, threw the yogurt container in the trash and returned to the library. The break had done her good. It was just a short walk, but she decided that she had vacillated long enough.

As soon as she got back to the library she would open and inspect the contents of the manila envelope, which until now had remained sealed in her briefcase.

Chapter Twenty-One

Lila, in her Subaru, drove aggressively down Main Street to Marston's office during the worst of late afternoon traffic. She scarcely noticed the cars or the heat.

Impatiently she waited in Duval's outer office. And while she waited, she once again reviewed in her mind the content of the materials Ben Willey had provided which carefully detailed what Edgar Steele and unidentified others were up to. The contents of the envelope were almost unbelievable, yet there was no doubt in Lila's mind as to their accuracy. She had opened the envelope not knowing what to expect. She knew what she discovered in the envelope that afternoon in the library would affect the future of Congressman Duval, along with many other people and perhaps even herself.

Impatiently she waited.

Finally when most of the staff had left and she and Jack Marston were together in his office, she wasted little time getting to the subject. Holding the envelope out for Marston to see, she said, "This is the envelope that Shirley gave me yesterday. I opened it and looked at everything."

Marston frowned, "I thought it was restricted material?"

"I don't know where to begin — Jack, be prepared, this is strong stuff: It involves Duval's campaign," she paused before continuing, "as well as you and I."

Marston looked up, staring at Lila for a moment, alert, his mind racing. Lila and I? How could that be? He'd scarcely given the envelope a thought since Lila had asked for it the other day. But campaign related? He'd never considered a connection. Shirley Hogan had told him yesterday that she had given the envelope to Lila, but neither he nor Lila had mentioned it; it hadn't seemed that important. Then.

But now, remembering the break-in into his car at Lila's condo at Jay, and the car that had followed him on his trip up, all the coincidences suddenly became part of a different kind of pattern. When you did that, it all began to make sense when you considered the campaign. And of course, you had to consider the campaign. No wonder Ben Willey had been trying to contact him. It was to alert Duval ... about what was coming.

When Lila had opened the envelope at her desk at the University library, she studied each of the documents carefully — shielding the materials from the eyes of any passersby. Now at Marston's office, she once again removed the various documents and pictures from the envelope and placed them on the floor in front of both of them.

Marston felt the blood drain from his face as he realized what he was seeing. His initial fleeting look at a couple of the documents had him shaking his head, incredulous to what was unfolding before his eyes. These things just didn't happen ...,

"There's something more you need to know...," Lila said.

She had wanted to find the right time or at least the right way to tell him. But there was no right way, and when Ben Willey's name first surfaced she seized upon a pause in the conversation.

"I've misled you on something, something important." Lila took a deep breath. "I was not related in any way to Ben Willey ... I'd never even met him. I was asked to do this by the CIA and it seemed harmless. I have done a little work for them in the past and this time they asked me to help prevent a security breach ... as they explained it. I came to see you about Ben Willey at their request. They figured that if I said I was his cousin, you would be more sympathetic to the situation."

Marston stared at her, dumbfounded.

She went on, "They told me he was a nut case that had left the Agency with materials that were classified, and that I could help him stay out of trouble by keeping Congressman Duval, or anyone else in his office, from looking at the contents of the envelope. I believed them."

Lila looked at Marston, the strain in her voice the only giveaway as to how she felt. Marston was little aware of the emotions raging beneath her calm demeanor. She continued, pleadingly: "I couldn't figure what to do."

Marston, overwhelmed, said nothing, and looked away.

Tentatively she reached for his hand, and said, "You and I, Jack, that was real. You have to believe that was real."

Marston let her take his hand, turned back, and nodded, and said, while revealing nothing, "Yeah, I know."

They talked into the early evening hours. They talked about the materials they were looking at. They talked about how to use the materials, and how Duval could fight back. The sun remained high above Whiteface Mountain in the New York Adirondacks, even this late in the day its reflection still sparkling off the lake. Neither Lila nor Marston noticed.

At one point Lila recalled for Marston that when they were walking up Church Street on the way to lunch, she had seen the man who broke into Marston's car talking with Edgar Steele immediately after Steele had left the office.

"We know Steele's part of this, and he's Richards's right hand man — I can't believe it, but could Richards...," Marston left the thought incomplete. He found himself more bewildered than angry, torn between his pleasure in finding evidence to prove the existence of a character assassination plot on Alan Duval, and the sinking feeling that what he had thought was something special between Lila and himself was only part of a game.

Lila Maret was now sitting cross-legged on the floor in front of him. She was not looking at him. Her head was down, and papers and photographs were scattered on the floor between them.

"Shirley told me she gave it to you," he replied, not looking at her, but instead staring at a photograph of Alan Duval wearing nothing but a strange smile. Duval was standing completely naked beside a beautiful black-haired woman, who was about twenty-five years old and also totally naked.

"I wondered why you didn't mention it," he said as though to no one in particular. He shook his head; looked at Lila as though for the first time, trying to find a way to explain it to himself, or make it as though it never happened.

Finally Lila returned his gaze, her eyes glistening as she said, "I know how it seems to you — God, do I know. I haven't slept — and if the CIA knew I had shown you this stuff," she said, waving her hand at the contents of the envelope spread out in front of her, "they could ...." she paused, looking directly at Marston, and began again, "Jack, I know what it looks like, but it wasn't all an act."

Marston got up from his chair. He was holding a memo authored by Ben Willey that was enclosed in the envelope, addressed "To Whom it May Concern." The memo, along with the other materials, explained how Willey had come upon the documents, and how it appeared to him that Duval had been set up. The photographs and other documents were evidence of the efforts to shake up the campaign of Congressman Alan Duval for U.S. Senate. Smiling wistfully, Marston looked at Lila Maret. Sitting on the floor as she was, appearing somehow even smaller than before.

"This is crazy — I don't even know — first I have to show Alan. Maybe he and Godine will have some ideas. Who do you go to with this kind of stuff? The U.S. Attorney, or the FBI, or," he concluded, answering his own question as he stared at Lila, "maybe there's no one to trust. Christ what a mess!"

"I better leave," she said, and stood up.

"No, don't go, we both need to get used to what happened — we both got suckered."

Lila flinched.

Marston continued, "What's got to come first right now is Duval and the campaign. We need to set that straight. I'll need your help to explain all this. Stay and watch the news — God knows what they'll have tonight."

But the six o'clock evening news ended strangely silent on the story that had rocked the Duval campaign the previous evening. There was a brief recap of the previous evening's story, but nothing new. Following the broadcast, Marston spoke by phone with Duval, who'd already arrived at Mt. Washington. Marston not trusting that the telephone was secure, purposely left out the details of what Lila had found in the envelope. Instead, Marston told Duval he had something that could be of help and they needed to talk right away.

Duval had arrived at Mt. Washington earlier that day. By leaving the state in advance of when he'd planned, he managed to avoid the Vermont press and get some badly needed rest as a bonus. When Marston hinted at what he'd found, Duval told him to head for New Hampshire right away.

While Marston was on the phone Lila remained sitting on the floor, waiting quietly. She'd gone out earlier to get sandwiches, chips, and coffee at the deli across the street. Wrappings and empty cartons were scattered about Marston's desk and on the floor.

When Marston hung up the phone, he walked to the window and looked out on the city as daylight began to fade and the coolness of the evening insinuated its presence. He turned and looked at Lila, now standing a few feet away. He said, "Alan thinks I should go over there — tonight. He wants to see the stuff, of course."

"Will you tell him everything?" she asked, realizing the inevitable answer almost as soon as the words were out.

"Yes." He said this simply, then with a sad smile continued, "You know we're in this together, whether we like it or not."

"Do you believe me, Jack, when I say it wasn't an act?"

He felt a stab of pain at her question. Looking away for a moment he replied, "I don't know Lila," then with a half smile concluded, "but that's what I want to believe."

◆ ◆ ◆ ◆ ◆ ◆ ◆

Brill heard every word.

Early in the day on Tuesday, Augie Brill had decided to experiment. In his bag of electronic gadgetry he carried a special listening device he'd picked up a few months ago but never used. He thought when he first tried it that from the angle of his second story location to the fifth floor across the street he would be lucky to pick up even a few words. Instead, he could hear perfectly into Marston's office. Curiously however, he found he could hear virtually nothing in any other part of the office.

But he learned everything he needed to know. The envelope was in the hands of Lila Maret and Jack Marston and, more importantly, they had opened it and now knew what Steele was plotting. This would be very bad news to Edgar Steele when Brill called to let him know. Brill hustled down the stairs and out the door toward the phone booth.

He called the Washington number he had been provided and, as usual, was told to hang up and wait for the call-back. Within minutes the pay phone rang and he was talking to Steele. Steele was returning the call from the Mount Washington Hotel where he'd checked in earlier. Brill described what his surveillance had now revealed. Steele, surprisingly was not upset that Marston and Maret had the envelope in their possession, but rather was reassured that he now knew its whereabouts. Because of what happened in Maine when Brill was assigned to track Ben Willey, Steele's main concern was that Brill not be so aggressive in going after it that he risk being discovered, and jeopardize the whole operation. "Hey," he said, "I want you to continue to watch Marston, and continue listening in on that office. Don't try to follow Marston to New Hampshire. It's a real break that you can overhear what's going on in that office — stay with that. I've got another idea for getting the envelope!"

Brill shook his head, disappointed. He was sure he would only need to wait for Marston to leave his office with the envelope in hand to do what was necessary to take it. But Brill also knew the rules. It was the money down the line that he was waiting for, and if Steele had another way to get the envelope, so be it.

From the chair in his room where he was sitting while talking to Augie Brill, Steele could see the afternoon sun reflecting off the still snowy summit of Mt. Washington. He held the phone in his lap another moment; his briefcase on the bed nearby. He stayed still, thinking.

He picked up the phone and dialed his first call to Washington, D.C. His next call was to the governor's office in New Hampshire. He got through easily, and within moments had reached the person in that office that he needed to talk to.

He smiled to himself, enjoying the sensation of power as he manipulated the players. The drama was heightened for Edgar Steele by the history of his surroundings. It was here, in 1944, that the Bretton Woods Conference took place and established the International Monetary Fund. The conference established the postwar rules for the conduct of international finance; rules that remained unchanged for over fifty years.

He hung up from his last call, almost shaking with delight. He had always liked the phrase from Shakespeare's *Julius Caesar*: "Cry 'Havoc' and let slip the dogs of war!"

The dogs would be loosed the following day when the next and most important part of the story of Duval's ill-fated South American trip became grist for every paper in the land — from the *New York Times* to the *National Enquirer*. He put his briefcase away, the phone back on the stand, and walked again to the window where he stood looking out on the mountain still visible in the fading light. He could have described to no one the extraordinary pleasure he felt at having defeated Vermont's Senate candidate, Alan Duval, with the election still almost five months away.

And, to be able to bring such a player as Congressman Duval to his knees meant that he, Steele, could do it with others whenever it was necessary.

Steele's stomach signaled. Time for dinner, he concluded.

Perhaps a very rare filet this evening.

Chapter Twenty-Two

Jack Marston and Lila Maret left the building together, Lila was heading for her car, Marston to the Quick-Stop/Deli located across the street to get coffee in preparation for the long trip to New Hampshire.

"That'll work better," Marston was saying, "I'll be able to talk with Duval and explain what's happened. You should probably come over ... maybe tomorrow night, but I'll call you on that." Suddenly the moment was awkward.

Lila reached out and touched Marston's arm. "Call me?"

Marston smiled, "I'll call, Lila ...," he said turning his head away. Then turning back and looking into her eyes with a wry smile he continued, "Right now I ... I don't know," he shrugged. "But I will call." He reached out and with his right hand squeezed her shoulder, then abruptly walked away.

Lila watched as he headed down the street and around the corner to the garage where his car was parked. He was carrying his battered old briefcase by the handle. As usual, the briefcase was full of reports, unopened correspondence, magazines he intended to read, and a motley assortment of road maps. But stuffed in there along with everything else was the padded manila envelope with the photographs and other incriminating material, and several pages of explanation written by Ben Willey. Lila had suggested copying the materials, but Marston hadn't wanted to take the time.

Augie Brill watched from his vantage point in the old building across the way. Even in the daylight he was sure he could have taken the briefcase from Marston without attracting attention. Still, Brill believed in the "golden rule," namely, that whomever has the gold makes the rules. And Edgar Steele had the gold!

Jack Marston liked driving at night. Years before, when he traveled the three northern New England states for Chrysler, he often planned these longer trips after sundown when the air had cooled and the engines of his automobiles, as though welcoming his consideration, ran both quietly and efficiently. Tonight, before he got on the road to New Hampshire, he would need to stop in Underhill to pick up some clothes and secure the house for a few days.

Marston quickly charted in his mind the best route to Mt. Washington. As he had done in the old days, he would take Route 15 to Route 2, then immediately after he passed St. Johnsbury, he would jump on I-93 toward Littleton, New Hampshire. At Littleton he would follow Route 302 all the way to the Mount Washington Hotel. Except for the new stretch of interstate, Marston had spent countless hours on these roads.

After spending a few moments at the house in Underhill, picking up a few things and letting one of the neighbors know he'd be gone a while, he was back on the road. In a strange way he was looking forward to the trip. He set the air-conditioning on low and rolled up the windows. At first he turned on the radio, but the Vermont public radio station was on one of its more exotic kicks. Marston decided against listening to the discordant sounds of some ugly city being depicted in music considered avant garde, and congratulated himself for remembering to bring some cassettes. He unzipped the small carrying case and picked the soundtrack from *Brigadoon.* Slipping it into the player, he listened to the mechanical clicks as the player positioned the tape, and then the beginning of the familiar overture. He turned up the volume.

After listening to *Brigadoon,* he would play the tape of *Paint Your Wagon,* an underrated musical he hadn't heard for some time. By the end of both tapes he would have arrived in Littleton. Maybe he'd stop there for more coffee.

The miles sped by; the music was welcome; the car was running well. He was glad he'd stopped to put air in the tires — there was nothing so irritating as having a car handle badly on the winding, northern New England roads.

His mind raced in rhythm with the car. Emotions visited that hadn't been by for a long time. When Lila had revealed that she had deceived him, he had, at first, felt anger, but then came sadness. He continually replayed it in his mind, along with memories of their weekend at Jay Peak. It would have to wait.

Then his thoughts turned to the terrible situation Duval found himself in. He was concerned that Duval, Godine and even he, might have overlooked something as they prepared to fight back against the dirty tricks that had been introduced into the campaign. It was that way in campaigns: you never really had time to look at all the options. Never enough time to analyze. Decisions are made from the gut. Focus groups can give some answers within twenty-four hours — but you don't get twenty-four hours. Good politicians have to have good intuition, or they are soon out of business. It's the way the game is played.

He arrived in the St. Johnsbury area, checked his watch, and found he was ahead of schedule. The road was much improved from the time he had first traveled it many years before; it had been widened, curves banked, and in one section an additional lane added. These changes would shorten the trip to Littleton by at least twenty minutes. No police cars were in evidence. Undoubtedly financial pressures on state government had lightened the midweek evening patrols. He continued along at five or ten miles above the speed limit.

On I-93 now, he was approaching the New Hampshire border. He'd avoided thinking about Lila for awhile. Then it all returned and again he saw her face. She changed his life in one short weekend. He remembered the quiet time as they had lain in bed talking, moments before the intruder had broken into his car. He felt a kind of pain, a sadness — a regret not unlike the emotions provoked by great music. He couldn't avoid the issue much longer. He should have asked her more questions. But he had been speechless when she told him. Marston shook his head and slapped the steering wheel with his right hand.

Just then the tape ended and silence filled the car.

He knew he needed to think about what Lila had said, not just blot it out. Time to put in another tape. Perhaps more serious music this time — Beethoven maybe. Serious music for serious thinking. The Creatures of Prometheus. He wondered if music experts considered Beethoven's only effort (not counting his *Ritter Ballet* credited incorrectly to Count Waldstein) at ballet to be a serious one. He laughed at himself. At least he could still do that ... The music began.

Littleton was in sight on his left; the lights of this pretty New Hampshire town blinked in greeting as he passed by. The turn onto Route 302 was just ahead.

Lyle Foote had always wanted to be a policeman.

He had never quite been able to pass the tests to work for the local or state police. He thought the tests were stupid. They didn't really prove what a man could do when he was in a real police-type situation. That didn't matter now. Four years ago he had been made a deputy sheriff of his county, and as his uncle said, he could do everything the other cops could and not have to put up with any bullshit.

On this night he was sitting in his big Ford with the lights on top, the spotlight on the driver's side, the heavy-duty suspension, and a siren he wasn't afraid to use. He had pulled the car off the road into one of his favorite spots, out of sight among some mid-sized pines off Route 302. Working from this vantage point, he had stopped and arrested over twenty-five speeders in the past four months.

It was after nine o'clock. This was later than he usually stayed out, but this was a big deal. He'd never had this kind of a call before. When the orders came in he'd put on his complete uniform including his hat, and told his mother with whom he lived that he was on assignment and would be home real late. He had said it matter-of-factly, as though this sort of thing happened often. He'd told her to call his uncle, her brother, at the feed store where he worked and let him know he might be late in the morning.

Now he lit a Marlboro, tilted his hat a bit lower, and slumped in his seat. He waited.

He was parked east of Littleton and west of the quaint town of Bethlehem, New Hampshire — a haven for Hasidic Jews who returned there each summer. It was as though they were biblically directed — year after year for as long as anyone could remember, they came to vacation and join with old friends. Fires and the ravages of time had destroyed many of the large inns and hotels that formerly lined the streets of Bethlehem. But still, one could not travel through town without observing evidence of its unique role in the lives of so many who had chosen to summer there as their parents and grandparents had done before.

Such things didn't interest Lyle Foote. He didn't care a whit about tourists, any of them. Lyle worked days at the feed store with his uncle, a job his mother had gotten for him (although he didn't know that). And he did a good job. But if you asked Lyle, it was the police work that he cared about. Law enforcement was what was important to him.

The Dodge zoomed by.

Lyle spotted it: The Dodge was speeding, no question.

He started the Ford, and swung onto the two-lane highway. Originally he planned to follow the car for a short way to make sure he had the right one, but the license plate was immediately visible.

Lyle Foote smiled to himself. Then he reached down to turn on the blue lights and the siren. The flashing of the lights and the frightening sound of the siren never failed to invoke in him that wonderful feeling of power. He felt another surge of pleasure as the Dodge ahead began to slow up. He remembered the beer ad, something about "It doesn't get any better than this." They had that right.

He passed and parked in front of the Dodge, blue lights circling eerily through the darkness of the trees and into the sky beyond.

Chapter Twenty-Three

Helen Grearson was born in Bath, Maine, and like her ancestors before her would probably die there. But her life had been different from that of her ancestors, different than a lot of people's. Helen had spent two tours of duty in Vietnam as an army nurse, and that had changed everything. Everything.

Nowadays in the early morning she liked to walk along the shore of the Kennebec River. There was a sense of things coming alive, as though for the first time. She loved the smells of the outdoors, the sight of birds anxiously diving for breakfast, and the respite for her soul. The river was a symbol of peace, of permanence, of something lasting. As a child, she had never tired of hearing its story. It was the history of the eastern frontier, of Native American Indians joining with the French to challenge unsuccessfully the English domination of northern New England. She especially loved to hear stories of the Kennebec River, which rose in Canada and flowed many miles down through Maine and out into the Atlantic. It was as though this history could never have been written but for the river.

Helen Grearson stood just under six feet tall. But unlike many tall women, she did not try to diminish her stature by slouching. As long as anyone could remember, the Grearson women grew tall. And like the others in her family, she stood full erect and never minded the stares that her striking figure provoked. Beautiful? No, no one ever said that. But her presence was never overlooked, and to Fred Younger, a young lieutenant she met in Vietnam, she was a goddess.

Fred had somehow become a part of that war. He never should have been there. It wasn't just the questionable logic of the Vietnam War, but rather that Fred was a man meant never to be near any kind of war. He was a quiet man, trained in geology, whose advanced academic work had been interrupted and put on hold. Helen was a talented surgical nurse, constantly in demand. When she had gone to Vietnam she had been prepared for the tragedy of war. Yet as time passed, and she watched the endless number of torn young bodies being carried into the hospital, she began to look for a logic to justify this war. She questioned her part in the peculiar scheme of things that found her halfway across the globe from her native Maine, repairing the rent bodies of young men who were also questioning and bewildered.

So it was when Helen and Fred met that night in downtown Saigon, each of them found in the other a place to retreat from the horror around them.

They sought quiet areas, away from the noise of wartime Saigon. An odd couple maybe — Helen standing a full two inches taller than Fred, but two people desperate in their love and loyalty to one another. Their love was the most important thing that had ever happened to either of them.

When the war was ended, Helen returned to Maine and bought a small place along the river before the prices had become impossible. The area was now settled by a mix of natives and affluent wanderers who somehow managed to peacefully coexist on the stretch of river running from Bath, Maine down to Fort Popham where the river meets the Atlantic.

But still she heard it in her dreams — a single shot, a sniper's bullet had gone through Fred's right eye when he was returning from patrol one night. He died instantly. Helen was not there; she couldn't have heard the shot. Yet from the first time she learned of his death, it was in her dreams each night. From deep in the clutches of sleep, a single shot would ring out and sear through her soul. She would sit bolt upright in bed, destined to be wide awake for at least an hour or two, and often for the rest of the night each time this happened. Eventually she ended up in the psychiatric ward of a stateside veteran's hospital.

She thought she would never work as a nurse again, but therapy had helped. The pain eased, but remained nearby. Soon she was working again — the work perhaps better therapy than any treatment. But Fred's death and the torrents of useless bloodshed had forever changed her. The pain of remembering would be forever her companion. She returned from Vietnam almost twenty years ago, but for Helen it seemed as only yesterday.

She worked twelve-hour shifts at the Maine Medical Center in Portland, three days on, one day off, and then three more days on. On every third week she had seven full days off. It was on her week off that she was walking along the river and came upon Ben Willey lying unconscious on the shore of the river, a hundred and fifty yards up river from her small cottage. Ben had nearly been taken out to sea by the Kennebec River when it rose up on the banks with the approach of high tide.

At first she had thought he was drunk. Then she saw the blood — lots of blood. After a quick examination and some emergency triage to his wounds, she first moved him out of the danger of the river. Then she went over to what she correctly presumed to be his car, shut off the radio, took the keys and closed the door.

She glanced in the direction of her cottage, which was located out of sight among the pines below. Without further thought, and by applying a fireman's lift, she lifted Ben Willey into her arms and carried him with surprising ease along the edge of the Kennebec. She pushed open the door of the cottage and lay him on the bed in the spare bedroom. Her two dogs, English Setters named Max and Greta, watched curiously; her tiger cat Pillow, a stray she had adopted, sat licking herself on the windowsill, refusing to dignify the intrusion. Helen proceeded to clean the wound, checking to make sure there weren't other lacerations she might have missed. She dug out the antibiotics she kept on hand and applied them to the wounds.

Her patient was already breathing better. Part of the problem was the heat. One could last only a short time in the direct sun where Willey had lain. He might need some blood, but she'd wait a little longer. She didn't need a doctor — a doctor would just get in the way. She'd handled worse than this and knew she didn't need the help of any intern from the hospital; she'd have to tell them what to do anyway. Helen was not reticent about her considerable medical skills, to the consternation of the physicians and other nursing staff at the Maine Medical Center.

In the kitchen she drank a glass of water for herself, then she dampened a cloth with cold water to wipe her patient down. Again she checked his pulse. It was stronger now, beating evenly. Hands on her hips, she looked at him and smiled to herself — he was doing well.

She'd wait a while before taking him to the hospital. She probably wouldn't even have to bother.

◆◆◆◆◆◆

The steady rhythm, the hypnotic hum of the road, and the darkness of the night was broken by blue police lights spinning their eerie glow behind him. It seemed to Jack Marston that the white police car had come out of nowhere.

"Damn! What in God's name are the police doing chasing cars on a quiet Tuesday night?" he muttered to himself. Some "Rambo" deputy he decided. He slowed the Dodge and pulled the car onto the shoulder, put it in neutral, remained inside and rolled down the window.

Lyle Foote approached the car slowly, with his hand on his holster, ready to pull the gun.

"Out of the car, hands on the roof, spread your legs," Lyle directed.

Marston sighed as he shifted into park, and got out of the car as he was told. He had been stopped by overzealous "deputies" before. The only thing to do was comply and keep quiet. Lyle patted Marston up and down, gingerly looking for weapons.

"I may have been a little over the limit, officer, but I don't —"

"Shut up, you're in bigger trouble than a speeding ticket, Bud." Lyle was enjoying every minute; it was going just as he had planned. "Stay like that with your hands on the car. I have a search warrant here."

Marston swore. It hit him — this wasn't about speeding. What a dunce! He should have thought about this and been prepared. Silently he cursed himself for his carelessness.

Lyle Foote opened the back door and was leaning into the back seat. Both of his hands were busy pawing through Marston's briefcase.

Marston knew what he had to do. Get away if he possibly could — run for it. He had to get to Duval. Most importantly, he needed to tell Duval what was going on. If they arrested him here, they might hold him where no one could find him for at least a couple of days. By then it would be too late to rescue the situation, if it wasn't already. The deputy was probably under orders to detain him, at least for a while.

Marston glanced at the woods behind. He could get lost in there in minutes. The deputy didn't look too brainy ... Still, Marston's mind was racing, if he ran away they could call him a fugitive. But they'd have him dead to rights on this thing anyway, claiming the envelope was CIA property. Marston had been around government long enough to understand the frightening power of the "Company" and held few illusions that the courts or anyone else could help him once he was in custody.

He bolted for the woods.

"Hey!"

Lyle Foote shouted as he reached for his gun.

"Hey!" he said again, then fired into the air.

Foote took a step or two toward the woods, then stopped and didn't try to follow. Marston was already out of sight, having sprinted even faster when he heard the gun.

Marston was thankful for the light provided by the nearly full moon. He shielded his eyes as he ran, hoping to ward off any protruding branches, totally unaware that the deputy hadn't tried to follow. Marston was praying that the woods wouldn't become so thick they would prevent him from putting some distance between himself and the deputy.

Lyle Foote smiled to himself and holstered the forty-five, muttering aloud to no one in particular, "They said he might do that, and if he does let him!"

Foote took the keys from Marston's car, popped the hood and reached under to disable the car. Then he slammed the hood down, dusted off his hands, and returned to the police car. Once inside he placed the envelope out of sight under the passenger seat and turned off the flashing lights.

He was looking forward to making the phone call to the special number he'd been given. They'd said to simply say "Code One, Littleton," and they would put him through. He liked that.

He headed for the phone just outside Ed's Gulf.

Marston stopped and listened. He'd been running as fast as he could ever deeper into the woods. He seemed to be climbing. He had no idea where he was, but he knew he was running away from town. He could hear nothing. Breathing heavily he decided to rest and then figure what to do next. He sat on the ground and leaned against the base of a tree.

He wouldn't last long in the woods. In no time they'd have dogs sniffing after him. He'd be safer in the middle of Littleton if he could get there. Besides he needed a phone. He had to somehow get to Duval. Would Duval's phone be tapped at Bretton Woods? Most likely.

Lila. Should he call Lila?

Who else?

Maybe they were watching her? Still he had to try. It wasn't likely they'd be watching her. Worth the gamble, he decided, if he ever got clear of the woods and could find a phone.

Marston knew he had traveled only a short way past Littleton on Route 302 before the deputy had pulled him over. He decided to backtrack, then cross to the other side of the road to get into downtown Littleton. He was sweating; it was hot for this early in June. Marston was glad he'd put on a short-sleeve shirt for the trip, dispensing with tie and jacket. It would also serve to make him less noticeable when he got into town.

He got up and started to move again, angling this time back toward the road. He remained deep in the woods, not yet trying to cross the road. As he walked through the woods, he became aware of the "piney" scent of the evergreens. The night was bright, and from the light of the moon he saw mushrooms sprouting through just beyond a marshy area bordered by soft moss. He wondered if he was heading toward a pond. If anyone was following he didn't want to be hemmed in by a pond. No sign so far, but if they weren't following now they would be soon. He decided it was time to cut back   directly toward the road. He had to cross the road sometime, it might as well be now.

He was still a couple hundred yards away looking in the direction of downtown when he spotted the road. The traffic seemed light, and there was no apparent police activity. Glancing at his watch he realized that he had fled from the deputy less than thirty minutes ago. He wondered why the "locals" hadn't appeared on the scene right away. Then he remembered. State, local, and county police spent almost as much time fighting with each other as they did chasing the bad guys. Jurisdictional jealousy probably saved him.

So far.

Or maybe, just maybe they didn't want to catch him! It dawned on him, as a fugitive they figured they had him neutralized, they had the envelope and the evidence that Duval had to have, plus they'd have a big story for television the next day. Whatever happened, it was bad news for Duval.

He crossed the road hastily, without incident. He found himself in a residential area consisting of widely scattered homes on large two and three-acre lots. He wished there were more people around. He wasn't used to playing the fugitive and felt as though a thousand eyes were upon him. In reality he was dressed appropriately and would cause little notice. It could be tricky, though. If he crossed the open lots, people might think he was a potential intruder and call the police. If he walked along the street in this part of town, he could easily run into people looking for him. He traveled on a small connecting road for a while until he saw a sign to the hospital. He knew when he came to the hospital he would be just a short way from downtown. Years before he had lost his way and gotten off the track and now he remembered turning around in the same hospital lot. He smiled at the detail of this memory. Memory was man's uncertain computer.

The dog came out of nowhere. A Doberman — unchained. Marston froze. Slowly, but deliberately, the dog approached, barking ferociously.

Marston was on the edge of one of the large lots, with an average-sized two-story house about hundred feet away. He remained frozen in place as the sleek black animal charged.

With the dog only a few feet away, Marston raised both hands, and hollered as loud as he could. The dog skidded to a stop, then began a quiet growl which emanated from deep in his throat.

"Ivan!" A ten-year-old boy came trotting toward the dog. "He won't hurt you, mister. He likes to walk loose some times when I take him out."

"Okay ... good," Marston replied a bit foolishly, relieved, but shaking from the after-effects of the rush of adrenaline. Marston was remembering the first time someone had told him to disregard an attacking Doberman. At age six he had done so, and the small scar on his forehead gave testimony that a dog's owner is not always correct in interpreting a dog's intentions.

But Ivan was now under control and off in another direction.

Marston knew the thumping heartbeat would subside in a few minutes; he continued toward town, passing by the old hospital and hoping he'd seen the last of any animals, friendly or otherwise.

That same evening Lila Maret arrived at her Jay Peak condominium and changed into short cotton pajamas. She put together a salad, some cold ham, a square of Vermont cheddar cheese, and a couple of pieces of French bread, which along with a tall iced tea she placed on a small wooden tray which she then brought out onto her deck. She had barely touched the food she had brought to Marston's office earlier; her stomach had been in knots.

Lila loved this time of night. She could still see the outline of the mountain against the fading light of the summer sky. But after preparing the food, she found she wasn't as hungry as she anticipated and nibbled absently at the salad.

She thought back over the day. She knew that she'd had to tell Jack that she misrepresented herself to him in order to get the envelope. It was one of toughest things she had ever had to do. It didn't make it any easier that he reacted more with hurt than with anger. She hadn't expected him to lose his temper. And he didn't. Outwardly it seemed he barely heard her. He bottled it up, his reaction at first was almost a mystery. Anyone would be hurt. She understood, even expected this.

But now where did she stand with him? She could tell nothing from anything he said or did. This guy held it all in, you didn't know what to think. Maybe she should run the other way? But she knew she wouldn't — that is if he didn't decide to forget the whole thing.

He was different from anyone she had known. It was trite but true; he was comfortable to be with. And she trusted him. Maybe that was the biggest fear. She knew she cared for him, a lot ... maybe loved him. A scary word for Lila Maret.

She went to retrieve the notes she had taken in the morning at the library. As an experienced writer, she knew that sometimes when she felt she was going nowhere with her work, she needed to take a second look. Let it rest a little. And when she did this she often found she had been too self-critical. She hoped this would prove to be true of the morning's research.

The sun had dropped behind the mountain and it was becoming difficult to see, a slight chill imbued the mountain air. She could have brought out a sweater but she needed to turn on a light to see and if she did it would attract the black flies, so she brought the dishes in and settled back on the end of the sofa, notes in hand.

The phone rang.

Startled, she answered.

It was Marston, the strain in his voice apparent.

"I'm in Littleton and ...," and he explained as much as he could.

"Yes, I understand,..." she said and listened as Marston continued on, not very coherently, about what had happened.

"Your phone could be tapped so be careful," he cautioned, then changing the subject asked, "Do you remember that place we talked about when we discussed the article 'Fields of the North Country?'"

She hesitated a moment, then nodding to herself, replied decisively, "Oh, yes ..."

"Just drive by there, I'll be in there somewhere ... watching for you. If anyone is following you — but I don't think there will be, try to lose them. Okay?" he asked. For a moment he was overwhelmed and discouraged by the possibilities that someone could be listening to his every word. Then they would simply have someone waiting who would identify Lila's car when she came into town and there was little he or she could do about it. He had to hope. And to stay well out of sight until Lila got there to be sure she was not followed. Like a damn spy novel, he thought. He liked to read them; he never planned on living one.

Lila picked up on the discouragement in Marston's voice, "Jack, hang on. I can do this. Stay out of sight ... it may take a while, but I'll get there. I will get there," she affirmed.

Marston smiled to himself, noting as he had before the resilience and determination Lila showed under pressure. "God knows the pressure's on now," he muttered to himself.

Marston had called Lila from the same phone Lyle Foote had used less than a half an hour before. Hanging up the receiver, and outside the phone booth now, he paused and looked around. Main Street in Littleton was mostly deserted. Lila could drive from Jay Peak to Littleton in about two hours, maybe less, Marston figured. A few cars passed him as he stood there, mostly cars full of young people driving up and down the main street looking for excitement.

He reentered the booth; he had to make another call. He would have liked to call Duval at the Mount Washington Hotel, but by now he figured Duval's phone was tapped for sure, otherwise how had they tracked him down. They might or might not monitor Lila's calls, but in the case of Duval there would be no doubt. They would expect him to call. Then he had an idea. His spirits rose. He thought of another way to make contact.

He dialed New Hampshire information, and said, "In Manchester, Operator."

When he received the number he dialed again, using his government credit card and hoping desperately for an answer.

Chapter Twenty-Four

The tallest among the giants of the Presidential Range, Mt. Washington, is a thrilling sight from wherever one looks upon it. As he always did, after checking in earlier in the day at the venerable Mount Washington Hotel, Congressman Alan Duval stood at the window taking in the magnificent view looking east toward the mountain. From his room he could see the upper part of the famous cog railway that operates daily in the summer delivering tourists to the top of the mountain.

When he had checked in at the desk he had been alone, without staff. He decided at the time not to seek out Bill Richards who probably was already here as well, until Marston arrived. Marston was all the staff he would need for the meeting. If he needed any technical materials, he could call one of the committee staff in Washington. Chuckling to himself he remembered what one of Vermont's best loved senators had once said only half in jest, "The member of Congress is becoming a constitutional impediment to the staff!" He had been around long enough to understand the accuracy of that statement. Congressional staff was ever ready to do the thinking for the member and anything and everything else anyone could imagine!

He didn't want to run into other invitees to the conference and so he made himself comfortable in the room with newspapers he'd purchased in the lobby. Approaching the noon hour he ordered lunch to be brought up, and following that was able to get some badly needed sleep.

When he awoke later in the afternoon, he showered and changed into some casual slacks and a golf shirt. He remained in his room, and opened the large briefcase that seemingly never emptied of mail and staff memos mostly concerning pending legislation. He spent the balance of the afternoon immersed in work.

Later, shortly after he had ordered dinner in the room, he received the disturbing call from Jack Marston. Marston hadn't been able to say too much. The call proved unnerving. After hanging up, he had sat on the edge of the bed, his hand remaining for several moments on the phone.

Once again he rose and walked to the window to take in the view. In the waning June light, the colors of the early evening created a scene of indescribable beauty. Duval had been here before and was never surprised at how new the experience seemed each time. His favorite vantage for looking at New England mountains was the view facing East, during the soft hues of the afternoon light. An amateur photographer, Duval wished at times like this that he could devote more time to the hobby. Then he paused, smiling ruefully. If things don't get straightened out soon he'd have time to take all the photos he'd ever wanted!

The suite he occupied had been completely refurbished, but still the room had the dignity provided only by older hotels. An older hotel perhaps, but probably the most famous one in northern New England. He knew the history well: The hotel had come on hard times and had a number of owners, each rescuing the hotel one more time in celebration of all the grand hotels of the north country, of which so many had become simply a memory.

With time on his hands — something he wasn't used to, Duval called John Godine at campaign headquarters. He discussed with Godine possible reasons why TV still hadn't run a follow-up story on the South American trip. There were, as far as he could figure, no good reasons for the delay. That was the odd part. What the hell were they waiting for?

He glanced at his watch, then walked to the other window which looked out on the golf course, deciding as he did that he'd take a walk around the grounds. He'd have time before Jack Marston got there.

As he started to the door the phone rang.

"Yes," he answered crisply, not particularly wanting to reveal his name in case he didn't want to talk to the caller. He smiled when he heard the voice on the other end, and after exchanging a few pleasantries said, "Why yes, sure Nick, ... yes, it happens I can do that. I'll leave right away ... I've got to leave a note for Jack Marston to tell him where I'm going ... you remember Jack?"

Nick Sikoris assured Duval that he remembered Jack Marston. Chuckling to himself, Duval decided that Sikoris probably remembered every politician he'd ever met. An old friend of Marston's and later of Duval, Sikoris had been a key figure in at least seven presidential primaries in the granite state. When Nick Sikoris called, few practicing politicians could afford to turn him down.

Enormously wealthy, Sikoris had real estate holdings world wide. No one really knew how wealthy he was. Skillful as he was in real estate development, his passion was politics, and he had established residency in New Hampshire, living there most of the time simply because from there he could have more effect on presidential politics in America than from anywhere else in the world. Little New Hampshire was so often the king-maker in American primary battles, and Sikoris wasn't above using his money and influence to affect the outcome. And not just the primary of his own party. When he thought he had a chance, he would use his money to shape the choice of the other party as well.

Not many people knew this.

But Jack Marston did. And as a result so did Congressman Alan Duval.

Duval grabbed his car keys and went down to the front desk where he scribbled a note explaining to Marston that he was going to North Conway to have a drink with Nick Sikoris. He left the note at the desk for Marston to pick up when he checked in.

◆◆◆◆◆◆◆

Back in Littleton, Marston waited in the shadows.

It hadn't taken him long to find the old ballpark. Remech Field was built in 1904. Marston had played semi-pro baseball there over thirty years before. The ballpark was located just a few hundred yards up the hill from the center of Littleton, and with the help of the bright moonlight he could see the many changes in recent years. Home plate was located in what had formerly had been right field, the small, neat grandstand he remembered was boarded up, and the manicured perfection was no longer in evidence having given way to shaggy neglect. The lush trim ballfield that had once been his favorite over all others was now only a memory from another time.

The huge pines in the outfield that provided a rich backdrop for the batter at home plate were still there, however, and had grown even taller. Marston could see them against the darkening sky, swaying gently in the summer breeze as they had for so many years. A six-foot- square press box supported by long stilt-like legs presided over the field as it had for over forty years. The enclosure was built especially to command a view high above the field, towering over what had once been third base. Touched by a wave of nostalgia, Marston reflected that the field was still there, the stage was set, but the players he had known were scattered far and wide, never to return.

"We all play different games now," he thought to himself, "and what a game I've gotten into."

Earlier, after finishing his phone calls, Marston had ventured a few hundred feet up Main Street, then took a side street left up the hill walking briskly toward the old ballpark where he had told Lila he would wait. Not wanting to give away the location where he would be waiting to anybody who might possibly have tapped onto Lila's phone, he explained where they could meet by referring to an article they had discussed on old ballparks that were still in use in northern New England entitled, "Fields of the North

Country." Lila and he spent time discussing Remech Field and Marston knew Lila would recognize what he was talking about when he mentioned the article.

He found a spot to wait out of sight behind the old grandstand where he could see the road unobserved. They agreed that if when she arrived it seemed she was being followed, he would simply stay in the shadows.

At first the chance to finally get some rest was welcome. The adrenaline he had been operating on dropped to normal and he was at first tired and then overtaken by a nagging uneasiness. He began to dwell on the seeming hopelessness of Duval's situation now that he had lost the envelope to the deputy. Every few minutes Marston would stand and pace a few yards in one direction and then retrace his steps to where he started, sit down again, and think for a while longer.

At one point he dozed off only to awaken with a start: Car lights were approaching. He strained to see. He glanced at his watch and settled back. It couldn't be Lila. It was only an hour since he had called. The car passed. A sedan, New Hampshire plates. He stood up. He couldn't afford to fall asleep again. He felt vaguely hungry.

Night deepened. Clouds began to thicken and obscure the nearly full moon. The lights from the city were fading. Over an hour and a half had passed since he phoned Lila. She should be arriving — if nothing prevented it. Still he waited.

A half an hour later another set of car lights approached. A Subaru wagon. He watched. The car passed slowly by. He wanted to run out, but stayed back out of sight. No one seemed to be following. The Subaru passed out of sight up the hill. Marston stayed back, obscured by the shadows. A few moments later the lights of the white car came into view from the opposite direction. The car slowed. Marston looked up and down the street, poised to run.

He saw nothing.

After once more looking both ways, he got up and ran; when he reached the car he yanked the door open and got in.

Route 302 out of Littleton snakes back and forth, up and down, as it winds east through the White Mountains on its way to the Maine shore of the Atlantic Ocean. Hundreds of years earlier Route 302 had developed as an Indian trail through the mountains.

Since that time, the mountains of northern New Hampshire have been safe haven for summer tourists for well over a hundred years. In the nineteenth and early twentieth century prior to the invention of air-conditioning, literally hundreds of summer hotels provided relief from the summer heat for visitors from America's great eastern cities. Whole families would move up for the summer, while the male breadwinner commuted on weekends, riding on the railroads which financed the hotels in the first place.

Lila negotiated her way through Littleton without incident. She drove with both hands on the wheel, her arms extended, her eyes straight ahead.

"The road narrows up ahead," Marston noted nervously as he glanced at the speedometer.

"I know the road, Jack," Lila snapped, wishing she could recall the words as soon as she spoke.

"Sorry," he said, wondering if they would ever get it right again.

A few minutes later when they passed the city limits and were out of town, Marston began to relax. He told Lila the full story about how he had been stopped, lost the manila envelope to the Deputy, and finally escaped into the woods. When they stayed on that subject the conversation flowed nicely.

But on each of their minds loomed Lila's confession made earlier in the evening that she had not quite played it square. When Marston called for her help a couple of hours ago, Lila had welcomed the call. She knew her deception concerning her involvement with the CIA had hurt him badly. She wanted to somehow reconcile this, and get it out of the way, but it remained between them, still unresolved, as the white Subaru flew through the New Hampshire night.

She could have understood anger and harsh words. With that she could hope to move to forgiveness. But this strange man had barely reacted outwardly and left her lost and confused scarcely daring to hope for the forgiveness she desperately wanted.

When he climbed into the car back at Remech Field her heart jumped. He looked at her for a long moment, his eyes strangely sad and yet ... but he merely said, almost formally, "Thank you, thank you, Lila, I appreciate this," much as though he were thanking a waiter in a restaurant, or expressing gratitude for an unsolicited political contribution.

Just a mile or two out of town, Marston said, "Change of plans; I called a friend, Nick Sikoris, who will contact Duval for us at the hotel — we're going to North Conway."

"North Conway?"

"They'd be waiting for me at the Mount Washington Hotel. I can't show up there. I got word to Alan through Sikoris. Sikoris called to invite Alan over for a drink at a restaurant just this side of North Conway. Hopefully they won't follow Alan when he leaves the hotel — although I'm not sure they care whether they catch me or not. I'm probably a better story as a fugitive!" He shook his head, "Christ!" he exclaimed, slamming his right fist into his open left hand.

Remaining silent for a few moments he continued, "They'll have tapped Duval's phone and overheard the call he got from our friend Sikoris in North Conway. They'll assume it's just financial stuff for the campaign. When I called Sikoris, — thank God he was there — and asked him to call Alan, as usual he jumped right in and said he'd help. He had heard the first news story, so of course he was curious.

"Who is he?"

"Strangely enough he's a millionaire political junkie."

Marston looked at Lila and smiled. He went on to tell her the strange and interesting story of Nick Sikoris, whom they would be meeting shortly. Lila glanced at him, feeling the warmth of his smile. She took her right hand from the wheel and grasped Marston's hand, squeezing it once, and drove on through the night with one hand on the wheel.

Neither spoke for a while, both contented to listen to the hum of the tires and to enjoy the warm June night as they traveled east through the mountains. Finally Lila said, "You know we continue to talk about 'they' Jack, but who do you think 'they' are?" Before he could answer she continued, "I mean, we know about Steele, but there must be more than just Steele involved."

"I have no idea, but this is big league stuff."

"You said Richards wouldn't help Duval ... admit he had asked Duval to cover that meeting in Colombia. Is he part of it?"

"It sure looks it — the head of the CIA for Christ's sake — mucking around in this kind of stuff ...," Marston said, once again shaking his head, as if that would somehow make it all go away.

The little Subaru tracked the New Hampshire roads easily. Normally Marston was strongly partial to cars sporting American nameplates, and had resisted the American love affair with Japanese cars. But still he admired the way the car performed on the mountain roads. He and Lila rode silently for a while.

Again Lila broke the silence and said, "Somebody doesn't want Alan elected to the Senate, which is not unusual. But the set-up, the frame if you will, seems to be well planned. If Ben Willey hadn't upset things by getting onto this, it would be all over by now."

"Poor Ben ... that's the tragedy here. He risked everything to warn us and

I blew it ... losing the Goddamn envelope to that stupid deputy."

"Does Alan still have a chance, Jack?"

"There's a chance ... there's always a chance if you get a break. But," and here he paused for emphasis, and spoke slowly saying, "we do need a break! It better happen soon. The tabloids are going to eat this up. Even if Richards is on the level and can be prevailed upon to back up Alan's story that he was meeting with Tomarra at the administration's request, so much crap will have come out ... the pictures, the implications of some sort of drug dealings ... after a week of that the truth won't have a chance."

Lila replied, "What I can't understand is how anyone has the courage to go this far in disrupting an election. It's like something that would happen in a banana republic!"

Marston shifted in his seat and said, "The soldiers-of-fortune renegades in and out of government got away with murder and more in the eighties. That set the tone. Lie, but face the camera with a smile!" His anger mounted as he continued.

"It's not what you do any more, but what it looks like! And Congress sat still for all of it. The guys involved were too well loved or too popular to be opposed. We are asked to protect our political institutions. But instead of protecting them we've paralyzed them! So much for political courage in the nineties."

"But how does that connect to what's happening to Duval?"

"This crap is the logical next step for the zealots, for the superpatriots. If they were not called to account for their sins in Iran-contra, the banking scandals — maybe even the 1980 election — if crime elicits no punishment then the next order of business for the 'loonies' is getting what they would call 'right-thinking' people in Congress and making sure independent-minded people like Duval are defeated."

Marston leaned back and said nothing for a few moments, then continued quietly as though resigned to what he was saying, "It completely bewilders me how people who are often so enormously successful in other ways, can fail to recognize the destructive nature of what they espouse politically. The reality is they don't really trust democratic practices and institutions, and spend all their time trying to control the process itself."

Chapter Twenty-Five

Nick Sikoris and Alan Duval were talking quietly in one of the back rooms of Vic's Galley. Sikoris had served as a silent partner in the restaurant when it started, and continued to maintain the partnership as a favor to Les Dimoras, his active partner in the business. The restaurant is located on Route 16 which heads north off Route 302 toward challenging and historic Tuckerman's Ravine, a unique ski bowl located on the eastern slopes of Mt. Washington.

Tuckerman's Ravine has attracted rugged eastern skiers dating back to the early nineteen thirties. Hardy collegians, particularly from Dartmouth and Harvard, traveled to the area for the ultimate challenge in the new and growing sport. No chair lift or other uphill contrivance could be constructed to service Tuckerman's; it has been skied since the early days of the sport only by those willing to climb, and those whose skill could match the breathless challenge.

Lila drove the Subaru into the parking lot along side Vic's Galley. Sensing it was what he wanted, Lila said, "I'll wait here."

"Yes, for now," Marston replied and went inside alone while Lila remained in the car. The hour was late, the restaurant nearly empty except for a few customers lingering at the small bar off the main dining room. Muffled noises from the kitchen, busboys scurrying to and from the dining room signaled closing time.

"I am so glad to see you, my friend," Sikoris stood greeting Marston as he walked in, "It's been too long."

Marston mostly avoided hugging friends, male or female, but Nick Sikoris would have it no other way and grabbed Marston's hand, wrapping his other arm all the way around. Sikoris was of average height, with large shoulders, a thick neck, thinning black hair, and a pleasant round face that belied his strength, both physical and intellectual. Marston said, "We always meet when there's trouble of some kind, Nick, I appreciate ..."

"Never mind appreciate! We are friends — what can I do?"

Marston glanced at Duval, who remained seated at the table. Marston never failed to be surprised by the world-embracing enthusiasm and confidence Nick Sikoris brought to any situation. Marston smiled and shook his head saying as he took a chair, "You'll never change Nick — and thank God."

Sikoris grabbed the chair at the head of the table, sat down and leaned forward. "Now we need to go over the whole story. We will see what we have, then figure what to do."

Marston had first met Sikoris over twenty-five years ago. At that time Sikoris had become interested in taking over two failing auto dealerships, one in New Hampshire and one in Maine. Sikoris had sought out Marston, who was then with Chrysler, and was able to help arrange financing so that Sikoris could buy the two dealerships before they went under. Sikoris had sold them both a few years later in a highly lucrative deal, one of many for the Greek financier. Sikoris had come a long way since those days, but had never forgotten Marston's role in convincing Chrysler Corporation that Sikoris had the talent to put the two dealerships back on their feet. Since that time, Marston had seen Sikoris mainly when he had been involved in one or another presidential primary being played out in the small towns and hamlets of New Hampshire. When Marston called, Sikoris was available. It was as simple as that. He was always ready with political contributions if Marston asked. For his part, Marston was careful not to abuse the friendship. They had never spoken with one another about the enormous wealth that Sikoris had amassed. Marston made no pretense of understanding the world of international finance and real estate, and Sikoris said little about his holdings to his friends and contacts in the north country. He was able to manage much of his financial empire operating from a computer installed at his home near Manchester, traveling once every couple of weeks to a New York office, and on rare occasions, overseas.

Sikoris ordered sandwiches and coffee. Marston, who had eaten little throughout day was eating and talking at the same time. With sandwich in hand, he began to describe in detail everything that happened since Lila Maret first came to see him. As he recounted the events for his listeners, the only noises were the occasional click of Sikoris's cup as it returned to the saucer; the low hum of the ventilation system; and the distant voices and occasional laughter emanating from the bar.

Duval and Sikoris listened intently, interrupting only for clarification. When he got to what happened Saturday evening at Lila's Jay Peak condominium, Marston omitted any reference to his relationship with Lila. Although in telling the story it became clear to the others that he had stayed at her condominium on Saturday night before returning home to Underhill on Sunday.

"Before I go any further," he said, as he came to the subject of Lila's admission to the CIA link, "I want you to know I screwed up royally, and I'm willing —"

"Never mind that, Jack ... this isn't about blaming anyone," Duval interjected.

"Anyway, earlier today Lila Maret told me she had originally come to see me at the request of the CIA — specifically our friend Edgar Steele. The reason, of course, is that after she opened the envelope, she saw the whole picture. And to confirm Steele's role in this, Lila saw him — Steele — on Church street in Burlington talking to the man Lila is sure is the one who broke into my car at Jay Peak. Materials in the envelope incriminated Steele and perhaps the CIA, and laid out the whole story on how you were to be politically destroyed."

First there was silence. It took a minute to sink in. Duval was stunned. "The CIA? My God Jack, what...?"

"We should let him tell the whole story, Congressman," Sikoris interrupted..

"Yeah, go on Jack," Duval replied, his face still registering outrage and shock at the idea of the CIA interfering in anything involving a legislative office.

"In the beginning getting the envelope was just a simple job, incidental really, and was represented to her as a way of helping a disturbed agent, Ben Willey, stay out of trouble. She knows now it was all a scam. Lila feels terrible about her part in this. She really does."

To Duval, the story seemed like something out of a movie. He could only shake his head, muttering, "What is public life in this country coming to — what next? My God!"

When Marston had phoned Sikoris earlier, he told him of his encounter with the deputy in Littleton. As he was relating the incident, Duval interrupted asking, "How'd you get here ... if they have your car?"

Looking at Duval, Marston replied, "I had to call Lila — or steal a car. She knew everything anyway."

"Is she outside?" Sikoris inquired, and when Marston nodded, Sikoris, looking at Duval continued, "I think we bring her in, Congressman."

"Of course," Duval replied absently; then almost as an afterthought and more as a statement than a question looked at Marston, and said, "You trust her Jack?"

"Yes. Yes I do, Alan," Marston replied, surprising himself as he said it.

"Go out and ask her to join us, maybe she can help."

Nick Sikoris took advantage of the momentary break and excused himself. Marston followed behind, but before he left the room, Alan Duval said, "Wait, Jack," and rose from his chair, approaching Marston,

Standing beside his longtime aide, Duval put his arm around him and said, "I want you to know that if you trust her, I trust her." He then flashed the boyish smile that had charmed Vermonters from the onset of his political career, and continued, "And if you love her, I love her." With this, he squeezed Marston's arm and said, "We'll find a way, Jack. We'll find a way."

◆ ◆ ◆ ◆ ◆ ◆ ◆

It was vintage Duval; the decisiveness, his loyalty, and especially his capacity to trust were becoming a rarity in media-dominated political life where image, not substance, has become the measure.

"Thanks, Alan," Marston said, wanting to say more but wisely sensing he had said enough.

He left the room to find Lila.

Lila Maret, with Marston at her side, entered the room with hesitance, sensing the tension her presence engendered. But Nick Sikoris, gracious as always, seized the moment to offer Lila iced tea, or coffee, "...or a drink perhaps or maybe some food," Lila declined everything.

"Lila," Sikoris went on, "I know being here among strangers is difficult for you, but we need to hear from you in your words how you became involved in this matter. We need to know what the people who ... recruited you to seek out Jack Marston told you, what they asked you to say and do. In your own words — we are all friends here." Sikoris's manner was gentle, his words supportive; his skill in dealing with people apparent. The others looked on, saying nothing. Sikoris had taken charge.

Lila responded to the questions without apology, in a straight forward manner, easing the tension. As Marston listened to Lila tell Sikoris and Duval what happened, it became apparent to him that she had acted reasonably, that her deception truly did start out as a minor action and she truly had been a victim of circumstances.

She told how she had been approached while working on a travel article in Maine to seek out Jack Marston and recover the envelope. Sikoris then asked her to trace her history of work with the CIA, and the nature of the assignments she had been given.

"Was Edgar Steele your only contact at the CIA?"

"Yes, he's the only person I know there."

"Didn't you become suspicious when Steele asked you to blatantly misrepresent yourself to a representative of a member of Congress?"

"I can only say I am — was — naive. In all honesty, I felt I was helping someone stay out of trouble. They said that this man Willey had worked for the Agency for thirty years and had just retired, but that for what he had done he could end up in prison for years. It seemed such a waste ... and I figured that the man had just gone around the bend."

At that point a waiter came into the room, leaned over and whispered to Nick Sikoris. While the waiter stood by, Sikoris said, "You have a phone call, Congressman, from a Mr. John Godine, from Burlington, Vt."

Duval stood up, "Yes, good, I'll get it," he said, and left the room.

He returned a few minutes later, fatigue showing on his face. Godine had relayed to Duval that the late news had rerun the story of Duval's unreported meeting in Colombia with drug lord, Arturo Tomarra. The updated story, carried on eleven o'clock TV news in Vermont, offered some additional details, not reported on the six o'clock news, including an accurate account of Duval's exact itinerary while visiting Tomarra. The TV station offered free air time for an unedited press conference if "Duval wants to clear the air." The balance of the story dealt with information that had been emerging about Tomarra's drug dealing over the past two years. His drug involvement had been unknown in the United States at the time of Duval's visit — a fact that the television account of the story neglected to mention, neatly skewering Duval in the process. The station also announced that they had been provided other information including some "damaging" photographs, but reported that since they were unsure of the source and the authenticity of the photographs, they would withhold this information for the time being.

The restaurant was now quiet, the hour late. The wait-staff had left.

Conversation was at a low point, nothing new was being said. Sikoris, sensing they had accomplished all they were going to, said, "I think we have done all we can for now. However we must find a place for Mr. Marston and Miss Maret to stay. We must keep you," he said looking at Marston, "out of sight until we can determine your legal status. I can do that fairly easily. I have a place you can stay. Secondly Alan, you will come home with me tonight; tomorrow you and I must travel to see Senator Everett Stone. I think he's in Maine, but wherever he is we must see him, he is key. Finally, you must then return to Mt. Washington and see your friend, Bill Richards. He may be a key also," then smiling he continued, "perhaps a badly bent key!"

It was well into early morning when the group, now totally exhausted, left the restaurant.

◆ ◆ ◆ ◆ ◆ ◆ ◆

Back in the Subaru once again, Jack Marston and Lila Maret were heading north on Route 16 to the ski chalet Nick Sikoris had arranged for them to use. Built in the early sixties before the condominium craze had hit the north country, the chalet was located at the end of a dirt road, two or three miles off the main highway.

As they traveled through the night, Lila and Marston talked about the news story the Vermont TV station had run that evening. "At least they're showing some responsibility, by not showing those pictures," Lila said.

"Yeah," Marston replied cynically, "the bastards win both ways — they titillate the public with part of the story, indicate they have some pictures, then self-righteously withhold them. I don't call that showing responsibility. Chances are they're more afraid of a law suit than they are acting in a socially responsible way!"

"Whoever is sending out the material must be sending it all over I assume — someone will run the pictures — especially the one where he's standing naked next to that young girl."

"Woman, not girl," Marston interjected.

"Okay ... woman." Lila glanced at Marston wryly, and continued, "The local TV station offered Duval unedited coverage of a press conference if *'he would accept the challenge and clear the air.'* How will he handle that?"

Marston ignored the question, saying instead, "Whoops! There's the sign where Nick said we're supposed to turn off the main road." Lila had driven past the turn, and had to travel another quarter of a mile before she could turn around. On the narrow bumpy dirt road heading to the chalet now, Marston reflected on Lila's last question, remembering the quote Godine had read over the phone:

"This television station will continue to monitor and screen this story responsibly. We are concerned about the source of the information. It has not been made available to us. But it is also the responsibility of Congressman Alan Duval to meet with the press as soon as possible and clear the air."

As though to no one, Marston said, "I can't abide a sanctimonious press, but they try." Then returning to Lila's question he said, "I agree with Sikoris, — thank God *he* had some energy left at the end so we'd have some idea what we're going to do next. He's right of course: we've got to know where we stand once and for all with the people that can help us before Alan talks to the press. Normally we'd kill for an unedited press conference, but not yet, not like this. Alan has to talk to Richards face to face and make sure once and for all whether he will, or will not, admit asking Duval to take a side trip to visit Tomarra.

"I hope Sikoris can work out a meeting with Senator Stone. They'll have to travel to Portland or maybe Brunswick where Stone lives. It's a good thing Sikoris has as much influence in the other party as he does in our own. He can get a meeting with Stone ... I'm not so sure we could get it on our own hook. Stone has a reputation as a straight arrow, but he's got a self-righteous streak that makes him hard to talk to."

Then looking at Lila he said, "My job," he smiled at Lila correcting himself, "Our job — they'll be onto your role in this by now — is to stay out of sight!"

Coming to the end of the narrow dirt road Lila pulled in to the driveway and parked the car. True to his word, Sikoris's chalet was unpretentious, and belied his great wealth. He had purchased it for the use of his children and their friends who used it mostly in the winter. Sikoris had little use for the trappings of wealth or conspicuous life-styles. The chalet would do the job and it was a sound investment, as Sikoris explained it. "Fancy" was for other men's children!

Unlocking the chalet they found the lights and raised the thermostat controlling the electric heat. Marston returned to the car to bring in the groceries they had bought at an all-night Quik-Stop. They were both exhausted but the mood was light. Finally, with the groceries out of the way they found themselves standing together quietly in the middle of the kitchen, each waiting for the other to speak, the silence itself suddenly intrusive. In a very deliberate way Marston walked to Lila and put his arms around her. "Thank you for ..."

Lila put her hand over his mouth saying, "Never mind 'thank you.' Don't you see?" She looked out the window, although there was little to see since the moon had now disappeared, "Once again, it's you and I and," she smiled, "the mountains!"

She pulled his face down to hers, and they both knew that for a little while everything would be all right.

Chapter Twenty-Six

Marston awoke with the morning sun streaming in the window. Lila remained in bed, asleep under a thin cotton sheet in the rumpled bed. Naked, Marston walked to the window and looked out and found the early signs of another bright, summer day. Through the open window he felt a hint of crispness in the air with the warmth of late June a promise lingering just behind. He glanced back at the small figure lying with arms splayed and for a moment considered returning to the warmth of the bed.

Instead he slipped into his shorts and went into the kitchen where he found an old percolator. He measured out the coffee, added the right amount of water, set the pot over the burner, and turned the gas on in the stove. He then went into the bathroom.

While showering, he thought back on the strange series of events of the previous day. It had indeed been a bizarre one. The heavy needle-like spray of hot water from a pre-energy-conscious era bore down on him bringing him fully awake. Strangely, he didn't feel tired, although he and Lila hadn't gone to bed until after two-thirty AM, and it was some time after that before they slept. He smiled. He felt better and he knew why: he had let go of the hurt.

In the strange way decisions are made as we sleep, Marston found that Lila was someone he wanted, and he wasn't going to give her up. His doubts were gone. Somehow, probably in the dark shadows of sleep, he found his answer. No nagging questions of trust remained. He had decided. He wanted the raven-haired Lila if she would have him.

Checking his watch as he finished drying himself with a huge red towel that he found in the bathroom closet. It was six-fifteen. He went to the telephone.— he knew the number by heart — and dialed.

As he listened, he wondered idly how many rings it would take before Shirley Hogan answered the phone. Two, he guessed. He pictured her buzzing around the downstairs of her small Burlington home, wondering who in the world would be calling this early.

"Hello?" A question was in her voice as she picked up the receiver after the second ring.

"It's Jack, Shirley."

"What's up?" she replied immediately sensing things amiss.

"I'll tell you as much as I can in a few minutes," said Marston, who proceeded to explain what had happened on his trip to Mt. Washington, how he had been stopped, escaped, and ended up hiding out. He didn't say exactly where he was. Shirley, stunned at first, said little. She wanted to help but didn't know how. She paced around the kitchen at the end of the extra-long cord, while bracing the phone between her ear and her shoulder as she poured orange juice and took out a cup and saucer to hold her morning coffee which just finished brewing.

She was alone this morning as was often the case during the week, her husband, a long-distance truck driver, was halfway to Atlanta.

"... you can contact me if necessary at this number, but whatever you do don't call me from the office. They must have a tap on those phones or they wouldn't have been able to pick me up so easily last night."

"I'll call from Mickey's if I need to — and I probably will," she said referring to a nearby deli, popular at lunch-time. Shirley paused a moment, her voice softening, "Take care of yourself," concluding more gruffly, "you hear!"

A couple of hours later Marston had dressed and was toying with a small table radio, his third cup of coffee growing cold beside him. Lila sat on the sofa with her ever-present notebook in her lap, a pen in hand. Mostly she sat there as though waiting for inspiration, occasionally glancing over at Jack.

Things were at a standstill. After the breakneck action of the previous day, Marston felt like he should be still moving, doing something; his legs ached from inactivity. The trip spanning Vermont and New Hampshire the previous evening had metamorphosized into the kind of thing one sees in films. But now matters were at a standstill; he could only wait, and for the normally patient Jack Marston, the change of pace was severe. He found himself walking back and forth, first to one window and then another, checking for he didn't know what, then abruptly sitting for a few moments.

The morning dragged on. Marston walked out on the deck with its glorious view to the east across a broad open valley. Glancing at his watch, he noted he had been up a little over three hours.

The phone rang, just as he once more walked in from the deck.

Lila and Marston's eyes met. Lila stood up. While Sikoris, Duval and Shirley Hogan knew the number, Jack hadn't expected a call. "Let me," Lila said and picking up the phone. "Yes?" Listening for a moment, she smiled and handed the phone to Marston, "For you, it's Shirley."

"Hi, Shirley?" he said with an offhandedness he didn't feel.

He listened for a moment, then exclaimed, "What! Alive! Damn ... I'll be damned! He called you at the office? I'll leave right away — Lila and I — tell him if he calls again we'll ...." Shirley apparently finally was able to get Marston to listen as she explained that Ben Willey had called, and what he had told her. Marston, his mind racing now, thanked Shirley, then slowly and deliberately cradled the phone.

"Ben Willey's alive!" Marston blurted out, suddenly looking at Lila Maret as though he had forgotten she was there.

"Alive? Alive?" Lila replied twice, a disbelieving look on her face. "Where?"

"He was attacked and badly hurt when he got to Maine last week. Knifed, he told Shirley. Then somebody found him and took care of him. He's been hiding out ever since. Says he's mending pretty well. That's all I know for now," he explained. "It's enough. He called my office in Burlington looking for me. Unfortunately whoever's trying to get rid of Willey probably now knows he's alive — if they have the office phone tapped and I'm almost sure they have. All they know though, is that he's somewhere near Brunswick and he wants to see me. The good news is they'll probably let up on Duval until they can be sure Willey is out of the way, the bad news is they're probably trying to find Willey right now, to get rid of him! But we're going to Maine. We're going to find him first!"

"If he told Shirley he was in Brunswick, did he say something more so you can find him?"

"Yes and no. When he called the office he told Shirley to tell me to meet him at the 'the hottest spot in town — between two-thirty and three.'"

"The hottest spot in town?"

"Hard to believe that I remember it after all these years, but I do. Willey was from Brunswick you know, and when I knew him at the University of Vermont he was always bragging about the museums at Bowdoin. They have a world-famous museum that features the Peary expedition to the North Pole. We used to kid him about spending time in museums, and tell him that they were the hottest thing in Brunswick."

A disbelieving look came over Lila's face as she said, "You're going to meet him at a museum you talked about twenty-five or thirty years ago?"

Marston replied matter-of factly, "It's got to be one of those museum buildings on the campus. I don't know which one, but my guess is that if I get there, Ben will spot me. Hell, he's been in the CIA, he knows all about this stuff — I don't! He'll make sure I'm not being followed. I won't have to find him, he'll find me," Marston said.

Within minutes they were out the door and back in the white Subaru, zipping east toward Portland where they would veer northeast to Brunswick in search of the elusive Ben Willey!

An hour earlier that same morning, Congressman Alan Duval and Nick Sikoris departed the latter's home located in the hills outside North Conway. Together in Sikoris's Chrysler they headed for Portland, Maine to meet with Senator Stone. Sikoris was at the wheel. Despite his wealth the Greek millionaire shunned chauffeurs and liked to drive himself. As he explained to Duval on the way, the twenty-five years that had passed since he drove well worn used cars didn't seem so long ago. It wasn't that he needed to remember, but that he enjoyed the luxurious feeling of heading down the road in the beautifully engineered Chrysler. The pleasure he derived from automobiles came from having hands on, and not from being carted about in the back seat as if he were unable to manage.

Duval was pleasantly surprised at how easily and how quickly Sikoris had arranged the meeting with Senator Everett Stone. Stone's reputation was that of a remote, difficult patrician whose name and family money combined with good luck had landed him in the Senate. He had managed to stay there by hiring first class political operatives who knew how to take every advantage of incumbency and were second to none in dealing with the media — two important requisites in modern political life. Now in his fourth term in the Senate, Stone was unlikely ever to be seriously challenged unless in the unlikely event that a major scandal erupted around him — and this was not apt to happen to the squeaky-clean Senator Stone, at least if one believed the Washington press.

Duval found himself wondering what it was that Stone cared about. While some politicians appear more often than not to simply want re-election and nothing else, Duval knew that for most people serving in Congress, there was, underneath it all, a basic reason they had chosen politics. Often there's an idealistic streak or a cause that motivates people. But with Stone it would be hard to know what those motivations were. Perhaps the forthcoming meeting would reveal more about this strange man.

When Duval and Sikoris were ushered into the well-appointed offices on the fifth floor in a downtown bank building in Portland, Senator Everett Stone didn't stand up. Sitting in an overstuffed leather chair behind the large oak desk, Stone appeared small somehow diminished by his surroundings. The assistant who ushered them in took a seat on the large sofa off to the side, his hands crossed in his lap, his face impassive. It was quickly apparent to Duval that the appointment had been pressed on Stone by his operatives in deference to Sikoris and the enormous wealth he represented. Stone didn't apologize for failing to get up, but simply reached his gnarled hand across the desk, shaking hands first with Sikoris then with Duval.

"Well?"

Duval noted the dark flash of anger that passed quickly over Nick Sikoris's face. Charming and gracious in all his dealings, Sikoris took affront at Stone's lack of manners and was further irritated that the assistant who showed them in, a man named Charles Abrams, remained in the room.

But Sikoris, ever the charming deal maker, opened in his usual gracious way, by pointing out that the business they were to discuss was confidential, and gently implying that he would prefer that Stone's assistant leave the room.

"Mr. Abrams will stay," Stone said, his eyes darting from Sikoris to Duval then back to Sikoris, and it was clear to Sikoris and Duval that Stone meant it.

Accepting the rebuff impassively, Duval mustered his dignity and began, "Senator, I have reason to believe that I have been the victim of some kind of ..." He hadn't wanted to say plot, and events made it clear that it was more than a bureaucratic snafu. Still looking for the right word he continued, "... operation, than we have every reason to think is being engineered by top officials in the CIA."

"Oh my," Stone responded leaning forward in the leather chair and looking reprovingly at Sikoris.

Duval reflected that Stone might as well have said aloud, "Why have you brought this loose cannon here?" But Duval pushed on, describing his trip to South America, and the special mission he had undertaken at the request of the CIA on behalf of the administration. Following this he told of the news reports that had made it seem as if he was meeting secretly with a known drug dealer, and the implications of further scandal.

He went on to tell of the events that followed, of the envelope that had been sent by Ben Willey which would be sure to clear his name, and how the envelope had been taken from Marston's car in Littleton as Marston was bringing it to the Mount Washington Hotel. He explained how Marston had escaped from the deputy and was currently staying in Sikoris's chalet to remain out of sight until things were resolved.

"The problem is that I have talked to Richards who is a friend of mine — we served together in the House not long ago — and he won't admit publicly that he asked me to represent him on my visit to Tomarra. He won't admit that he asked me to do this! Senator, I need your help!" he concluded.

Through all this Stone sat deathly still, without expression — except for his eyes, which were constantly moving. Stone replied hastily, almost too hastily, "I don't interfere in operations. You got yourself in trouble, and it would be inappropriate for me to bail you out even if I could. Richards has his reasons, I'm sure. Members of Congress ought to stay out of day to day operations ...," and here he scowled, peering as if over imaginary glasses, first at Duval, then at Sikoris. His beady eyes snapped back and reattached themselves to Duval, and he said, "... then this kind of thing wouldn't happen." His eyes once again shifted to Sikoris.

Duval could scarcely believe his ears. Stone had always been considered fair — a man who lusted for nothing more, who was content with what he already had, and a man that could and would call them as he saw them. This man speaking to them, the tiny man in the great leather chair, whose eyes darted about like a man cornered, was not at all what Duval had expected. Something was askew or there would have to be a new rap sheet on the silver-haired patrician from Maine.

Sikoris, sitting back and observing both the conversation between Stone and Duval, and Stone's assistant Abrams who remained in stoic concentration on the sofa, concluded in his own mind that Stone had known what was coming and had followed a script prepared in advance. A master at engineering agreements and finding ways to resolve seemingly diametrically opposing views, in this situation Sikoris decided to not even try. He would leave a simple message with Stone, and with the administration through Stone that he was unhappy, but he would go no further. No sense showing his hand here.

Meanwhile, Duval's boyish charm had no effect on Stone. He said finally, "Is there no way I can get you to inquire on my behalf?"

Stone stared at him and replied, "Very well, because Mr. Sikoris has taken an interest, I will inquire of the director's assistant for such matters, but the director ..."

"I'm sorry Senator Stone, but we know the assistant — Edgar Steele, if we're talking about the same man — we know Steele is involved, and our only hope is that this is being done without the knowledge and approval of the director."

As if acting on signal, the assistant, Abrams, stood up, "Gentleman, I assist Senator Stone by staffing the Intelligence committee, and all of this ... this unsubstantiated information is way out of line. The senator respects you, Mr. Sikoris," he continued, pointedly ignoring Duval, "but we are very close to breaching the ethics code by discussing operational matters. Senator Stone is too gracious to call a halt, but I must insist."

Duval stared for a moment at the intrusion, then slowly got up and walked to the door, shaking his head imperceptibly. Reaching the door he turned, hands on his hips, and said with half a smile, "Senator Stone, I never realized ... I never realized ...," and then left the room.

In the elevator alone with Sikoris he continued, "... but now I do. It's scarier than I thought. Jesus Christ, they've even gotten to Stone!"

Sikoris remained silent, his face troubled.

"Are you familiar with Brunswick?" Marston inquired of Lila Maret.

"Yes, yes, I've been there several times attending the music theater."

"That's a great theater. They run a solid program each summer — if you like musical comedy."

"Best summer program in New England, I think. One of the best in the country."

"Agreed ... where are you going?" he asked abruptly.

Lila had arrived in Fryeburg, Maine, and then, in the center of town, turned right onto Route 113.

"At this time of year this way is a lot faster ... less traffic than 302. We'll hook left onto Route 25, follow it to Exit 8 on the Maine pike, up one exit or so then cut down onto I-95 north. Fastest way I think"

"Do you always follow the 'road less traveled?'" Marston asked.

Lila glanced sideways at Marston, her long lashes sweeping across her face. "Only lately, friend. Only lately," she replied and reached for his hand, her eyes once more intent on the road ahead.

Less than two hours later they entered the city of Brunswick, spotted a diner and pulled in.

They grabbed a booth and through the smoky haze studied the timeworn menu in a glass case above the grill, white letters against a black background. Traditional diner fare: hot chicken, beef, or pork sandwiches, steaks that would have to be pulled from the freezer, and offerings of shrimp, or fish waiting to be dropped in deep fat.

They ordered coffee and hamburgers.

Ben Willey positioned himself in the center building on the second floor.

The few Bowdoin students around for the summer scarcely gave him a glance as he stood staring out the hall window looking for Jack Marston. Helen Grearson remained in the car parked out on the road, a couple hundred yards away, watching for anyone or anything that didn't seem right. Unbeknownst to Ben Willey, Helen carried mace as well as a small .22 caliber revolver in her purse. Like an experienced big, city cop, her eyes were constantly moving, first in one direction then another.

She had positioned herself so she could use the car mirror to see anyone who parked in back of her.

Willey, on the second floor of the museum building, waited.

They had purposely arrived early, and so it was over an hour before Helen spotted a car carrying two people which might be Marston and Lila. The car pulled up and parked perhaps seventy-five feet back of Helen's car. Helen picked up the walkie-talkie unit from the seat beside her and said, "We've got a white foreign car here with a man and a woman — I think its them."

"Got it."

Willey then slipped his unit back into the leather briefcase. Helen had suggested the radios as a precaution and Willey, gun shy from his experience with Augie Brill, had agreed.

Marston got out of the car and headed toward the building at the end of the green. The campus was virtually empty, classes having ended several weeks earlier. It reminded Marston of a movie he had seen — the beautiful green of the campus and the hero walking quietly forward when suddenly the tranquil scene was marred. Gunshots, then screaming. Mentally he flinched. Better forget the movies until this is over.

Back on the street and remaining in their cars parked within shouting distance, the two women eyed each other, Lila sitting in the car in back and looking straight ahead through the windshield, Helen staring into the angled rearview mirror. Strangers, yet both invited by fate to be major players in a game they hadn't known existed.

Marston entered the building and headed for the stairs, the hollow sound of the his heels echoing intrusively throughout the near empty building. He climbed the stairs, and within moments found himself face to face with his old friend.

"Ben."

"Jack."

The two men stood eyeing one another, perhaps more nervous than cautious, though each man seemed poised for flight. They shook hands almost formally. Then Marston placed his hand on Willey's shoulder leaving it there for a moment.

"I'm glad you're okay," he said searching for a way to begin. "What happened?"

"The abridged version is I was knifed and Helen — the lady you may have seen in the car where you parked — found me and patched me up." He smiled, "I know a lot more Jack, a lot more, but not all of it ... and I'm not sure where this is coming from."

"Edgar Steele ...," Marston tried to continue.

"Oh yes, Edgar Steele, but he's acting for someone and I can't figure out who." Willey looked around the empty hall and then out the window, as though expecting someone to intrude, but there were only hollow sounds and distant meaningless noises. The odor of strong cleaning chemicals permeated the building and reminded Marston of the last day of school when he was in the eighth grade, and of an afternoon class picnic, and Louella his eighth grade love whose name had slipped from memory for over thirty-five years until this moment.

"Ben, let's see if we can find an empty office where we can talk until we both know the same things."

Ben Willey nodded, and said, "Follow me, While I was waiting I found one with the door unlocked at the end of the hall."

Marston took the straight non-descript wooden chair, while Willey sat in the metal desk chair. Then they began to talk.

Each in turn told of what had transpired. Willey didn't comment when Marston told of how he had been deceived by Lila Maret when she first approached him. Willey in relating his story reproached himself for not being more careful and for causing the death of Charlie Gleason.

After about a half an hour most of what had happened to each of them was now shared.

"Kind of like the old days, Ben," Marston said breaking the silence, "Sitting here quietly — the only thing missing is the chess board between us."

"It's been a long time," Willey commented.

Again they sat without speaking for a while.

Finally Willey said, "I've been thinking of the best way we could stay in touch, with tapped phones and all, we have to be careful."

After talking about it for a few moments they agreed on ways each could be in touch with the other by telephone, using code words for when Willey called Marston's office, and in the case of Marston, he would call the Maine Medical Center who would relay calls to Helen Grearson.

"I think the best thing we can do Ben, is to stay out of sight and see if Duval has any luck with Stone. If not we'll have to rethink it, but I doubt even if you came forward with your story that without evidence anyone would believe you. The press already thinks you're a loony."

"I know — but we'll have to do something!'

"For now, staying out of sight is what you and I have to do!"

Forty-five minutes had passed when they finally stood up, and began walking back toward the street where the cars were parked. When they got to Helen's battered Chevrolet station wagon, Willey awkwardly introduced

Marston, who waived for Lila to join them.

The tension that was so heavy in the air prior to their meeting had lifted. No observer would have dreamed that these four very different people were anything more than two couples enjoying the campus. The diminutive, self-possessed Lila Maret looked curiously at the strong, but wary, six-foot Helen Grearson, then at the owlish-looking Ben Willey, and the experienced, quietly confident, political professional, Jack Marston. Her writer's juices were flowing. Unable to resist lightening the occasion she said, "Am I the only one who thinks this is a wholly unlikely quartet?"

The comment brought laughter, but was somehow a reminder to Willey not to let his guard down again, and he said, nervously, "We need to break this up."

So with that each couple hurried off, Ben Willey and Helen Grearson back to Helen's cottage along the Kennebec River; Marston and Lila, on their way to the secluded chalet in North Conway.

Chapter Twenty-Seven

It was mid-afternoon when Alan Duval and Nick Sikoris returned to North Conway from their meeting in Portland with Senator Everett Stone. When they were back once again at Sikoris's estate, Duval had only to pick up his car and be on his way.

The two old friends had said little on the return trip; Duval alone with his thoughts, thinking what he never believed he would; namely that withdrawal from the race was his only solution. Always a competitor, his anger at his inability to find a way to fight back was all he could think about. Sikoris, a man who had triumphed in so many situations, felt betrayed by Stone, a man from whom he had expected more.

Sikoris drove the big, blue, Chrysler up the long driveway leading to his estate. The morning sun had given way to clouds, and scattered drops of rain spotted the windshield.

"You are going to speak to Richards once more before you return to Burlington?" Sikoris insisted as the two men walked toward Duval's rental car parked in the large turnaround area beside the garages.

"Yes, Nick. I'm going to try one more time with him. When we first talked on the phone about the problem, I had the feeling he wanted to say more but couldn't — at least at that time. It's almost like he's in on it or they've got something on him ... hard to believe ... a decent guy when we served together."

"Then back to Burlington?"

"Either there or Montpelier. If this is the end of it, I want to get everyone together who helped me get started, you know, old friends as well as new,"

"Don't hurry this ..."

"I won't — and I appreciate your advice, but ...," and with that Duval raised his arms, then dropped them to his side. A final, despairing gesture.

He got in the car and drove away.

In the car now Duval was alone with his thoughts traveling back to the Mount Washington Hotel. The conference would now be underway. Duval had arranged to have committee staff on hand while he traveled to Portland with Sikoris. While the conference was still not yet officially underway, most of the work and the agreements were rapidly being put together; the conference itself, if all went well, would be mostly formalities.

Before he left Sikoris he called both his campaign office and his district office in Burlington. He learned nothing he hadn't known: namely that the political situation in the state was continuing to deteriorate. On the street there was an unconfirmed story that Jack Marston had resisted arrest and was hiding out. The press was hounding his campaign staff and press secretary for information or denials, and for the moment, neither were possible.

Duval's challenger in the primary, Paul Wellington, was having a field day in southern Vermont, obviously grandstanding, but egged on by the media and profiting from Duval's difficulties. Duval and Wellington had known each other for years; both attended most party functions and dinners. When a party leader, or office holder is politically damaged there are always more people ready to take his place than to rally or provide support, Duval reflected.

On Wellington's part, he was spurred on, as is often the case for someone who is running for the first time, by the heady experience of seeing his name on the front page, his picture staring back at him on the six o'clock news, and accolades from political well-wishers and hangers-on lusting for their own place in the sun.

The more seasoned politician, Brad Meacham, who was unchallenged in the primary of the other party, and would face Duval in November had, to his credit, been more restrained. A wise move, reflected Duval, Meacham was simply letting the press do the dirty work and he could stay away from the issue and capitalize on Duval's negative publicity. If the problem was somehow cleared up, he would be seen as having taken a responsible position.

Duval worried about Jack Marston. In Vermont politics for many years, Marston had probably never earned even a speeding ticket. Now he was in hiding, with a possibility of a felony hanging over his head for escaping from the deputy in New Hampshire. Duval shook his head, thinking to himself of the many people in political life who ought to be in trouble, but knowing full well that Jack Marston hadn't earned this and shouldn't be among them.

A light rain had begun; the steady hypnotic thump of the wipers on the window reaffirmed the direction of his thoughts. He kept the car at a steady pace as he negotiated the twists and turns of the winding mountain road. Duval stopped briefly at a rest stop, then got back in the car, and began the climb through Crawford Notch. He arrived at the highest point in the notch, formerly the site of the famed Crawford House, now but a memory; the railroad station still stood but now served as a gift shop. Across the road, the small glacial pond remained as it had since the ice age with not a hint of a ripple breaking the glassy surface. In this small pond Duval had once observed two enormous moose wading to cool down on a hot July day many years before. Cars had stopped all along the road; the moose had remained oblivious.

He slowed the car as he drove by. And stopped. He wished he had his car phone, wondering idly if the phone would work in this remote part of the world. He wanted to talk to Ellie. He wondered if he had ever told her about the moose he had seen here.

He wondered what life would be like, out of politics forever. It was almost scary; his obsession with the "game" was far greater than he had realized now that it was about to end. But Ellie would be there for him; she would take it in stride. They'd return to Vermont and live the good life in the Green Mountain state. And it would be okay.

It was quiet, still. Very little traffic passed him parked there on the shoulder. Quiet, yes, but still no moose, he chuckled to himself, and, in that instant — his mind making the leap — confirmed once and for all that he must withdraw from the race. Unless a miracle occurred and he received help from Richards, he would make the announcement tomorrow afternoon at the Vermont State House, in Montpelier.

"Was he as you remembered him?" Lila inquired, referring to Ben Willey.

"I saw him once four or five years back. But yes and no. It's curious how a person's mannerisms are such a clear trademark. Appearances change, and Ben's now decidedly more pear-shaped than he was when we were in school, but the gestures, the mannerisms — like when he's not quite sure of what he wants to say, they're dead giveaways. I think I'd know him if he was in total disguise! Anyway, I'm sure glad he's okay! Strange maybe, but it takes some of the sting out of the rest of this fiasco."

Lila glanced at him. Marston was taking a turn at the wheel. Lila had driven all the way to Brunswick and on the way back they interrupted the trip for a combination lunch/dinner in Fryeburg, Maine. It turned out to be a brief stop; each of them found themselves looking around uneasily when they left the car to enter the restaurant. Inside it seemed that the other customers gawked at them openly. Maybe imagination, or so they hoped. They ordered quickly, ate, and left.

Back in the car now, Lila said, "Seeing Willey seemed to lighten you up."

"Think so?"

"Know so."

All tension between Marston and Lila Maret had now disappeared, giving way to easy conversation. Especially on the return trip from Brunswick, Marston had relaxed, treating what was happening to them almost as an adventure. In the back of both of their minds was the 'no win' situation in which Alan Duval found himself. "Isn't there someone who might come forward at the CIA to vouch for Willey? Someone who will affirm that he's not crazy?"

"Lawson Nabors, an accountant who worked for Willey would do anything Ben asked, he told me. But then you get into one of those things where you play 'who's telling the truth?' The best you get out of that is a congressional hearing that will drag on forever. The worst of it is that if the leadership is involved they can control most of the media play; they have the experts, the money, the contacts, and God knows how many IOU's out there with the people who own the media. They'd eat Willey and Nabors alive. They've already got the story out that Ben was certifiably nuts — just as they told you when they roped you in. Same deal. They make it sound so logical!"

"Are they really that powerful? I know a lot of totally honest people in media who would kill to tell the truth?"

"Yes, we'd end up with some people on our side — members of the press — who'd want to believe us, but they would be the outcasts, the ones who are always looking for the off-beat, the ones who believe the conspiracy theories on the Kennedy assassination, the October surprise, or that little green people visit us regularly from Mars.

"By the time that we convinced the 'name' reporters from the *Times* or *the Washington Post* it would be history — another story nobody cares about. Who knows what would really happen if we try to challenge them just on the basis of Ben Willey's word? We could of course, that's up to Duval and Willey if they want to risk it.

"The real problem is that public opinion isn't worth a hell of a lot since the Iran-contra deal. Everybody lied, and they all went off scot-free, from the top down. Hell, Ollie North has made a fortune telling the public how he lied. Medals for lying are 'in.' In my opinion a simple guy like Ben Willey would be destroyed — those cats have had a lot of practice! We've had two presidents recently look us right in our television eye and say things so outrageous their most zealous supporters know they're lying through their teeth, and the public simply nods." He stopped for a moment and then continued, "You know, even as I say it, I think, this can't be true? But it is!"

Still six or seven miles from the chalet, Marston turned north onto Route 16 heading up a short incline. From out of nowhere a county sheriff's car zipped past. Preoccupied with his destination, its occupant never tossed a glance at the white Subaru. Marston and Lila exchanged looks, but neither spoke.

Lila persisted, "You don't have much faith in people do you?" Without waiting for his answer she went on, "If Willey doesn't come forth with the information he has, the press will continue to crucify Duval, and he will be forced to withdraw, won't he?"

Marston didn't answer. Finally, as he swung left onto the dirt road leading to the chalet where they had spent the previous evening, he replied with frustration and anger.

"That's what's really on my mind, I guess. I'm out in the middle of nowhere, hiding out like a Goddamn fugitive — I am a fugitive — and Duval's virtually all alone at Mt. Washington. The press must be all over him. Jesus, I need to be where I can talk to him ..."

"Look out Jack — up ahead!"

The two county sheriff's cars were parked in the yard, one on each side of the chalet. On one of the cars the flashing blue light broadcast its warning of danger, catching Lila's attention from nearly a half a mile away. Spotting the cars, Marston swung the Subaru into an opening in a hay field which had fallen into disuse. Partially grown over, Marston gambled successfully that the opening wasn't a mud bog. He drove in just far enough so by quickly shifting to reverse and backing up, he could swing the wheel about with only moments lost before he was charging back toward the main road.

Approaching Route 16 he hesitated a moment, then turned left heading north.

Lila was half turned in her seat looking back through the rear window. Marston remained intent on the road, nervously checking the rearview mirror, pushing the car to meet the demands of the road. After traveling a mile or so, still half turned in her seat, Lila said, "I haven't seen anyone following."

"I know ...," replied Marston.

"They'll probably radio ahead."

"I headed north figuring there'll be fewer police cars up that way. Only problem is that I don't know the back roads up this way if we need to use them. I almost never traveled this route, although this is the way to Tuckerman's Ravine. I skied there years ago ... I'm not sure how far it is to Gorham — that's the next major town to the north. We need to get that far in order to lose them, otherwise they can box us in."

"I've got a map here," Lila replied, rummaging around in the glove box.

Lila, quiet for a moment studied the map. "Twenty-four miles, Jack, according to this."

Marston thought a minute, "I wish it was less, but if we get to Gorham, we'll have a chance to lose them. We won't be hemmed in with mountains on either side like we are here. When we get to the intersection of Route 16 and Route 2, we can turn off in either direction and disappear on some back roads — they'd never have enough people to chase us down. We could even go up through Berlin."

"I've got an idea, Jack, when you get to Gorham, find a place to park this car for a while, then we can buy an old truck or something — a 'cheapie.' We'll put it on my credit card, get some old clothes and we'll be a lot harder to spot."

"Sounds good!" Marston said admiringly, "All we've got to do is beat them to Gorham!" He pushed the Subaru to the limit, continuing to test his driving skills against the challenging road through Pinkham Notch.

Back at the chalet where Marston and Lila had spent the night, a debate was taking place. From a distance the deputies who had just arrived at the chalet had spotted the white Subaru on the road to the chalet from a half a mile away or so. When they saw the car slow down, apparently after spotting the police cars, then abruptly turn around and head off in the opposite direction, they knew they had Marston in their sights. Deputy Sheriff Dan Riggins wanted to radio ahead to the state police. "Bud" Goslant, also a deputy, who had driven up in the car that had passed Lila and Jack Marston at the intersection, resisted. "Damn state police never call us unless the shit really hits the fan. This one should be ours ... hell, we'll be in *USA Today* if we nail this one. Screw the state police, I say."

Resigned that he was getting nowhere with Goslant, Riggins said, "Well, let's go. We don't even know which way they'll turn — you head north, if you don't spot them you'll have to radio ahead for the state police, I'll head south. Stay in touch as long as you can."

Accepting the apparent compromise without comment, Deputy Goslant jumped in the high-powered Ford, spun his wheels while turning around and within moments was back on Route 16 heading north, unaware that he trailed Marston by less than two miles. If he had radioed ahead the New Hampshire state trooper parked at the entrance to the Wildcat Mountain Ski area would have easily been able to spot the white Subaru. But it wasn't to be. Goslant had resolved long ago that it would be a cold day in hell before he called the state police on something this good, Riggins be damned! The long standing feud between the state police and the sheriff's department was a fact of life in the north country and in the case of "Bud" Goslant it rankled even more since he had been turned down for a job with the state police a couple of years before. Anyway, Goslant figured, his big Ford could easily over-take the little 'Jap' car — as he characterized it — if it was headed north. For "Bud" Goslant technology reached its zenith with the invention of the Ford V-8 engine — everything after that was nit-picking!

Thirty minutes later, Lila Maret and Jack Marston arrived safely in Gorham, turned left and headed west. Earlier, when they had seen the state police car parked at the entrance to the Wildcat Ski area they both held their breath, but the trooper sitting in the car scarcely glanced at them.

In Gorham, just beyond the town line, Marston swung off the highway onto a dirt road and headed toward the foothills of the great mountains beyond. After traveling a few miles on the washboard-like surface they found a place to pull off the road and get their bearings, safe once more from their pursuers.

Chapter Twenty-Eight

In the early evening of that same day that Marston and Lila were on their way to Gorham, having evaded for the moment the police detail that lay in wait for them at the chalet, Herbert and Greta Kleinerman were returning from their long weekend in Toronto.

As Kleinerman fitted the key into the lock and opened the door, the phone was ringing. Methodical as always he set his case down, hung the key on its hook, walked to the phone and picked up the receiver. He put the phone to his ear but heard only a dial tone. He replaced the receiver and went back out to the car and assisted by Greta, brought in the rest of the luggage which he left at the foot of the stairs.

Each time he undertook the rigorous job of directing a chess tournament, it tired him more than he remembered. He never considered that with every tournament he had grown that much older. On the plane ride back from Toronto he vowed to Greta that he would limit the number of tournaments he would direct in the future.

"You always say that — then you always go when they call," she replied.

Kleinerman hadn't answered his wife of fifty years as they sat together in the plane looking out on the vast expanse of the North American continent. Instead. as he so often had when he was tired, he recalled the difficulties endured in Europe by master chess players wanting to play tournament chess during the frightening turmoil leading up to World War II. Oh, they had been prima donnas too, some of them. He thought of Alekhine, the brooding, alcoholic, world champion; Botvinnick, the brilliant Russian who would achieve the world championship after the war; Capablanca the Cuban who made winning seem so simple and who would die so young; and Max Euwe, always the gentleman, who became world champion by defeating Alekhine, then later continued his career as a much sought after analyst and theoretician. These men had endured poverty, political manipulation, and finally a sad loneliness when their chess powers waned and they began to play the game as mere mortals do — Gods no longer. Whatever their quirks, they had wanted to play. They competed for material rewards that were pitifully small, enhanced only by the fawning admiration of the rich, and members of royalty who viewed genius as something one could own.

In Toronto, Kleinerman had once again watched the current crop of North American chess masters compete. Indeed some of them would develop to a point where they equaled or exceeded the masters of his generation.

Near genius, some of them. But so many acted badly, as though that kind of behavior was part of being a competitive chess player, complaining about the format, the accommodations, and of all things the prizes, the size of which would have boggled the minds of the masters who had introduced him to the game so many years before.

As director of the Toronto tournament it had been his job to keep play moving, on time, and to solve the petty problems brought to him by gifted young men no older than his grandchildren. He did his job well, everyone agreed. When it was over, the young players mellowed. The anxiety over public failure behind them, many of the young players had approached him to thank him. And he had smiled and accepted their thanks.

He and Greta stayed on Monday night in the two-room suite provided him as one of the perks of being tournament director, remaining in the beautiful hotel and attending an excellent concert that evening before returning to Maine the next day.

Now that they were home, Greta would go to the kitchen to make coffee. He knew that. He would go into the den and sit down among his papers and his books where he would gather his thoughts. He would pick up a pocket-sized chess board, and concentrate on the sixty-four squares, formulating a position in his mind.

And Greta knew that.

Together so long, one always knew, and that was good.

Later, he sat back in his chair, set the pocket chess set aside, and brooded over the loss of his friend Ben Willey. His thoughts had never been far from Ben Willey since hearing the shocking news. The abbreviated news story had come over television on the late news following the concert. He had been unable to get any of the details. But with what Willey had told him before he left on his trip to Toronto Herbert Kleinerman knew he had to do something. But what? He had mailed the envelope that Willey had left with him. Could he do something more?

He reached for the pile of newspapers that had collected while he was away, hoping they would shed further light on Willey's demise.

But after a half an hour with the papers, he learned nothing more. He did find out, however, that someone had begun to spread the stories about the young congressman from Vermont. Willey had warned him of what might be coming when he showed Kleinerman the material contained in the manila envelope explaining how important it was.

The story about Duval ran below the fold on the front page in the Portland papers, so he imagined it was headline news in Vermont. As expected it was the story of the congressman's dealings with the South

American drug king-pin, Tomarra, along with implications of lots of financial hanky-panky with the promise of lurid incriminating photographs to be printed over the next few days. Willey had come to him, Kleinerman, to help head this off. And so as they agreed, Kleinerman had mailed the envelope to Duval on Friday when he lost contact with Willey. The congressman in Vermont should have something to fight back with now. But they hadn't tried. Why? He wondered.

Maybe the envelope never got there?

The first story had broken on Monday, and Duval should have had the envelope by then. But Duval had not answered the newspaper charges directly — only weak quotes appeared from his obviously confused staff. Kleinerman sat thinking for a while. Greta came in with the coffee. He didn't ask, he knew it was decaf. It was always decaf in the evening.

The next morning, Kleinerman called the Vermont office of Congressman Alan Duval and asked to speak to Duval or whomever was in charge.

"I'm sorry, Mr. Kleinerman, the congressman is out of town." Shirley Hogan had hung up a short time ago from talking with Jack Marston, and she said, "You'd want Mr. Marston, but Mr. Marston — he's — not — here, there's no one here right now — maybe I can help?"

Kleinerman also paused, thinking it over again, deciding just how much to say over the phone to someone who wasn't in a position of authority. He continued, "I have some business to discuss with the congressman. I think it is important for him. I think I can clear up some of what is being said."

Shirley Hogan's heart jumped. She had been coming into the office early and staying late, desperately seeking ways to help both Duval and now Marston. She picked up the foreign accent in Kleinerman's speech and not wanting to cut him off if he could be of help, but not wanting to say too much fearing, as Marston had warned, that the phones might be bugged, she asked, "Where are you calling from, Mr. Kleinerman?"

"Brunswick, Maine, I live here."

"Oh!"

When Kleinerman said "Brunswick", a shock like a bolt of lightning rocketed through Shirley's nervous system. Brunswick was the town in Maine where Ben Willey had supposedly been killed, and where he had called from earlier trying to reach Jack Marston! She thought for a moment. She didn't want to say too much, but this man might, just might, have something that could help. She said, "I'll tell the congressman you called. You can leave a number — if you want to try again." Then she said almost pleadingly, "Please ... please try again." She had done her best, without giving away too much, to let the caller know that he would be able to reach Duval.

Kleinerman understood. "Thank you, I shall call again after ... say ... one o'clock ."

He hung up and went into the kitchen. "We'll go to Vermont," he said to Greta, who was wiping an imaginary spot off the shelf.

She nodded. "I'll put some things in a bag — then we'll go."

At quarter past ten that same morning, Kleinerman was backing the car out of the garage, with Greta at his side, headed for Vermont.

As the garage door descended and Kleinerman backed onto the street, the phone in his study began ringing once more. Again Ben Willey who was calling had just missed connecting with his good friend.

When Kleinerman failed once more to answer, Willey put down the phone, turned to Helen Grearson and said, "Still no answer: I don't understand it; Herbert Kleinerman is very organized — God I hope they haven't found out I went to see him and have hurt him in some way."

Helen Grearson smiled at Ben who had sat back down on the edge of the bed. "You need to rest," she said, "Your friend said to stay 'dead' for now, and I order you to." Again she smiled, her head resting against the pillow, a cotton sheet covering her.

Willey turned to look at her, then crawled back under the sheet and without any change in expression, said, "You call this rest?"

"Of course, this is why nurses are better for you than doctors!" She reached for him, and he turned to her, carefully, still conscious of the damage wrought by the knife of his assailant.

The romance began the night before. Helen had come into his room, checked his wounds which were mostly healed, re-bandaged them, touched his forehead with the back of her fingers, then his cheek and she said, looking at him closely, "No fever."

Willey surprising her, and himself, had replied uncharacteristically, "That's all you know!"

Helen had come to his room prepared for bed wearing a purple robe tied with a white rope-like sash. The robe, open at the throat, exposed the top of a matching gown. When Ben answered her in the way he did and she saw how he was looking at her, she stood perfectly still. Ben touched the sleeve of the satin robe with the back of his fingers, moving the back of his fingers against the soft fabric, then he carefully wrapped his hand around her arm, not pulling her to him, but remaining with his hand gently holding her arm. She had stood looking at him for a long moment, then without a word climbed into his bed without removing the robe.

They stayed like that for a long time, barely touching, not moving, a quiet tension building. There were no words. And then they knew it was time. Helen shut off the light, darkening the room, then removed her robe and gown. Turning toward Ben, she said, after a first lingering kiss, "You'll have to be careful, so let me."

And then Helen was leading him from that lonely place they both knew well; crossing dangerous territory into memories of pain, sadness, and disappointment. Then at last they were together.

The soft rain that was falling had stopped, and the night air was cool. The dim light from the moon cast exaggerated shadows of the branch of a tree which crossed in front of the window just outside the room; the branch swayed back and forth in gentle rhythm, rubbing against the side of the house generating small sounds; the moon captured reflections of Helen kneeling over Willey; herself gently moving, swaying, as though in cadence with the nearby Kennebec, flowing to the waiting ocean.

And after they were still. They lay together; for now without words. A few moments later Helen left the bed and went into the other room. When she returned, Willey lay motionless, Helen's statuesque body was hypnotic in its effect on him. She turned on the small stereo system; then returned to the bed. They lay together like this again, this time listening to the haunting melody of *The Moldau* by Smetana.

They fell asleep holding hands.

◆ ◆ ◆ ◆ ◆ ◆

Duval arrived back at the conference site at the Mount Washington Hotel in the early evening. From his room, he sent a message to his Washington staffer Gina Caravagio. Caravagio, who was not yet thirty years old, had been the best choice to staff the conference because of her background which included extensive research on the European Common Market. She was fluent in French and Italian, and could understand German and as well as some of the Slavic dialects. Within minutes Caravagio knocked and entered Duval's room.

"How's it going down there?" Duval inquired.

Caravagio hadn't spent a lot of time working directly with Duval. She had been on staff only a few months and was usually holed up in the back office researching and drafting legislation. It was an awkward time for the brilliant young woman to be talking with her boss whom she greatly admired, while the terrible stories about the unexplained side trip Duval had supposedly taken in South America swirled about. Caravagio fought to maintain her poise as she replied, "Officially, of course everything starts tomorrow, but the staff energy that's going into this isn't going to leave the principals with many items that haven't been either decided or nearly so. It's very well organized, staff is staying on subject, in fact I think they have reached fundamental understandings on all the phase one proposals."

"Sit down Gina," Duval said, changing the subject. "Have you seen Bill Richards around?"

"I saw him earlier this morning on the porch, and then at breakfast. Of course he wouldn't be attending the sessions yet, and I haven't seen him since then. One of his staff people told me he likes to climb around on the mountains, knows this area pretty well, apparently. He told me he thought Richards was going to sneak off and hike out on one of the trails."

Duval looked at the earnest young woman and realized for a moment how soon people lose their innocence upon arriving in Washington. He knew that Gina Caravagio wanted to believe that he, Duval, was innocent of the charges against him — wanted to with all her heart. The young woman was hanging on desperately to the notion that most of the people in Washington were good people, and that the charges against her boss would soon be explained. This in the light of a Washington that had destroyed the dreams of the Kennedy generation, and was doing its best to insure, through one public malfeasance after another, that such ideals would never again take root. Sadly, reflected Duval, the America approaching the twenty-first century would be a "me-first" America.

With all the selfish, self-serving, egomaniacal behavior one found in Washington, Duval was happily surprised at the number of young, talented people who tried, through it all, to make the world a better place. Sometimes it seemed as though every one of them applied for jobs in his office. Caravagio was one of these idealists.

"I'd hope to see Richards," Duval said absently, then continuing, "Can you get word to one of his staff?"

"Easily. He should be back by seven I would think— just an hour from now — the French are hosting a reception this evening. I'm sure he'll attend that."

But William "Bill" Richards, Director of the CIA for a year and a half, didn't appear back at the conference by seven ... or seven-thirty... or eight o'clock.

Duval remained in his room waiting.

Shortly before seven-thirty, Peg Slattery, Richards's personal secretary for many years, became very worried. Without consulting anyone she enlisted some young staffers to go out and search for Richards along the trail he'd said he'd be hiking. And in another half an hour, with still no word, the New Hampshire State Police were informed, and word of Richards's seeming disappearance had circulated among conference participants. The language differences had the affect of generating wild rumors, one of them suggesting that Richards had been kidnapped by terrorists.

Duval had dinner sent to his room. He initially planned to return to Vermont before dinner, having figured out how to best proceed with his plans to withdraw, but wanting just once more to talk to his friend Richards about the stories that were destroying his career. It had been Richards who got him into this he said to himself for the hundredth time. Face-to-face he knew he could convince his old friend to help.

While he nibbled at dinner he called Washington and found that Ellie had gone out. He wanted to hear her voice. He needed to tell her what he was planning. He called the campaign office in Vermont to check on the local news. TV didn't lead with the story on Duval, thanks to a gory murder, born of human passion and acted out on the streets of Winooski, Vermont. But the reprieve was temporary, for the next story was a challenge by Paul Wellington asking Duval to withdraw, "in the best interests of the party." Duval's likely November opponent, Brad Meacham, continued on a self-serving higher road asking that Duval "just explain this thing."

Then wondering about Marston, Duval dialed the number of the chalet Sikoris had made available to Lila and Marston. No answer. Curious, thought Duval. Where would they go? They'd agreed to stay out of sight unless they could help.

Replacing the receiver, Duval frowned. Maybe they'd gone for walk, he tried to convince himself. He looked again at his watch. Almost eight o'clock. Gina Caravagio had been keeping him posted on the results, or lack of them, of the search being carried out for Bill Richards.

He paced. He turned on the TV. A half an hour later he snapped it off and sat down to revise what he had written for his withdrawal speech that he would give the next day in Montpelier. For the umpteenth time he walked to the window and looked out. The shadows lengthened. This long day — not a good one, was mostly over. But where in hell was Richards? What could have happened he asked himself, knowing too well that he could have fallen while out on the mountain, had a heart attack, or ... God, they wouldn't harm the director of the CIA ... or would they? What's going on? The room seemed to get smaller; Duval felt edgy, nervous. He needed exercise, but he couldn't leave the room without some word.

An hour and a half later the long summer day had finally surrendered, and darkness set in. At eleven o'clock with still no word on the whereabouts of Richards, Duval finally decided to spend the night and return to Vermont in the morning. He was undressing for bed when the phone rang: It was Caravagio.

"They've sent for dogs. If he went hiking where he said he was going to, the dogs will find the trail."

"Right, Gina. Call me if they find anything — I don't care what time it is!"

Sleep had never been a problem for Alan Duval regardless of what was happening around him, and within moments of darkening the room, he was asleep.

◆ ◆ ◆ ◆ ◆ ◆ ◆

Back in his room, at the Mount Washington Hotel, Edgar Steele was satisfied that his talk earlier with Richards had accomplished all that was to be expected. Richards had given Steele plenty of room to operate when he'd been appointed Richards's Special Assistant. As well he might have, given both the White House support for Steele's appointment as well as the letters and phone calls of recommendation that came in from some very big names — names in some cases even associated with the legendary Alex Koenig.

But when Richards had asked Steele about finding ways to help his friend Duval — even to the point of confirming Duval's story about interrupting his trip to a conference in South America to take a side trip on behalf of the administration three years ago — Steele now knew that Richards had become a problem that needed to be solved.

He smiled to himself. He felt absolutely nothing. No regrets, no sadness, no anger. Only a pleasant sense of accomplishment. He had his talk with Richards at three o'clock this afternoon in Richards's suite. The director was only half listening, and gazed impatiently out the window at the mountains clearly anxious to leave and get some exercise on one of the hiking trails. Steele concluded his conversation with Richards by conceding that Richards should go ahead and confirm Duval's story.

He smiled as he left, patting Richards on the back, and warning him to be careful. "You're a very important asset to the administration, and to the country," he had told Richards as he was leaving.

As soon as he was alone, he ran down the back way, picked up his rental car and drove to a parking area on Route 302 at the head of one of the hiking trails. In the car, he slipped on some running shoes, flipped the lock on the car, and hurried ahead on the trail that Richards had told him he would be hiking. Richards had even told him enough about the trail that Steele had gone to the one spot where the walking trail could present difficulties if one wasn't careful.

And there he waited.

But not for long. Twenty minutes later the director of the CIA walked past the place where Steele had patiently secluded himself.

Steele used no weapon, said nothing, but simply came from the side and pushed Richards off the trail, over the edge, and down the shear embankment. Richards fell over a hundred and fifty feet before he struck anything. When his body struck the rocks, it bounced another hundred feet or so before coming to rest nearly three hundred feet away.

Richards, at the last moment before being pushed, had seen Steele and his face displayed a sudden comprehension which quickly gave way to sheer terror, as he fell through space understanding as he did that his life was now ended here on the granite ledges of a New Hampshire mountain.

When Lila and Marston arrived in Gorham, rather than trying to travel any further they parked in a secluded grove for over an hour, a couple miles outside town. They hoped any immediate police cars in pursuit would continue on, and Gorham, while a small town, was probably the best town in this rural area for them be easily assimilated.

After biding their time for an hour or so, they drove closer to town, while continuing to avoid the main roads.

On the very outskirts of the business section, Lila parked. While Marston remained in the car, She walked to the business section of town, and found an old-fashioned general store where she picked up clothes for both of them. With the clothes she had chosen, she hoped they looked different enough that they would be difficult to identify.

When she returned, they once again drove out of town a short ways, pulled to the side of the road, and went into the thick woods far enough so they could change clothes without being seen.

Then, following up on Lila's earlier idea, they returned to town and drove around until they found a used car lot. Lila, again leaving Marston to wait, went onto the lot and within a half an hour drove back in a full-size Ford pick-up truck to where Marston was waiting.

Then they switched places, with Marston taking the wheel of the truck, while Lila followed behind in the Subaru. Marston soon spotted what he was looking for — another auto dealer who had cars waiting for service scattered haphazardly on a back lot. Marston drove the truck out back with Lila following. She pulled the Subaru in among the cars waiting for service and parked. Leaving the car there unlocked, she then jumped in the truck and they headed back toward the business area of downtown.

"Nobody will ever spot us in this garb unless they're really looking," Lila said.

Looking at Lila and at his own new attire Marston chuckled and said, "If nothing else, we can become lumberjacks — we've got the clothes, the truck ... you didn't buy a chain saw by any chance?" he said with sly grin.

Semi-seriously Lila said, "They've got them back there," pointing to a hardware store. Lila had tried her best to look like a woman right out of the woods, decked out in baggy slacks, a checkered shirt which she tied at the mid-rift, exposing some skin, and a hat advertising grain from the local feed company.

She looked more like the parody than the person, mused Marston. There's no way to obscure ... what was it ... her spirit ... something. For himself, he had a similar outfit, except that his short sleeve shirt proclaimed him to be a "Harley" owner, his hat was the twin of Lila's. He hoped they looked like tourists trying to go native, since he was sure that trying to pass as natives they would fool no one, although he hadn't the heart to tell Lila.

Marston liked the truck. Lila had done a good job of picking one that seemed mechanically sound. She had paid fifteen hundred for it and it ran smoothly. The combination of rust and "fender benders" would limit the future life of the rig, but it would solve their immediate problem.

"Let's go back and get something at that restaurant we passed — just across from the park. I'm hungry. Besides we have to decide on a game plan. I never thought we'd get away so I wasn't worried about it!"

"You aren't used to having such a talented partner!"

"Glad I have, though," he laughed, and put his arm around Lila as they entered the restaurant.

Inside now, they ordered coffee while they waited for their food to arrive. They positioned themselves to be able to see out the window onto the main street. The only police car they had seen so far belonged to the local police, no sheriffs or state police cars had appeared.

"Hard to figure. They should be closer than this, but ..." Marston shrugged, relieved for the moment that they weren't any closer.

Chapter Twenty-Nine

"No word yet," Gina Caravagio reported by phone.

It was six thirty in the morning, but Alan Duval was wide awake waiting for the call from his young staffer.

"State and every other kind of police are all over the place. Rumors galore. One policeman I talked to who seemed to have his head on straight said that he figured Richards fell somewhere. It seems the trail he intended to take is safe enough, but if he got off it and tried to keep going in the dark, a fall would be very possible."

"They've got dogs, right?"

"Yes, they're out there now, although there was a light rain through the night which makes it harder for the dogs to get a scent."

"Thanks, Gina — hang in there for me. I won't be able to join the conference today as I planned. I'm heading back to Vermont. Cover for me here. Any word on Richards and you call the Vermont office immediately. I'll be in constant contact with them. Okay?"

"Yes sir ... Sir, anything else I can help with.?"

"Just keep me informed about Richards." Duval picked up on the plaintive tone in Gina's voice; seeking reassurance, but for the moment reassurances were something Alan Duval didn't have the capacity to give.

Duval had showered, dressed, and was knotting his tie when the phone rang again.

Talking faster this time, her voice showing the strain, Gina Caravagio said, "The dogs have tracked his scent to the edge of a cliff that drops way down into a real nasty area. They figure he must have fallen there, but it's going to take some time to get down in there to ... to find the body..."

"Stay with it Gina ... and keep calling. As long as I remain here I want to know everything you know."

Duval hung up, held the receiver down for moment began dialing the first of several calls to Vermont. After talking with John Godine, Marlene Brownell, Eddie Fine, and several others, he tried again to reach Jack Marston at Sikoris's chalet in North Conway. Still no answer. It didn't make sense. Where was he?

Duval decided he couldn't wait any longer. He grabbed the bag he'd never unpacked along with his briefcase and skipped down the back stairs out to his car hoping not to be seen.

It worked, no one noticed. He drove down the long drive past the golf course and out toward the main road, but pulled off to the side for a moment and to take a long look back at the majestic hotel. To Duval, the scene encompassing the beauty of the hotel with the mountain as backdrop conveyed a message from another time, another generation, that said simply: this is how you do it, this is how man should build and blend his world with that of nature.

Back on Route 302 heading to Vermont, Duval's thoughts were on the things he had to do and additional people he ought to call prior to his formal withdrawal from the race. Most of all, he was wondering how to explain the withdrawal. He had watched many a politician resign or bow out under pressure of scandal, and there seemed no right way. He didn't want to appear to confirm the terrible rumors, but simply withdrawing from the race would, in effect, do this very thing. One thing was for sure, after withdrawing from the race he would persist till he found the source of the trouble foisted on him. He knew it went beyond Steele, but to where?

As he became accustomed to the road, fighter that he was, Duval's thoughts returned again and again to finding ways that would make it possible to continue the race.

His last hope hung on the possibility that Richards might be found and would come forward and verify his explanation of the South American trip. Caravagio's last call hadn't left him with any expectation that this would happen. Still, he decided that he wouldn't actually make the announcement until he talked with Richards or he was certain that Richards was dead. He held onto this last slim thread as he drove through the crisp early morning air on his return trip to Vermont.

At the same time that Duval was speeding toward Montpelier, his key advisors, minus Jack Marston, were meeting in his Burlington office. Jack Godine, Eddie Fine, Marlene Brownell were joined by Shirley Hogan who was the only one present in recent contact with Jack Marston. The phone rang; Shirley picked it up.

"Oh yes, Mr. Kleinerman."

She listened a moment and continued, "Congressman Duval will be in Montpelier this afternoon, he's returning from New Hampshire. He's planning to make an announcement in Room 11 of the Vermont State House, probably around four-thirty PM." She hesitated then said, "That could change, however." She listened for a few more moments, then continued, "When you get into Montpelier go directly to the State House and find the lt. governor's office — it's in the west end of the main lobby. As of right now that's where we'll be meeting prior to the announcement."

Godine and the others had heard part of the conversation and looked at Shirley expectantly. A slightly puzzled look on her face, she said, "That's the man that I told you about who called from Brunswick, Maine ... he has a kind of accent ... claims he can help clear Congressman Duval!"

"How?" they asked in unison.

"I don't know ... says he talked with Willey about a week ago ... I told him to meet us in the State House, before the announcement."

"What could he know that would help, I wonder?" Marlene Brownell asked.

"Don't get your hopes up folks, our only hope is Richards and it's a hundred to one he's dead!" Godine said looking up from the withdrawal speech he was writing and which he knew Duval would ignore, preferring instead to ad lib as he always did on important matters.

Jack Marston and Lila Maret parked their newly acquired truck in front of an unrented room in the motel three doors down from their own, on the outskirts of Gorham. They decided the motel they had selected was as safe a place to stop as anywhere while they got their bearings. They had spent the night, and early in the morning Lila went out and picked up a fast food breakfast for each of them.

Marston was sitting in a chair looking at, but not seeing, the flickering images on an aging black and white television set. He turned to Lila, who was sitting on the bed propped up with a couple of pillows, and said, "How did they know we were staying at the chalet? The police were waiting for us, right at the chalet. Nobody knew where we were, except Duval ..."

"Well, Sikoris knew."

"Oh, I know but ... Christ, not Nick. It couldn't be Nick — he and I go way back — he's — oh no, not Nick!"

Lila said nothing, Marston's frown gave away his troubled thoughts.

The morning dragged on. They were able to learn little from either the television or the small radio Lila had purchased in town. Marston paced for awhile, then sat down, only to rise after remaining less than a minute or so in the chair, and begin pacing again. He cursed the events that left him stranded in Gorham, New Hampshire, miles away, unable to help his boss and friend Alan Duval who was in the fight of his life.

Finally, he slammed his hands down on the credenza, and said, "I'm going to call Shirley."

"At the office?"

"I need to know what's going on — I won't say where we are."

"Can't they trace calls."

"Mostly no, they can't. That business about tracing calls is more 'story book' than a readily usable police technique. It can be done with advance notice but it is very expensive and takes time." Marston walked over to the phone and dialed the office number.

Shirley Hogan answered.

"Jack!! Are you okay?"

"We've had to move, but we're okay here so far."

"Jack — the congressman is planning to withdraw. He's announcing this afternoon in Montpelier."

Marston said nothing at first, not surprised, but he felt once again the overpowering helplessness resulting from his inability to be on hand and to assist his longtime friend. "God, I wish I was there, Shirley!"

"Jack, a Mr. Kleinerman called from Brunswick, he ..."

" He's the one who mailed the envelope, Shirley, probably wonders what we're waiting for."

"He said that maybe he could help ..., I think he intends to come to Montpelier."

"The old guy did his part Shirley, it's yours truly here who screwed up ... what time is the press conference, maybe I can make it."

After getting the details, he hung up. He stood with his hand still on the receiver, and said, "I've got to go and be with him. It's over. He's announced a press conference in Montpelier. Whether they want to arrest me or not, I've got to be there."

"I understand. I'll go with you," Lila replied and busied herself packing her few things.

"If they decide I'm still a fugitive after Duval withdraws, which I doubt, they may arrest you for helping me."

"I know."

"But my guess is that all the charges will mysteriously disappear as soon as Duval withdraws." Then Marston exploded, "Goddamn it, there must be a way out of this!"

Lila walked over, put her arms around him, and said, "All we can do is go over there and let it play out — pray for a miracle, Jack," she said.

Augie Brill, who had returned to his listening post across from Duval's Burlington office had heard all he needed.

Following Kleinerman's second call he hustled down the stairs then up one block and entered the phone booth next to the convenience store. As always, he called Steele's number, identified himself and the number he was calling from, hung up and waited. Five minutes passed before the phone in the booth startled him with its harsh ring. It was Steele.

Brill relayed what he had had picked up from his listening post.

Steele said, "I know. I've tapped into both ends of that conversation through another source. Something strange is going on. I want you to get to Montpelier. Go over and get the feel of the place. Duval will be around the statehouse when he gets there. Check out the statehouse. Your job is to prevent this guy Kleinerman from getting anywhere near Duval. If he has a brief case or any papers, take them. As far as I know he couldn't — just don't let him near anybody. Take him out if you have to."

Brill was glad to hear from Steele. He'd been out of touch. He said, "How'll I know this guy?"

"Old guy, maybe seventy-five. He'll have Maine plates on his car. He'll probably try to park somewhere near the State House. My sources say his wife will probably be with him. You shouldn't have any trouble. Just get rid of him, and then you split, disappear for a while. Okay?"

"Yeah ..."

"I'll get the money to you after — to the safe deposit box we set up."

Fifteen minutes later Brill was at the wheel of the Honda on I-89 heading for Montpelier, his task clearly in mind, and an additional fifty thousand dollars awaiting the successful completion of the dangerous assignment.

Brill had never been to Montpelier and although he had plenty of time, he left early, wanting to get the feel of the place and figure how he would actually accomplish what he'd agreed to do. Leaving I-89 on the outskirts of Montpelier he pulled off onto the side of the road just before entering the small capital city. He walked around to the back of the car and opened the trunk where he kept the small bag. Inside his case he found a second knife, along with some tape which he used to strap the knife inside his shirt. The other knife, the one with which he had wounded Ben Willey, was strapped to the inside of his left leg just above the ankle. He looked for a moment at the disassembled plastic revolver that he had brought with him but never used. He thought about it a long moment. No, guns were just trouble, he reaffirmed, leaving the gun where it lay.

Back behind the wheel, he drove into town.

What was important now was that he get a feel of the city so whatever happened he'd know where he was and where he was going. He consulted a map, then drove all over downtown Montpelier determining where he might position himself for what he had to do, and, of equal importance, how to escape once the job was done. It was a small town, hard to disappear in, he decided. But within a half an hour, he knew as much as most natives about the layout, and was comfortable that when he accomplished what he came for, he could get away safely.

Next, he returned to get a closer look at the State House which has served as Vermont's seat of government since before the Civil War. He noted the entrances on all four sides. Brill's task was to identify and eliminate his target before they could gain access to the building through any one of the entrances. Complicating things for Augie Brill was the absence of parking in the immediate area that would allow him to do what he had to do and still make a fast getaway. Luckily for him, while he was looking around with his car double parked and idling, a spot opened up on Court Street within a hundred yards of one of the side entrances to the State House. Brill quickly moved the Honda into the spot and parked.

Jack Marston and Lila Maret were in the truck they purchased the day before and were traveling west on Route 2 toward Montpelier. Lila was trying to make the scratchy radio work. She finally narrowed it to two "am" stations where the reception was clear enough to hear the news if there was any to be heard.

They had been traveling for about a half an hour listening to the combination of contemporary music and static in competition with the wind and the noisy engine when the program was interrupted and the radio blared,

"This just in, Director of the CIA, William Richards is dead. Richards, who was attending a conference at the Mount Washington Hotel in Bretton Woods, New Hampshire, died apparently of a fall while hiking in the mountains yesterday afternoon. More later."

Jack and Lila looked at one another. For a moment neither said a word.

"Why am I not surprised?" Marston said finally, and not waiting for Lila to reply continued, "That was Duval's last chance. When I talked with Shirley, she said that Duval was still hoping in the back of his mind that Richards would come forward and support his story."

"Maybe he planned to, maybe that's why he's dead."

"God that's right ... probably killed? Murdered!"

"Sure, they've played hardball all the way, why not murder?" Lila asserted.

They rode in silence for several minutes when Marston finally said, "I just can't believe that Sikoris is involved in this."

"Maybe ... maybe he told someone he trusted that we were staying at the chalet ..."

"And that's how they found us? No way. That friendship goes too far back — it's something else."

Chapter Thirty

From where Augie Brill parked he could spot anyone who might enter the Vermont State House through three of the four entrances. Anyone unfamiliar with the building, as Kleinerman certainly was, would be unlikely to use the west side entrance Brill had decided, after walking around to take a look. Brill sat motionless, except for the ever-present cigarette between his fingers moving like clockwork every fifteen seconds or so to his mouth. His hand would pause at his mouth while he took in the smoke, and then move woodenly to withdraw the cigarette, with an almost marionette-like quality to the movements. The resulting smoke curled and settled lazily in the car, barely any of it escaping through the half-open window.

The sweet smell of the many June flowers planted on the grounds around the State House was everywhere, but Brill never noticed. His eyes were narrowed, watering slightly from fatigue. He had slept little these past few days. And he was suffering from inaction. But his assignment up until now, had been to stay put — and observe. This he had done. But now with Steele's latest call he had an assignment — an assignment that he welcomed.

While Brill sat there, looking for an older couple in a car with Maine plates, Jack Marston and Lila Maret, still dressed in the odd assortment of clothes they had acquired in Gorham, drove right by where Brill was parked. They had passed within just a few feet of him. But just as Brill failed to identify them as they passed by, neither did Lila and Marston spot their nemesis as he sat in the car, waiting.

Pulling the truck to a stop and idling in a no parking area at the corner of Governor Davis Drive, just a few yards ahead of where Brill was parked, Marston said to Lila, "I'll drop you here, and you can keep an eye out for Duval, Godine or any of the others. If you see Duval before I'm parked and back here, let him know we've arrived. I want to see him — and make sure the press conference is still scheduled for four-thirty in Room 11. That's late for a State House press conference — they like to leave early over there. They might have to change it."

Lila removed her cap and threw it in back and tucked her shirt inside her jeans. She leaned back against the door, opened her arms in a pose and asked, "I look okay?"

"Fine," Marston chuckled, noticing again how the outfits Lila had selected for both of them were so out of character. He continued with characteristic humor, "It'll give the press conference a populist touch!"

Lila climbed out of the truck just a few steps from the east entrance to the State House. Marston drove the old truck down Governor Davis Drive and turned right onto State Street. A couple of hundred yards up State Street he found a parking place just off the corner of the broad green expanse of the State House lawn. He was parked diagonally several hundred yards across the well- kept grounds from where he had let Lila out.

Waiting for Marston, Lila walked slowly toward the front of the State House taking in the elegant landscaping, the well-tended flowers and the glory of the Vermont June day. Marston, who was out of the truck now, could see her from across the broad expanse where he parked.

Inside the State House in the lt. governor's office, Duval, Godine and the others had already arrived. The lt. governor, Lou Ann Chandler-Aiken, was a longtime friend of Duval's and she had repeatedly told him to feel free to use her office any time he was in town. It was ironic, mused Duval who was standing apart from the others and looking out on the State House grounds, that the first time he was able to accept her gracious offer it would be to withdraw from public life.

Lying on the desk next to him was a single sheet of paper typed by Godine which was to be Duval's statement of withdrawal. Duval had set it aside without reading it. He philosophized to himself how easy it was in this modern age to reduce every event, every happening, to a mere dollop of words typed on paper. And all of it in a single paragraph. Questions please, he mused.

In the scheme of things he supposed it wasn't such a big deal. But it was wrong. An injustice. An injustice to himself, his people, but more than that, it was the unchallenged corruption that angered him. Unchallenged corruption — good title for a book, he decided.

Godine and the others had heard the news on the radio on the way over from Burlington that Richards's body had been discovered in a ravine. Duval was made immediately aware of the fact as soon as he arrived. The last slim thread of hope was now gone. Duval, for his part, had taken the news of Richards's death almost stoically. He had expected the worst and was unable to generate either grief or anger.

The conversation in the office was muted from the time they all arrived. Earlier Duval had finally reached Ellie and she insisted on flying up from Washington to be with him. But anxious to get it over with Duval had decided not to wait for her arrival before he made his announcement, and then go ahead and meet her in Burlington after the press conference.

Godine, Fine, Brownell and Shirley Hogan occupied a couple of soft chairs and the sofa on the other side of the room, and engaged in quiet conversation. Duval alternately sat quietly, then rose and paced to and from the window, finally announcing, "Let's go out there now. The room's all set up. Everybody who's coming's already here. Christ, let's get it over with!"

But Shirley Hogan argued with her boss, perhaps for the first time ever, "Congressman," she said, "we know Jack Marston's on his way. He'll be here shortly. This is too important a thing for you to do without Jack here. We're talking about a lifetime of friendship, Congressman," she pleaded. A few more minutes won't matter."

Duval looked at Shirley Hogan long and hard, and reflecting upon the courage it took for her to stand her ground with him he said, "You're right, Shirley, we'll wait."

Earlier she had tried unsuccessfully to convince Duval and the others that they should also wait until Kleinerman arrived. Shirley insisted that Kleinerman had said he could help. But she failed to be convincing, and neither Duval nor the others placed any importance upon his call. Godine had said more heatedly than intended, "For God sakes Shirley, what we need is real evidence. We can get lots of testimony; what we need is the hard stuff like the material Ben Willey put together exposing what was being done! We don't need some half-baked academic telling us what to do!"

Still at the window scanning the grounds now, Duval almost overlooked Jack Marston who was some distance away and was walking briskly up the main walk from State Street toward the State House. Just as Duval was about to mention to the others that Marston had arrived, he saw his aide stop abruptly, then apparently begin shouting something, and then break into a run, as he veered over toward Court Street. Within moments Marston passed out of Duval's line of sight.

Meanwhile, Herbert Kleinerman had parked his car fifty yards away from where Augie Brill sat waiting. Accompanied by Greta, who was hurrying to remain only a half step behind, Kleinerman walked spryly up the sidewalk with briefcase in hand, his destination the Vermont State House.

Augie Brill who was still sitting in his car had known only that he was looking for an older man in a car with Maine plates. He spotted the tags immediately, and when Kleinerman got out of his car where Brill was able to see him, he knew he had his man. Brill touched the knife taped to his ankle. He got out of his car and pretended to check the time, and straighten his jacket, all the while keeping his eye on the approaching couple.

Brill fingered the knife which he had now removed from its case still taped to his leg, and held it in the palm of his hand, his finger on the button that would expose the blade and bring the weapon alive.

An old man he decided, sizing Kleinerman up. He wouldn't need the knife. A quick thrust with a two finger fist below the heart, and the paralyzing chop to the neck would easily disable the old man. The woman was nothing. He would grab the briefcase and be in his car in thirty seconds. The black-haired woman who had been hanging about was now standing over in front of the State House too far away to cause any trouble.

The approaching Kleinermans were now only ten feet away.

The TV cameras were set up in Room 11, inside the State House. Reporters, camera persons, a couple of lobbyists without anything to do now that the legislature was out of session, and a couple of stray tourists attracted by the cameras waited for Congressman Duval to appear and make his announcement. The invitation and press release had not said that Duval would announce his withdrawal, but members of the press and others there were unanimous in agreeing that that was the motive for calling the conference.

Each day Vermont newspapers had been clamoring for Duval to clear up the scandal and innuendo surrounding the South American trip, and in the absence of his willingness to do this, the press, posturing with familiar sanctimony, suggested that they would have no choice but to oppose Duval's re-election.

Duval was now late, but the press were used to waiting. The light-hearted, nervous banter covered, for at least some members of the press, a regret for what they would have to report, although such feelings were not to be admitted. The adversarial nature of the business of the fourth estate had to be respected by professionals, if not always enjoyed.

At that moment most of those assembled saw Reg Gibson, the State House security officer running past the door. He headed down the hall to the east entrance. As they started to follow, hesitatingly at first, State House Sergeant at Arms, Sawyer Kirby, waved at the group saying, "Come on! Some kind of trouble out here!" They ran for the east entrance.

It happened too fast.

Lila saw the attack on the old man. Horrified, her eyes focused for the first time on the attacker's features — she recognized him instantly. She knew Marston was too far away to help; still she shouted and waved for him. Now both she and Marston were running toward Court Street where Brill was standing over Kleinerman who was down on his hands and knees on the sidewalk.

Chapter Thirty-One

At the last second Kleinerman sensed or saw the first blow coming at him and he parried it with his briefcase. Brill followed with a chop to the neck jarring Kleinerman off balance, knocking him down, but not unconscious. The aging Austrian, on his hands and knees, was trying to rise while still clutching the handle of the briefcase. Then the case broke open and papers poured out. Brill came at Kleinerman again, but Greta Kleinerman had other thoughts. With scarcely a hope of stopping him, she threw her arms around Brill. He shook her off, but again she tried; finally Brill angrily slammed his elbow back into the small woman's midsection. Greta Kleinerman collapsed and lay motionless on the sidewalk.

But her effort had taken a critical few seconds, seconds Brill could not afford. He looked up and now running toward him was an enraged and determined Lila Maret with Jack Marston keeping pace fifty yards behind. Brill grabbed for the knife he'd slipped in his pocket, but as he did so people began pouring out of the side door of the State House led by the uniformed State House security officer.

Brill paused for only a moment. He had little doubt that he could take care of Kleinerman, Marston and Maret. But he couldn't do that, collect the papers and materials that had spilled out of Kleinerman's briefcase, and avoid the new threat from the security officer and the group now pounding down the walk. The contents of the briefcase might be critical. But Brill hadn't lasted this long by taking risks in such situations. He was a survivor.

Leaving the briefcase and papers scattered about, Brill ran for his car, jumped in, started it up, and in moments was racing east on Court Street where he disappeared from sight.

Marston leaned over the dazed Herbert Kleinerman who said simply, "The briefcase ..."

Marston grabbed the briefcase and collected the papers scattered about.

Lila leaned over Greta Kleinerman, who was still not moving.

The room was buzzing. It was after six o'clock, over an hour and a half since the altercation on the corner, but the press crew assembled in Room 11 of the State House had been directed to ignore deadlines. Five television stations had cameras on site and were broadcasting live. Over a dozen reporters were on hand, nervously milling about, joined by State House employees and a gaggle of political junkies.

The late afternoon events were unprecedented, and the rumor mill was fast at work. The usually unexcitable and detached Vermont State House came alive with excitement, and phones rang persistently in the few offices that remained open. So far no one had been given a clear explanation of what had happened to precipitate the assault on the elderly couple from Maine.

Alan Duval, Godine, Fine, and Brownell now joined by Jack Marston and Lila Maret had reassembled in Lt. Governor Chandler-Aiken's office. Shirley Hogan stood guard in the outside office. Jack Marston, with Lila Maret's help, was reassembling the papers and other materials that had tumbled from Herbert Kleinerman's briefcase.

The group had learned only moments before that these papers would, once and for all, expose the plot to discredit Alan Duval, totally exonerating him and leaving his way clear to continue his bid for the U.S. Senate.

Duval and Godine were off to the side discussing the revised statement that Duval would be making to the waiting press corps, and, through the magic lens of the waiting cameras, live to the people of Vermont.

The lt. governor's phone rang. Godine reached for it.

"That was the hospital," he said when he hung up. The group was quiet for a moment, waiting. "The Kleinerman's are both resting comfortably. Mrs. Kleinerman has a couple of broken ribs, but neither of them are in any serious danger."

"Good news, John, good news," Duval said, once again beaming a broad smile.

"Alan, it's all here. Everything. Before we go in let's make more copies of some of this." Marston said, handing papers to Shirley Hogan in the outer office who then headed for the copier.

Ten minutes later, at exactly six-thirty-seven PM, John Godine, walked into Room 11 of the Vermont State House and announced that Congressman Duval was on his way.

The room became quiet.

Duval appeared.

The congressman walked to the wooden rostrum which was surrounded with microphones of varying size and shapes. The cameras with their bright lights followed him, film rolling, as soon as he walked into the room.

He nodded; the room quieted; he began.

"Thank you for waiting. I have a statement to read and then I will take questions. I believe what I have to say will be of interest to those of you here today as well as to all Vermonters.

"Within the past few days Vermont newspapers and television stations began to run a story concerning a trip I made to South America, almost three years ago. The press alleged that I took a secret side-trip to meet with a renowned drug trafficker. There were other allegations made. I knew of course that I was not guilty, but because I could not prove my innocence, and to spare my family, my friends, my party and myself further embarrass-ment, I had intended to come here today to announce my withdrawal as candidate for the U.S. Senate.

"Circumstances have now changed. I am now able to offer you proof of the fact that my activities in South America were entirely appropriate and duly authorized, and more importantly, I will offer as well, information as to how this effort to compromise me came about. It is fortunate, not so much for me, but for our system of government that strong courageous people can still make a difference. The person most responsible for the turn of events today which I will describe, must, for a while, remain anonymous to insure his safety. Once we can determine that the person I'm referring to is no longer vulnerable in this matter, then I'm sure there will be a fur-ther public statement."

For the next twenty five minutes Alan Duval explained the circum-stances that led him to take the side trip to Colombia. As he was deliver-ing his explanation, Jack Marston was handing out copies of Ben Willey's memo that explained what happened, and the materials that had been used for the set-up.

As soon as he finished the questions came fast and furious.

"Who framed you? Was it Richards?"

"I guess you all know that Mr. Richards was a friend of mine, a man with whom I served my first term in Congress. I believe you know too that he was found dead this morning, apparently after he fell or was pushed off ..."

"Are you saying Richards was murdered?"

"I have no information you do not have, but his death certainly seems suspicious."

The questions after a while became redundant, simply going over ground Duval had already covered. Mostly they wanted to know who had put the material together that showed how the frame occurred. Obviously it was somebody on the inside, and why had Duval taken so long to reveal that he had been framed.

"The material was delivered to me by Herbert Kleinerman, whom you witnessed being assaulted just two hundred yards from here, and was very nearly unable to deliver what he had traveled all the way from Brunswick,

Maine to give to me personally."

"Where'd he get it?" another member of the press inquired.

"A copy of the material was left in his hands for safe keeping. He mailed it to me as he was asked when, and because, he lost contact with the person who gave it to him. This is what they had agreed upon. I won't go into detail.

"What no one knew until a few minutes ago, was that he made a copy of all of this material before mailing his copy to me. He hid this extra copy in his house. No one except Kleinerman knew it existed. And but for that, the plot to discredit my candidacy would have been successful! Thank God for his foresight. It was this copy that his assailant was after when Mr. and Mrs. Kleinerman were attacked earlier this afternoon."

"How did the Kleinerman's assailant know what he had?" a reporter asked.

"We assume that some of our phones were tapped, and that when Kleinerman called my Burlington office and said he believed he could help, he revealed enough so they knew he needed to be stopped."

Finally at seven-twenty-one PM, Congressman Alan Duval — who less than three hours earlier had been expected to end his political career — left the rostrum in Room 11 of the Vermont State House, confident once again that his message to Vermonters would carry him to the United States Senate.

Chapter Thirty-Two

They had agreed to meet on the weekend following the November election.

Sunny November days in the north country are rare, but when the sun does appear, the beauty of November's purple can exceed the more obvious glories of the familiar orange and red colors of October, at least in the eyes of many Vermont natives.

Ben Willey and Helen Grearson traveled from Maine to join Jack Marston and Lila Maret who had come over from Underhill to meet at the Rabbit Hill Inn, in Lower Waterford, Vermont, located along the Connecticut River near the New Hampshire border just off Route 18. The beautiful up-scale inn is yet another of Vermont's wonderful secrets. A tavern was opened for business on this site in 1795, and a tavern or inn has existed on this site now for over two hundred years. The inn and restaurant are open to those seeking gourmet food and a peaceful setting amid beautiful surroundings of the Vermont countryside.

While awaiting dinner to be served the foursome sat in a small room off the dining room, enjoying some wine, and rehashing the events that had brought them together five months ago. Fast friends now, they were quietly celebrating Alan Duval's election to the United State Senate the previous week

Conversation was lighthearted as Lila Maret expounded on the advantages of late fall vacations in northern New England.

"Yes, Lila," replied Jack Marston who was lounging on the corner of the large sofa, "It's fine when the sun shines, as it is today — but we only see it two or three days in November!"

They all laughed.

They bantered back and forth for a while kidding about the weather, and about the newlyweds, Helen Grearson and Ben Willey. Lila and Jack were explaining the logic of living most of the time in Jack's bungalow in Underhill, while retaining Lila's Jay Peak condo for getaway weekends and vacations. Finally the conversation turned to the unlikely events that had brought the four of them together.

"It's so difficult for me to believe this sort of thing can happen in this country. It goes against everything we learn when we are young. What motivates seemingly successful people in government to undertake such crazy escapades?" Helen Grearson inquired.

For a moment no one replied, then Ben Willey spoke up. "People want to please 'the Prince.' It may not be in Machiavelli's treatise, but as soon as one group controls the government, people gravitate toward that power. They want to fan the flame of that power, stoke that energy. It has nothing to do with what one or another leader wants to accomplish — it has to do with pleasing the powerful."

Nodding his agreement, Jack Marston said, "For so many 'the game's the thing,' moral and political principles get lost in all this." Then looking at Ben Willey he continued, "You are a unique and courageous man, my friend, except for what you did, Alan Duval, a very decent man, would be lost to Vermont and the nation. He would have had to withdraw from political life."

And with that Marston lifted his wine glass in a toast to an embarrassed Ben Willey.

"By the way, Ben, who put out the report of your death — I never think to ask." Marston inquired.

"It seemed to me that I'd be out of harms way if that report appeared. It's amazing how easy it is to announce your own death in the newspaper. Actually my good friend at the agency, Lawson Nabors put out the story when I asked him to, then once one paper runs it they all dutifully repeat it."

Changing the subject Jack Marston said, "It's been five months Ben, do you still feel Bill Richards was not involved?"

Slow to answer as always, Willey replied, "I don't think Richards was involved in any serious way. He had a lot to worry about in that job and probably the operation got under way without him. When Duval asked for his help, he stalled, I'm sure, in order to find out what was going on. At any rate, despite the Agency's statement to the contrary, I'm convinced Richards was pushed to his death up on that mountain ."

"Who do you believe sicked the police on you at the chalet?" inquired Helen.

"We can't prove it, but Duval and Sikoris both told me they mentioned it to Senator Stone when they went to Portland." Marston replied.

"So somehow he's connected to this whole affair?" Helen continued incredulously.

"How are the Kleinermans doing?" inquired Lila

"Entirely back to normal. He's planning to direct a chess tournament in Minneapolis in a couple of weeks," Helen Grearson replied.

"Amazing man, Herbert Kleinerman," Marston said.

"Amazing woman, Greta Kleinerman," Lila said quickly.

"Very true," Marston agreed, "Without Greta Kleinerman grabbing onto the man who attacked them we would have lost the copy Kleinerman made of Ben's materials."

"What do you suppose prompted Kleinerman to make a copy of all that stuff?" Helen wondered aloud.

"It's the way the man thinks," Willey replied, "Systematically. With him everything is a system, I never anticipated he'd copy that material. But as I think about it — that's his way, always have a back-up position. When I saw the copier in his den at his home I wondered how often he would ever have occasion to use it. Apparently when I asked him to mail the padded envelope to Vermont, he decided he'd feel better if he copied the material before he left for Toronto. Then when he read the newspaper accounts of Duval's troubles, he put two and two together and decided that somehow the copy he had sent to Vermont had never arrived, or gotten into the wrong hands."

"Ben, what about the statement put out by the Agency that implied Edgar Steele had been under observation ... the hints at mental instability?" Marston inquired.

"Drivel, utter drivel. I would think they could do better than that or say nothing. But it works nicely since Steele is no longer with us to repudiate any of it." Willey replied.

"What about Steele?" Lila asked.

"Brilliant, no question, but probably a sociopath. Whoever masterminded this affair had to get rid of Steele when the evidence that I put together surfaced — imagine — shot while trying to escape. And apparently the public believes it." Ben Willey shook his head in disgust.

"The capacity of the American people to swallow what its government says has increased in leaps and bounds over the last twenty years — this is just another example," Marston interjected.

"Far more information, far less critical analysis," Helen interjected, her mind for the moment reverting to memories of Vietnam.

"Is it finally over, or will we learn more?" Lila inquired.

"It's over for us. They won't bother us further. We can't hurt them now. But this didn't begin with Edgar Steele, or even Bill Richards. Somewhere, probably right in the middle of our own government there is one or more very powerful people who want to determine the future direction of this country. If we look closely I bet we'll find other elections, upsets, that came about as a result of the kind of revelations that almost defeated Duval." Willey paused, momentarily embarrassed by the uncustomary long and emotional statement.

"It didn't end with Watergate." Marston replied.

"No, it didn't end with Watergate." Willey reiterated.

They went in to the dining room.

Epilogue

They decided to meet at the younger man's home; Alex Konig and the older man arrived separately. They were greeted cordially and ushered into the elevator and within moments the three men were seated comfortably in the plush living room.

The three had not been together for months, not since the gala birthday party where they'd met and Alex Konig had outlined his plans. Drinks and cigars were offered and declined. Suppressing his impatience, Konig sat impassively while the other two discussed in great detail the possibility that the Redskins might win yet another Superbowl.

Finally the younger man turned and said, "Well, Alex, I see you've brought us some new members to the Congress. People who, thank God, we can depend upon."

"The new members should be very easy for all of us to work with," replied Alex Konig.

"I'm aware you had problems in Vermont, Alex — that something went wrong. Can you tell me what happened there?"

"A curious twist of events, and probably the wrong person was selected to carry out the program in the field."

"Steele, wasn't it, the man shot and killed while trying to avoid being taken in by federal marshals?"

"The F.B.I. actually ..."

"Whatever, he was clumsy ..."

"Well," continued Konig, "the program worked in over a dozen races, and even with our failure in Vermont, there wasn't a hint of any fallout on either of you gentleman, or myself."

"That of course is the key, now and in the future," replied the younger man.

The conversation shifted and no more was said on the subject.

Twenty minutes later the younger man escorted Alex Konig and the white-haired chairman of the Senate Intelligence Committee, Senator Everett Stone to the elevator. They shook hands all around.

"Well done, Gentleman, well done," said the host.

Alex Konig stepped onto the elevator turned, smiled a rare smile, and said, "Thank you Mr. President."